TOO MANY WASTED YEARS

Edith is full of regret when her young man, fighting at the front as the Great War rages, is reported missing, presumed dead. For their last meeting had been quarrelsome when she'd refused his advances to make love ... During her grief she meets Alfred, a passionate man — and she's soon pregnant. They marry, but Alfred, although a kind man and a good father, lets money run through his fingers, and Edith spends her marriage regretting that he isn't her first love ... When Alfred dies, Edith becomes a housekeeper, and discovers what love really means — finally realising that she's always been chasing a dream.

Books by Susan Shaw
Published by The House of Ulverscroft:

ELEANOR
DREAMS OR REALITY

SUSAN SHAW

TOO MANY WASTED YEARS

Complete and Unabridged

ULVERSCROFT
Leicester

First published in Great Britain in 2006

First Large Print Edition
published 2007

British Library CIP Data

Shaw, Susan, *1950 –*
    Too many wasted years.—Large print ed.—
    Ulverscroft large print series: general fiction
    1. World War, *1914 – 1918*—Great Britain—Fiction
    2. Great Britain—Social life and customs—*1918 – 1945*
    —Fiction 3. Love stories 4. Large type books
    I. Title
    823.9′2 [F]

    ISBN 978–1–84617–635–7

Published by
F. A. Thorpe (Publishing)
Anstey, Leicestershire
Set by Words & Graphics Ltd.
Anstey, Leicestershire
Printed and bound in Great Britain by
T. J. International Ltd., Padstow, Cornwall

This book is printed on acid-free paper

1

For the umpteenth time, Edith peeped around the barn, each time more afraid somebody who knew her would be coming along. Oh! How she wished he would hurry up. What with the smell of hay which was overpowering and the butterflies churning in her stomach both with nerves and excitement, she felt quite sick. It was not safe here. She could easily be spotted but she just had to see him before he went away.

'Come please,' she whispered. 'Get here soon, Edward.'

But she had already waited too long. Her mother would be suspicious if she was late home and there would be ructions. One last look, that was all she could allow herself and then she must go. Tentatively looking around the corner she could at last see a figure in the distance.

'Let it be him,' she whispered in agitation.

She was quick to realise it was not Edward; the stranger's walk was too slow and stumbling. Pressing against the splintered wood of the old barn she just hoped the figure going past did not notice her. She knew she looked odd, furtive and suspicious lurking here like this and her mother would kill her if she ever found out, but she had to see him.

The air left her lungs in an explosive gasp as the man stumbled past without glancing left or right. She would have to go home; there was nothing else for it. Edward had let her down. Miserably, she crept out of the shadow of the barn and blinked in the sun. It took her a moment to believe what she could see. For there, barely twenty yards away, she recognised Edward's familiar, carefree stride. At last, at the eleventh hour, it was him.

Giving one last sneaky look to make sure there was nobody else around, she ran out of hiding to meet him. As soon as he saw her, he started running; his arms held open to catch her. With a sigh of relief she fell into them and looked at his strained face as she said, 'Oh Edward, I thought you weren't coming. I had to see you before you went. Where have you been?'

As he moved nearer he could not believe his good luck that his prayers had been answered and she had stayed. 'So many questions in one go. Sorry you've had such a long wait but it was difficult getting away from Mum. As it is I've had a few strange looks and harsh comments leaving her at a time like this, when it's my last few hours on leave for a while. But come on; don't let's waste the short time we have together.'

With this he pulled her towards the old barn never giving a thought that she might have to be on her way home. Edith wanted to savour this moment, it could be a long time before they met again. Even at the touch of his large, calloused hand her heart did a flutter. She loved him so very much. Why had everything to be so complicated? She wanted them to be together all the time and they should be able to declare their love openly. What did it matter that they were so young? Nothing else was important but the fact they loved each other.

'You're quiet tonight,' Edward said softly in her ear.

Edith jumped as his deep voice broke into her thoughts. 'I'm thinking about us. When do you think we'll be able to tell our families about walking out together?'

'Who's the impatient one now? This isn't the time to think about that. Just enjoy this moment we have together.'

'I will, I will, but I want it to go on forever. Not this pretence all the time and having to keep our feelings hidden.'

'I know love, but just be patient. We'll see what we can do on my next leave.'

Edith's face lit up at this thought. 'Do you really mean that?'

'Of course I do. Have you known me to promise you what I don't mean?'

'No of course not,' she replied not too sure about that. Then with a sob in her voice she added, 'But I'm going to miss you so much.'

'Now that's all the more reason to make the most of our time together,' and with no more ado he pulled her down on the bales of prickly straw.

Despite her discomfort of sharp spikes of straw sticking into her Edith could feel the passion building up within herself as he nibbled her ear and his rough hand roamed over her breast. It felt like a red hot fire inside her spreading down to between her legs. Some instinct made her know this feeling was wrong but try as she might she could not stop it. Her body moved of its own volition to press as close to him as she could. She sensed Edward's own arousal as he kissed and caressed her more and more, and a hard bulge pressed against her stomach.

They had done this before but Edward had always stopped short of going any further by saying, 'Time enough for the rest when we're married.' But each time he pulled away from her he did seem more reluctant.

Dreading it, yet knowing it was what he

should do, Edith expected him to move suddenly away from her. But he did not, his hand started to move up and down her leg until he was touching her where she knew it was wrong. It brought her abruptly to her senses as she jumped quickly out of his grasp. Showing both surprise and anger in her voice she asked, 'What on earth are you doing, Edward? You know this isn't right.'

The only answer he gave was to grab roughly hold of her and pull her closer to him in a tight hold as he started to kiss her again. Now panic started to build up in Edith afraid of what was going to happen as she was aware of Edward's strength. With one mighty push she moved away from him uttering a sigh of relief. Looking at him with puzzlement, she asked, 'What has got into you to-day? This is not like you at all.'

He looked shame faced as he said softly, 'I just love you so much.' Edith almost detected a sob in his voice as he carried on. 'I'm so afraid, Edith. What if I don't come back? I just want you this once, and then whatever happens we've been a proper couple. I'll always be able to carry this memory with me.'

Taking him into her arms, Edith cradled his head as she ran her fingers through his short coarse hair. 'I know, I know. But it wouldn't be right. I might end up with something else to carry with me. Me Ma always said she'd kill me if I ever got into trouble whilst I was unwed, just like Bessie down the road from us. I just daren't risk it, I daren't. I do love you, truly. But you'll come back to me safe and sound, I know you will. Then when we're old enough we'll be wed and it will all be proper like. It'll be far better to really love each other without any worry of the consequences.'

But there seemed no consoling him as he carried on begging. 'Please Edith, just let me this once. I'll take care so no harm comes to you.'

Even before she had time to answer he started to try to force his way on top of her. Now Edith was beginning to get really frightened, this was not the Edward she loved, he seemed crazed. She screamed loudly in his ear, 'No!'

Suddenly he moved away from her as he recovered his sanity. 'I'm sorry,' he said looking shamefaced. 'It's all this fighting and what you see at the front. I'm really anxious about going back this time.'

The last thing Edith wanted to do was to part on bad terms. She was fully aware of the harm that could do with them going back to fight with troubles on their mind. It took away their concentration and that could have dire consequences. 'I understand. I really do, but you must accept what I'm saying. Anyway I'll have to go in a minute; me Ma will kill me as it is for being so late home. Just come here and give me one last kiss and cuddle before you go. It'll be all right you'll see, then next time you're on leave we'll laugh about all the panic you had.' Although she tried to say it with conviction to make him feel better she still felt worried herself.

After one more kiss, with a great strength of will she tore herself away from him. 'I've to go now Edward.'

'I know you have. But always remember that I love you, whatever happens.'

As she took stumbling steps to walk reluctantly away Edith called back over her shoulder, 'I'll be waiting here for you, never fear.'

Just before she moved out of earshot she heard him shout, with concern in his voice, 'I hope your Ma won't be too cross.'

This brought tears to her eyes thinking how kind he really was. She turned, waved and mouthed back, 'I love you.'

With a great weight of sadness she put all her effort into moving home as quickly as she could. Getting nearer she slowed down; it would not do any good for her mother to see that she had been running. She ran her hand over her hair to smooth it hoping it did not look too much of a mess, and then she glanced down and saw some straw on her skirt. She tried to brush it off and only hoped there was no more anywhere else.

Just as she had anticipated, as soon as she cautiously opened the door her mother shouted irritably at her. 'And where have you been young lady? What excuse have you got this time for being so late home?'

Edith could have kicked herself at not having the foresight to get her excuse ready so stuttered the first thing that came into her head. 'It was such a lovely evening, a few of us decided to sit down on our walk home from the mill. We got laughing and joking and forgot the time, sorry, Ma.'

Her mother calmed down quickly, as she usually did, finally said grudgingly, 'H'm, well just make sure it doesn't happen again. Elsie's been asking for you. Go and see her whilst I dish up your tea although what it'll be like I don't know, most probably burnt to a cinder.'

Edith replied in a meek voice, hoping to keep on the good side of her mother, 'Yes, I'll just go and have a chat with her.'

At times it frustrated Edith that she had to give so much attention to her sister, Elsie, yet she did genuinely feel sorry for her. Elsie contacted rheumatic fever when she was younger and it had left her with a weak heart. Many a day she had not even enough strength to get out of bed and sit in a chair. Edith knew it must be a lonely life for her all day just lying in bed with nobody but her mother to talk to. Now she felt contrite when she knew she had been out enjoying herself illicitly and Elsie had been left on her own again. Although she was only two years younger than Edith, at times her astuteness made her seem older. As soon as she saw Edith her face lit up as she said laughingly, 'What have you been up to? Meeting some young man, I bet.'

Edith felt foolish as her cheeks burned hot with a blush and she did not want Elsie to know the truth in case she let the cat out of the bag to their mother. She was only sorry she could not tell her as she knew it would be the highlight of Elsie's day. Instead Edith tried to laugh it off by saying, 'I wish. I've only been chatting to my friends from work.' Then quickly trying to change the subject she added, 'If you look out of the window you'll see that it's a lovely evening, a shame to be indoors.'

These words made her feel a blundering fool as she saw the sadness come across Elsie's face as she so obviously wished she was out there enjoying it with the rest of them.

Edith tried to be cheerful and bring a look of happiness back to her face as she said trying to sound confident, 'You'll soon be strong again Elsie, then you can come with us whenever you have a mind to.'

With wisdom in her voice, far beyond her years, Elsie answered, 'I don't think so. I'm sure I'll always be stuck here. This is my life now.' Then she became the young girl she really was as she eagerly asked, 'Tell me what you were talking about and what it's like out there.'

This put Edith was in a dilemma how to answer, but she was saved from putting her foot in it further as their mother called, 'Come on, Edith, your meal is on the table.'

'I'd better go now before Ma gets furious with me. I'm in her bad books as it is. But I promise I will come back later and chat with you.'

As she ate her meal Edith sank deep into her own thoughts of the events that had taken place that evening. Her mother's voice broke into her dreams. 'I thought you said you'd had a good evening. You wouldn't think so by the look on your face. You look as if you've found a shilling and lost a pound.'

Having a guilty conscience she tried to cover

up her quietness by giving a nervous laugh, 'I'm tired that's all, Ma as it seemed hard today at work.'

'Not so bad as to stop you gallivanting though, young lady?'

'No, I'm sorry. It won't happen again.'

Softening a bit in her manner her mother looked at her. 'I know what it's like when the spring fever gets into you.'

These words brought Edith up sharply and she looked intently at her mother and could well understand how it had affected her too at times. Her mother was a pretty woman even now at her present age. It was not difficult to imagine that she had been beautiful as a young woman. Although at times she could be sharp with her, it was not really done with malice. When she listened to her friends she knew she was lucky in her mother; at heart she was a gentle and kind person. She treated them well and kept a very good house.

'Your Pa's late home tonight. Mind, he said he'd a big load to deliver today.'

Her feelings of sorrow for herself were brought abruptly to an end as her thoughts moved on. They lacked for nothing. Her father was the general carrier for all the local mills and there was always plenty of work for him. Too much at times, that was probably why he had always wished she had been born a lad. They even had a small-holding at the back of the house and always had a pig or two and plenty of hens. Aye, they were never short of food for the table. She knew she was lucky really even if her father was strict and treated her more like a lad. If only she could share her joy with them about Edward, then life would be really perfect.

2

Edith had always considered she was a happy go lucky person and was well contented in most things she did. But now she was restless, she suddenly disliked the confines of work, the routine of going home and helping her mother and father and even the normally enjoyable task of giving Elsie companionship was tedious despite the great love between them. Although she worked full time, her father still expected her to help him with the horses. Luckily, she did not mind animals and in some ways it had never seemed real work to her. Despite them being dumb animals she liked to talk to the massive cart horses as if they were her friends. Now she felt the resentment build up at having to do this.

She knew some of her friends at work had not been as lucky as her and were still stuck in the noisy weaving shed where she herself had first started work. Whenever she walked through those dust filled sheds and saw a young child stood on a stool to reach the loom, it brought back unhappy memories. She had been a bit on the small side when she started work and had needed to stand on a stool herself. How she hated those greasy looms and the smell. The noise was unbelievable; often she had thought that deafness would befall her before she was much older if it had been her lot to stay working there. Like all the other weavers, lip reading had come naturally to her because it was impossible to hear what was being said. Now, when people were out of earshot, as long as she could see them, she could work out what was being discussed. At least she had not been a weaver long enough to have impaired her hearing irretrievably.

She considered herself one of the lucky few when offered a job in the burling and mending department. It was still fresh in her mind, that remarkable day, when the call had come for her to report to the manager's office. To Edith it usually meant one thing when a worker was summonsed, that being their work was not up to scratch and the bosses were going to dock their pay. She knew her face must have shown fear to all her fellow workers as she walked nervously down the space between the looms to the office. She could imagine the trouble there would be at home when she told her parents about what had transpired. As hard as she thought she could not bring to mind anything she had done wrong. She had worked as hard as usual and was sure her work was up to standard. Nobody had made mention about there being more faults in her cloth than was expected.

With her hand shaking in fear she knocked on the office door and opened it timidly, when a deep voice had beckoned her to enter.

'Oh, Edith, come in and sit over here,' came an unexpectedly gentle voice back to her from the huge intimidating figure sitting there.

Her thoughts started to run riot, this all seemed very strange.

Mr Woodford, as if reading her thoughts by her expression paused a moment before speaking. This was one of the few times he enjoyed when he had something good to impart which took the person by total surprise. 'Now, young lady, we have a vacancy in the burling and mending department. How would you like to move there and be trained?' It was a joy to see the look of worry change to an expression of total disbelief on Edith's face.

Still in a daze at this piece of good luck she stammered, 'Me, move to burling and mending?'

Laughing, the usually sober faced manager studied her puzzled face. 'Have you gone deaf already? That's what I said. Now Edith, make up your mind, times money you know?'

15

'Yes, of course, I'd love to,' Edith said with no more ado; delight in her voice showing her true feelings about what she felt at this opportunity. She realised it must have been her father with being a carrier for the mill that had helped her get moved. Happen he had put a good word in for her. Coming back to reality with a jolt she heard the manager speaking once more. 'You'll start there on Monday next. I've picked a good worker to train you. Her name's Agnes. Aye, she'll take care of you. That's all, best get back to work now. We don't want the loom stood idle too long, now do we?'

'No, Mr. Woodford. Thank you ever so much for the new job.'

'That's all right. Just make sure you work as hard there as you've done in the weaving shed.'

'I will, have no fear on that score.'

Edith felt as if she was walking on air all day.

She knew she was one of the fortunate ones to live near a village that had a mill. Not all folk found it so easy to get to work, many had to travel miles. There were a great number of mills in the West Riding but most were nearer or in the larger towns. Her father's small-holding, where they lived, was outside a small village called Denholme, on the main road to

Keighley. Their house was a bit isolated being away from the village and it could be bleak in winter. Somehow or other she had still to get to work even in the bad weather. At times the snow would be nearly up to her knees, going over her boot tops, even when she walked in the middle of the road. Many of her friends from work lived in the small, grim, mill cottages around the mill and although they were nearer to work than Edith, she was still glad she did not live in one of those. There was barely room to swing a cat around in any of them. Nobody else she knew had a bedroom to themselves at home like she did. Their house, built of stone, stood on its own with some stables at the side. But their privy was still outside like it was with the mill cottages. Much to her relief they did not have to share it with other families. Her mother kept nattering at her father to have a bathroom installed inside, there was room enough. Besides, her mother argued, it would be far more convenient for Elsie. Her father always did the same thing, look up and say, 'Be thankful for what you've got, you're better off than most.' Edith did not agree; it was horrible sat out there in winter with the cold blowing around your private parts.

But her mother would never take an argument any further with her husband. Still,

Edith was thankful that their privy was hidden away so passers by could not see it. Each day as she walked to work she had to pass the row of privies belonging to the mill cottages. How anybody had any privacy there she just did not know.

Now on her way home, after being told she was going to train as a burler and mender, her thoughts were on none of that. The only notion in her mind was to get home as quickly as possible and thank her father for helping her get the promotion. As was her usual habit, she walked through the village with a group of workers, and a loud noise could be heard coming from them as they chattered to each other, glad to be away from the confines of the mill. But slowly one and another parted company as they went to their respective homes. Finally Edith was left to walk the last part of the lonely road on her own. That night the trek home seemed no distance as she dreamt about her new job. No sooner had she opened the door to the house than she shouted, 'Ma, are you there? You'll never guess what's happened?'

One look at her happy face and her mother knew it was not anything bad she was going to impart to her. Laughing back, her mother joked, 'You've been given a better job.'

Edith's face fell at the thought her mother

already knew and she was not going to give her a surprise after all. Seeing this, her mother tried to quickly reassure her as she thought she had caused her to be upset. 'I was only teasing. I didn't really think that had happened. Don't take on so.' Still not sure what to make of it all as she once more saw Edith's face brighten she asked rather impatiently. 'Was I right the first time, have you been promoted?'

'Yes, Ma, I'm to train as a burler and mender,' Edith said proudly.

'Why that's grand, lass, it really is. Just wait until I tell your Pa.'

'I'm sure he'll know already.'

'Oh I don't think so, lass. How can he?' Then a thought struck her. 'Oh, did you see him on your way home then?'

'No, Ma.' She did not want to say any more until she had seen her father as she was fair bursting inside waiting to thank him.

As soon as her father walked in, he took one look at her shining face and became curious. 'What have you been up to then today, lass?'

'I've been given a new job.'

'Have you indeed. Oh aye, doing what?'

'Come on Pa, stop teasing me. You know all about it.'

Taking a serious tone now he peered

intently at her, 'Now why should I?'

'Surely you put a good word in and helped me get it.'

He was getting impatient as his stomach was growling with hunger and he wanted his tea but had more manners than to start eating when speaking. Yet his daughter was making no headway in what she was saying. 'Get what? Talk sense and just finish what you're telling me.'

'I've been moved, well a week on Monday, to the burling and mending department to train there.'

'That's excellent news, lass, it really is. But it's none of my doing. I know they're well pleased with your work. Aye, you've earned your promotion yourself by your own hard efforts.' All thoughts of his hunger were now forgotten at hearing this good news.

'Do you really think so? Aye, that's even better if I have and I'm even more pleased knowing that.' Running out of the kitchen she shouted, 'I'll just go and tell Elsie.'

She heard her mother and father give a gentle laugh after her.

Elsie was just as interested as her parents and asked her lots of questions about the job but Edith only laughed. 'Hey, slow down. How do I know what it'll be like until I start? Not long to wait though, then once I'm doing it I'll tell you all there's to know each night.'

In fact, just as she had hoped she took straight to the job and Agnes, who was a plump, jovial woman that laughed at most things which life threw at her helped her tremendously. This gave her many a tale to recount to Elsie on the dark evenings. Not that the job was any easier than her old one in the weaving sheds but to Edith it was far more enjoyable.

This had all happened before Edward's going away but now she seemed to have no interest in anything including her job. Agnes was quick to comment on her sullen face. But even to Agnes there was no way she could admit the truth why she was so fed up. Agnes got the wrong end of the stick and it took a lot of persuasion from Edith not to ask for her to be transferred back to the weaving shed. 'Don't you like the job here, lass?' Agnes would ask at regular intervals.

Edith would feel a pain of fear in her stomach as she tried to reassure her. 'Of course I do. I think it's far better than weaving, I can tell you. It really is, honest.'

'Not everybody thinks so. I'd a trainee a while ago who hated it; begged and pleaded she did to be put back to the weaving. I've to admit you've picked up the burling quick enough, but the mending, learning the different patterns to cope with takes a while. Still, being in the weaving before helps, at least you know your weft from your warp.'

'Honestly, I love what I'm doing here. It's not the work, it's nothing to do with that, believe me.'

'Got problems at home, have you?' she asked curiously.

'No, all's fine there.' Then realising she could use this as a good excuse for her quietness she quickly added. 'Of course, we all worry about Elsie. She's getting weaker all the time. There's many a day she can't even manage to get out of bed and can only just manage to sit up in the chair. It's so upsetting to see. Here's me full of strength and her younger than me getting weaker and weaker and looking so thin and wan.'

'Aye, I can understand how it worries you, but life goes on you know. It's no good making yourself miserable over it, that won't alter anything. Now we've got that sorted out let's see a more cheerful face on you in future.'

Wanting no more recriminations from Agnes, Edith put a brave face on. But the cutting pain of missing Edward still went on inside her, she just became very good at hiding her true feelings. If only he would write to her, but she knew sometimes that was impossible. All she could do was wait patiently until he sent a message to her when he would be on leave again and they would meet at the usual place.

Sometimes at work, despite everything, she did forget her sadness. It was difficult not to, they were a boisterous lot in the burling and mending and the young and light-hearted part of her normal self surfaced and she joined in with them. At other times the job took a lot of concentration so thoughts of Edward were forgotten. It was at the moments when she was only pulling the material over the table and feeling and checking for faults which was easy for her to do it without much concentration that her mind would move away to other things. It was her hand that needed to do the work then not her mind. There was many a time she regretted not letting Edward have his way with her. At least she would have had that memory to carry with her. Shivers would go through her body as she remembered his arms around her, caressing her body that last time. Still, it might not be long before his next leave as he had been back at the front a length of time, and the next opportunity he begged for her body she would not stop him, whatever the consequences.

With weary steps, despite the banter, she

plodded home through the village and on the final trek of the journey to her home up on Keighley Road. She suddenly remembered her mother had asked her to call in the village shop for some flour.

She knew she had best go back to get it otherwise there would be trouble at home. Besides, her mother would no doubt start questioning her why she had been so forgetful if she did arrive home without it. She hoped the shop was not busy, full of the usual gossips. She would have a long wait if it was and she did not feel like being drawn into their fanciful tales, not that night. The bell above the door tinkled as she entered the shop and she felt relieved to see only the faces of Mrs. Greensmith and Mrs. Wilson. Both turned to see who was entering the shop and seeing it was only Edith carried on with their conversation with Mrs. Hartley, the shop keeper.

Edith did not want to listen in to what they were saying, but it was hard to close her ears totally. When she heard the name Mrs. Mitchell her ears pricked up and she became alert to their gossip. She thought maybe it was Edward's mother they were talking about. Happen she had received some good news that he was coming home soon.

Trying to listen intently, so she caught

every word that was said, yet not wanting to look as if she were being nosy, she turned to the shelf nearest her and appeared to be studying the food items there. She heard Mrs. Greensmith give an exclamation. 'Aye, poor Mrs. Mitchell, she received the telegram 'missing presumed dead'.'

Now Edith was silently pleading with them to get on with the story because she had to know they did not mean her Edward. She heard Mrs. Greensmith interrupt in her grating voice, 'He was her only son wasn't he?'

Mrs. Hartley, in her usual tone of knowing about most things, took it upon herself to answer. 'Aye, Edward was her only surviving child. She'd had seven others you know but none of them had lived past infancy. Now he's presumed dead. Oh! Poor woman, what will she do now? My heart goes out to her.'

Edith could not bear to hear more of what they were saying. Her Edward dead, impossible! She rushed out of the shop with a loud jangling of the bell and the three women stared after her open mouthed in amazement.

Mrs. Hartley recovered herself first. 'You'd have thought she'd have got used to hearing about death by now. Plenty of our young lads have already been killed. It isn't as if she knew him or anything.'

Mrs. Wilson added in bewilderment herself at the behaviour of the usually quiet and pleasant young lady, 'Aye, there's some funny lasses around these days, not like when we were young. Can't cope with death they can't. Been brought up too soft I reckon.'

Edith did not know which way to turn. She let her feet take her along the way they wanted to go. She ended up at the old, dirty barn where they had last met. Coming to her senses she quickly checked that nobody was around. Satisfied she was alone, she sank down onto the bales of straw and sobbed her heart out. It could not be true, it really could not. She loved him so, besides which, he had promised to come home to her. He would never let her down. How she wished she had given in to him. If she had, now she would have something more to remember him by. Quickly her mind changed track, remember him by, what was she thinking about? He would be sure to turn up soon, after all it only said presumed dead. Then again maybe it was not her Edward at all. This started to quell her fears, she felt more cheered and whatever she felt she would have to go home with a smile on her face. It would never do to let her mother see her like this. Besides there would be ructions because now she would not only arrive home late but without the flour her mother needed.

Picking herself up and dusting the straw off she realised it was time to make tracks home. As it was she had best think of a good excuse for not getting the flour and being so late.

As soon as she opened the door the expected words of reprimand came to her, 'And where do you think you've been until this time, young lady? I hope you remembered to get me my flour.'

Thinking up her excuse had at least taken her mind off the problem, so her sombre expression was not instantly noticeable to her mother. 'Agnes kept me talking at work, explaining how to mend a design I haven't seen before. Sorry, Ma, I was in such a rush to get home as I knew I was late, I forgot all about your flour.'

Her mother looked intently at her. 'Oh aye, pigs would fly if they had wings.'

'It's true, Ma, honest.'

'I'll say no more on the subject then. Just go and get your hands washed ready for your tea.'

Once she had moved out of the room and her mother's hearing she let out a sigh of relief that she had got off so easily. Now if only she could dispel her other worries as easily.

Little did she know her mother was busy finishing tea off with her own thoughts on the subject. She mumbled softly, 'Young madam. Who does she think she is telling me a tale like that? She's in for a surprise when I catch her out at what she's up to. She'll fair cop it from me.'

Edith felt even more frustrated by the fact she did not know how to get to the bottom of what she had heard. Who could she ask if it was really true and get more details about the situation? She could not go to his mother, when in all probability she did not even know Edith existed. It seemed as if it was going to be a case of keeping her ears open and gleaning any information from anybody at all who knew the family. None of this did anything to improve her recent moodiness.

Agnes complained. 'By, young miss, I thought you were bad enough before, but now you're like a bear with a sore head, that's for sure. What on earth is the matter with you girl? I told you before I can soon ask for you to be transferred back to the weaving shed if you'd prefer that.'

'Sorry, Agnes, it's nothing like that. I've told you often enough I love this job. It's far better than working in the weaving.'

Agnes just looked at her and gave an indignant, 'H'm you'd never believe it.' Being of a nosy nature Agnes still wanted to get to the bottom of it so she asked, 'What is it then, some fellow?'

Trying to hide her embarrassment, at Agnes being so near the truth, she gave a little giggle, 'Of course not, when would I have chance to meet a young man? No, I've already told you before it's just worry about my sister. She's getting worse you know?'

'Well, young lady, we all have our problems but we certainly don't bring them to work and behave like this with other people. We never know where we are with you, we don't. One minute as cheerful as can be, then next an old sore bones if I ever knew one. It's time you grew up and learnt how to control your feelings a bit more.'

With this Agnes looked over the top of her table to another work colleague, 'I'd better give her some lessons on cheerfulness, don't you think Lillian?'

Edith spoke quickly trying to stop any more being said on the subject. 'All right, all right I take the hint. I promise I'll be more cheerful from now on.'

Edith heard a few rather irate voices say all at the same time, 'Just see you do.' Now she knew she was well and truly in the dog house for grumpiness.

3

Edith understood that life had to go on and there were people in a far worse position than her. Young wives and mothers had been widowed and left to bring their children up on their own. In that sense she knew whatever had happened to Edward, at least she had not been left with a child in tow and the shame of being unmarried, which would have been too much to bear. But on the other hand she bitterly regretted their last time together. Edward had so much wanted to love her properly, yet she had stopped him. Now she had not even that memory to carry with her. If she had let him have his way when she sobbed quietly into her pillow in her despair, at night alone in her bed, she could have remembered those treasured moments. As it was she could only imagine what it would have been like to have been coupled with him and she knew that was not the same thing at all.

As Agnes had told her to do, she put her full attention into her work. It did take her mind off the other thoughts. She had not lied when she had told Agnes she was worried about her sister, Elsie. She did indeed seem to be getting weaker and weaker by the day and nobody seemed to have an explanation for it. Now this frail young body of hers, even on her good days, would not let her get out of bed. This was no way for a young woman to be spending her time. She knew it worried her mother and father, but whatever the doctor did it seemed to make little difference. Edith could see she was fading away before their very eyes.

Understanding some of what her sister was going through, she tried to spend more of her free time with her in order to give her companionship. But this did not stop Edith fretting to know more about Edward and it amazed her that once she kept her ears open to his name, how often she heard it mentioned. It seemed she had been right in assuming it was him they had been talking about in the shop. All sorts of rumours were going around that he was actually dead, then only presumed dead or that he was a prisoner of war. All this frustrated Edith because she could not get to the bottom of what had really happened to him. The only way was to go and see his mother but she had not the courage. To try to find some answers, which she so desperately needed within herself, whenever possible she visited the old barn.

She could not believe it was a year ago that they had last had the joy of holding each other.

Yet as she shut her eyes and tried to picture Edward, his image would not come. She shed many a bitter tear in frustration at this. She so wanted to remember him. He was so attractive and those arms when he held her had so much love and strength. But life often had a particular twist of fate and other events happened to Edith that suddenly took her mind off these thoughts.

It was one of the nights she ended up being late home again. She had spent too much time in the barn dwelling on her thoughts and memories. As soon as she opened the house door an unusual silence greeted her. She expected her mother to appear from nowhere to chastise her. But it did not happen. Then she heard a small break in the silence. Walking into the kitchen she could not believe her eyes when she saw her mother sat at the table, with head bent, sobbing.

Edith quickly rushed over to her expecting the worst, 'Ma, what's the matter? Has Pa had an accident?'

'No, it's Elsie.'

'Elsie! What do you mean?'

'I'm sorry, lass. She passed away quietly this afternoon.'

Edith screamed in anguish, 'No! Not Elsie, she can't have gone. There must be some mistake. Let me see her Ma, please.'

'You will in time, but there's no mistake, she's dead. Think on it this way, lass, at least now she's at peace and free from pain. These last few months have been hard on her.'

'Oh Ma, how I wish I'd not been so selfish in not spending more time with her. I knew she was getting weaker but I never expected this.' She let out a loud heartbreaking sob.

'Come on, lass, don't take on so. We all wish we'd done more when a loved one dies. I'm afraid I could see it coming but I didn't want to upset you any more than I need.'

Edith had never had to cope with the death of a close relative before. This was far worse than thinking about the possibility that Edward was dead. She had no actual proof about him but she knew, without a shadow of doubt, Elsie was no longer there. Hadn't she looked in the coffin and seen the waxen, cold body of her sister? Her mother was right in saying she was at peace. She had seen that look on her face. Yet in another way it did not even really look like her sister. Gently Edith had touched her to make sure she was really dead. As soon as she felt the icy coldness she knew it was true. Tears poured down her cheeks and she could not stop talking to her as if she could still hear. She told her the things she had always meant to but somehow or other had never the chance of doing so. Now it was too late.

She had learnt a hard lesson, not to put off things that you meant to do with the living. You never knew when people would die, young or old. It really sank into her what a thin thread it was that holds everybody between life and death. Yet here she was grieving so, as if she was the only person to feel this sadness. Now, for the first time, she truly appreciated what all the mothers, girlfriends and wives must be feeling for their men killed in this endless futile war.

Edith thought her heart would break when she saw the coffin lowered into the ground. There was a nice little graveyard by the Methodist Chapel they attended. Pleasant it might be but not for such a young girl to be put into the ground. Edith genuinely had a double reason to look so unhappy and sad. Since they all now knew at work about Elsie's death nobody questioned her sadness which she showed at times. Yet at other times her only way to deal with it was to snap at everybody in sight.

How hard she tried she could not get it from her mind that Edward must still be somewhere alive. But she had no way of proving it. All she could do was wait until he came home or so she thought.

For once she did as her mother had bid her and remembered to call in the village shop on her way home from work. Mrs. Hartley was just saying to her, 'Aye lass, I was right sorry to hear about Elsie. She was such a bonny girl when I last saw her. It's hard to believe she was as healthy as you until she caught that there rheumatic fever.' With this she turned to get the small order Edith had given her.

Edith jumped with a start as she felt a soft tap on her arm. 'Are you Sarah Ramsbottom's, that was, daughter?'

Edith turned to see a small gaunt woman stood at her side and starring at her. She had to think before she could answer, as it seemed funny to hear her mother referred to like this. 'Er, yes I suppose I am.'

'I used to know your Ma many years back in the mill. Did I hear you right that your sister, Elsie, has died?'

'Yes, we buried her last week.'

'Tell her Molly Mitchell sends her kind regards.'

Now Edith was really interested. Could this be his mother, Mrs. Mitchell? Taking the bull by the horns she plunged in, 'Haven't you recently lost your son, Edward?'

'Aye I have. But how do you know?'

Now at a loss for words Edith stammered, 'Oh I just heard the gossip. You know how it is in this village.'

'Too right, you've no need to tell me about gossip. Of course they haven't found his body as yet. He's only presumed dead. But I've heard nowt all this time. It must be true he's dead,' she said sadly.

'Oh don't say that, I'm sure there's always hope.'

Realising Mrs. Mitchell was giving her a strange look she quickly added, 'I'm sorry about your loss, I really am. I know what it's like with having just lost our Elsie.'

'Thanks, lass, that's most kind of you.'

She had really meant a lot more than she had actually said in words. Her sadness was not only for her sister, but for Edward as well. Even if she could not show it, at least under the guise of mourning for Elsie, she could also mourn for Edward.

So life went on in a humdrum fashion for Edith with nothing exciting happening to her personally. Then on 11am on the 11th day of the eleventh month the war ceased and there was an armistice bringing an end to the killings. This was the only time she felt any great pleasure that the war was actually at an end and there was rejoicing in the street. Now life could really start for her again once everybody was safely back home, or at least this was what she imagined it would be like. But the young men did not seem to suddenly appear back home as she had expected and her sadness would not go away. Then as usual, one Sunday morning Edith with her father and mother were all at chapel and it was going to be the local minister who was to take the service. Reverend Grindley was walking through the graveyard as Edith and her mother were tending Elsie's grave with her father standing by patiently waiting. 'Grand morning today, Reverend,' said Edith's father as he came by.

'Aye, a good morning to you all, tha's no doubt about it, which is for those of us who are still here,' replied the Reverend and continued to walk by and into the chapel.

'Well, Pa, did you see his face? It looks so gaunt.'

'Aye, I did, lass. It looks to me that he's been on a journey.'

'Wherever to, Pa?' Edith queried puzzled.

'Why no place in particular but maybe only in his head,' her father answered.

The service started with the usual hymns and prayer. Then it was time for Reverend Grindley's sermon and everyone was expectant of Hell and Damnation. But as he stood to speak a stillness settled over the chapel as never before. 'Well, on first sight it right gladdens my heart to see so many of you here today. Then I look around and there are so many we will never see again. Where are the choir lads? Some still to come home but not Eddy Wilkinson, Lesley Sewell or Barry Scales. Where are my two boys Malcolm and John? Where is that little scamp Barry Green? Why, it doesn't seem like two minutes ago I had to chastise him at Sunday School for throwing his prayer book at Lizzie Thomas, and so many more young and old, sons, fathers, brothers, cousins and friends. They will never sit with us in chapel again. They all sleep forever in Belgium or France. So if we could bottle all the sorrow of friend and foe here and all over Europe I think we would be overflowing with sadness for generations to come. It's the only commodity not in short supply. We must never forget them and above all we must never let it happen again.'

On the way home Edith's mother inquired of her father, 'What did you think of that sermon?'

'I just thank God we had no lads, Ma. It's bad enough our Elsie going.'

These words shocked Edith rigid as her father had grumbled so often in the past about her not being a lad. Now here he was saying he was glad she was not one.

38

After this, time passed in the same old way and once in a while Edith still needed to hide away with her own thoughts to try to put her grief to rest. Her last meeting place, with Edward, at the quiet barn gave her a sense of peace. But today that therapy was lacking and the loss of him seemed even more overpowering. Maybe with the war at an end there had been hope of hearing from Edward but there had been nothing, not a word and with this she had realised the full implication of the loss of both Edward and Elsie. Whatever the reason, the tears came fast and furious and she cried as if her heart would break.

Then she nearly did die, but not of grief, but fright as she felt a gentle tap on her arm and a male voice say in her ear, 'Are you all right, miss?'

She was so shocked her voice came out far more sharply than she intended, 'Do I look as if I am?'

'No, sorry but I wondered if there was anything I could do?'

'Now what on earth do you think you could do for me? Anyway, what are you doing here?' she asked abruptly as if it was her own private place and he had no right to visit the area.

'I'm on my way home from work. I usually walk home this way and I heard you sobbing.'

'Well it's kind of you to try to help me then, but I'm all right now.' With this she looked at him properly for the first time and gave a watery smile. Now her heart did a small flip when she realised what an attractive young man she was talking to and she wished she had spoken less harshly.

Suddenly she did not want to go but prolong her time with him. 'You say you were on your way home, where do you live then if you come this way?'

'Denholme Gate, do you know it?'

'Aye, I've an Uncle and Aunt who live at Denholme Clough, that's not so far away from there.'

'Do you live that way yourself?'

'No, I live the other side of the village.' Edith stopped abruptly as she felt she might have said too much about herself.

'Come up here often do you?'

'No, not really as I haven't always the opportunity. I'm not always like this you know.' Then to cover up her embarrassment she quickly added, 'My sister died a while back. Every so often it comes back to haunt me bad like, what's happened.'

'I'm sorry, I know what it's like to loose a close one. My brother died in the trenches.'

She gave him another watery smile. 'I'd best get home now. My Ma doesn't like me being too late in. Since Elsie died she's become even more protective.'

'Aye, I know just what you mean. Might you be up this way again when I pass by?'

'Happen so, you never know. I could well be. I like coming up here. Somehow after all the noise at work it feels so peaceful.' Laughing now she added, 'I don't always cry you know when I come here. But usually I do feel an inner calm and go home feeling a lot happier for that.'

'I know just what you mean. I like walking home this way because it happens to me too. By the time I reach home I feel as if all the stress and worries of work have dropped off me. Anyway, I'll watch out for you again when I come past.'

'Aye do that, I'm sure I'll be here again soon.' Suddenly she felt rather foolish hoping she had not been too forward at this first meeting.

With this they parted and went their separate ways but Edith walked home on feet that felt as if they had wings and barely touched the ground. There was no doubt she would be back there soon looking out for him. This seemed as if it was her day after all.

Her mother seeing her unusually happy face as soon as she walked in the door exclaimed, 'Well you look like the cat that's got the cream. Why's that?'

What had just happened to her was too new and fresh to tell her mother. Besides, she wanted to see if he was really serious about seeing her again. She was old enough to have a young man and as soon as they were walking out she would tell her parents. That would be soon enough.

'Oh, I don't know why I feel happy. Maybe it's because it feels a good day. You know how it is sometimes.'

Looking keenly at her daughter she answered, 'Aye, I do,' but she was already thinking, 'There's a lad involved somewhere here, to be sure.' Deciding it was best to leave the matter for the present she just asked, 'A good day at work was it? I take it the supervisor was in good humour today.'

Relieved that her mother thought this the reason for her cheerfulness, she was more than willing to keep the pretence up. 'Aye, she was today. You're right it makes life easier when you're on the right side of them.'

The minute she was out of the room her mother started to think and quietly muttered, 'I hope whoever he is he's a good man and he'll do no wrong to Edith. She's a good lass but I'm sure she lost a young man before in that wretched war. Not that she ever said a word to me but I saw it there in her eyes. Aye, she deserves a nice kindly lad and one who'll not be tempted by the sins of the flesh before they're wed.' She had lost one child to God, now she wanted her other child to be happy. She muttered a silent prayer to the Lord asking him to look after her and deliver her from all evil. Having done this she felt better in her mind. That was all she could do for her. She believed God would take care of her. Yet she could not stop doubt creeping into her heart here, when she thought about God taking her other young daughter. Not a kinder, gentler person was there than their Elsie had been. It came to mind what her own mother had always said to her on the death of a young one, 'God needs young folk as well as the old ones you know.' Reflecting on this she decided, how funny but it did seem to be the really kind ones who were taken away from them so young. Giving one last shrug she mumbled again, 'Aye, life's strange, you'd think it would be the bad ones who are taken first.' She gave a great sigh as much as to say, 'That's how it is.'

Each day took on a new meaning for Edith. She felt really alive again inside, as if there was a point in going on living. At times she wondered if this was a bit disrespectful to Edward, but still never a word had she heard properly about what had happened to him.

The only gossip she had heard was that his mother had moved away to live with her sister. So there seemed as if there was no chance of ever meeting up again with her to find out the truth of what had happened to him. No, she had faced reality, Edward belonged to the past. That chapter of her life was closed, now it was time to move forward with her own life. She wanted to as she felt ready now to move on with the next stage of it.

Her newfound happiness brought a few comments at work, 'Aye, whatever are you looking so pleased about. Met a young man have you?'

Not really sure if he were going to be her fella or not she was quick to reply, 'Course not, who'd I meet around here. It must be spring fever that's got into me.'

'A likely story, pull the other one. It'll be some bloke I'll be bound.'

Edith smiled to herself; let them think what they wanted. Maybe soon enough it would be true.

4

Edith now had a special reason to get to that decrepit old barn. It was with eager anticipation she visited it each time, only to come away disappointed. Then slowly her happiness started to evaporate as she began to think she was not going to see him again. Suddenly, when she least expected it, he was there. As she was moving away from the barn, with her head dropped down and feeling sorry for herself, she heard the longed for voice call to her. At first she thought it was her imagination working overtime.

'Hello there. I thought I was never going to manage to get here at the same time as you again. We've been so busy at work that it's made me late leaving most evenings.'

'Oh right! That's good if you've plenty of work. You must be luckier than most,' replied Edith at a loss what else to say to him.

'Aye, you're right there. Do you know after I'd left you I realised I'd never even asked your name?'

'I know, I thought the same thing. My name's Edith, what's yours then?'

'Alfred, bit of a daft name I think, but there

you are. It's what your parents land you with.'

'No, I like it. Do your friends call you Alfie?'

'No, it's strange but they all seem to stick to Alfred. Don't know why. Have you been up here often since I last saw you?'

Being a bit evasive because it would not do to appear too eager, she replied vaguely. 'Not really, I've been a bit busy doing jobs for my Ma and Pa.'

'That's good because I didn't like to think of you coming up here and waiting then I didn't come past.' Not sounding quite as confident and looking slightly embarrassed he carried on, 'It's good you've work to do for your Ma and Pa to keep you occupied.'

'Well, yes I'm used to working.' Then untruthfully she added, 'No, I've not been up here waiting, it's my first visit since last we met.'

'Good, good.' Here he seemed lost for words so Edith decided the only course of action open to her was to make a move. 'I'd better be on my way home now I've seen you.'

'Yes, all right.'

Her heart plummeted as he made no objection so she thought this was the end of all her eager anticipation. Then, much to her delight, as she turned to move away he quickly asked, 'Look, on Sunday there's a brass band playing in Foster Park. Would you like to come with me to listen to them?'

This was it then the date she had been waiting for. 'Aye, that would be right grand.'

'Shall I meet you at the main gate to the park at 2 o'clock?'

'Yes, but if I'm a few minutes late wait for me won't you? My Ma always wants me to help her clear up after Sunday dinner. Sometimes we're a bit later than other Sundays. It all depends what time we get away from chapel.'

Now looking at her eagerly he reassured her, 'Don't worry, I'll be there what ever time you arrive.'

Not quite sure how to say goodbye to him Edith turned hesitantly away, 'See you then.'

'Yes, goodbye, take care.'

Edith walked away feeling slightly dispirited that he had not at least given her a peck on her cheek but then she supposed that would have been a bit forward on his part. How she wished it was Sunday already, but at least there were only three days to wait until she saw him again. She was pleased that this time she had a proper date with him, no more wondering if they would unexpectedly bump into each other. But then her mind started pondering what to do about her mother and father. Should she tell them she was going to see him on Sunday? There again what if they stopped her going, because it was always a possibility with her father being so strict? She thought with regret that if only she had Elsie to talk to about it all, they could have talked it through and maybe come up with the best solution. But what if she told her mother only? But then she realised her mother would not keep it from her father as they had no secrets from each other and he would want to know where she had met him. Oh! It was so difficult to know what to do for the best. Aye, it may be safer to meet him this Sunday without telling them but instead say she was going to the park with one of her friends. She gave a little laugh to herself; well after all he was one of her friends. She could, at a later date, tell her mother she had met him in the park and he had asked her to walk out with him. Then she realised she might not have to say all this, after all, it would only be if he did want to meet her again after Sunday. She did not know whether he would be as keen once they'd had a chance to talk a bit more and get to know each other. Oh what a dilemma! Well she would have to wait and see but at least the problem about her mother and father was solved in her own mind.

She was glad Sunday dawned a lovely

bright, sunny day. She found it nearly impossible to keep her excitement subdued whilst they were at chapel. It seemed a never ending service just when she wished for a short one. Yet what it was about Edith had not a clue, as her mind thought about the rest of the day during the whole of it, in eager anticipation.

Her mother gave her a curious look when she saw her dressed in her best bright clothes, 'Anybody would think you're meeting a young man. Or is it just you and your friend parading yourselves in the hope of meeting one?'

Edith was in such good humour and thought it would do no harm in getting her mother slightly prepared, so she looked at her with a cheeky grin, 'You never know who you'll meet, now do you? After all, I bet you met Pa when you were least expecting it? Doesn't do any harm it seems to me, to be dressed ready just in case there's someone around who takes your fancy. It's about time there was.'

Memories were quickly brought back to her mother and she looked at her ruefully and said in a slightly sad voice, 'I know, you're at an age now when you want to meet that some one special. The war has taken so many from us. Aye, you do right. You go and have a good time and maybe you'll chat to me when you come back and tell me how you went on.' She gave a big sigh, adding with regret, 'I do wish I was young again.'

Edith felt guilty that she had not told her the full truth now as she had so understood her feelings. Still, the opportunity had gone and it was too late. She had best be on her way otherwise she would be late. Grabbing her bag and rushing to the door she called over her shoulder, 'Bye Ma, see you later.'

'Aye, have a good time but don't be late for tea. You know your Pa doesn't like his routine to be disrupted on a Sabbath.'

'I won't, don't worry,' Edith reassured her.

Her feet fair skipped along as she rushed to meet him. All her thoughts of behaving in a dignified manner were forgotten in her impatience to be there on time. Her main fear was that he would not be there. Maybe he had not really meant it. She had no need to have thought like that because as soon as she turned the corner and saw the large wrought iron gateway in the distance, she could not miss his eager face peering around looking out for her.

She gave a quick wave as he glanced towards her. He saw this and rushed forward to meet her. As soon as he was at her side he

50

asked, 'The service wasn't too long at chapel today, was it?'

'I don't know about that, it seemed never ending to me.'

'I just thought you'd made good time and wern't late after all. But forget that now, let's go and have an enjoyable afternoon, shall we?'

'Aye, that'd be grand.'

'Come on then, I think the band's due to start at any minute.'

Edith was not really sure if she wanted to listen to the music. She would much rather get to know Alfred a lot better but if that was what he wanted to do then so be it.

He was right in his assumption that the band was due to start. By the time they had reached the newly painted band stand there was already a large crowd forming. Not being that tall Edith could not see much of the bandsmen, although she decided it did not really matter that much as she would still be able to hear them. They played well enough, she had to admit, but she kept stealing a glance at Alfred, as if by looking she could find more out about him. As she peered once again his glance met hers and he quickly asked, 'Have you had enough of this? Do you want to go to a quiet area of the park then we could have a chat?'

'Aye, I'd like that. Don't think I haven't enjoyed the music, I have, but I'm ready to have a sit down now.'

'That's fine by me. Let's go over to that far side in the shade of the trees.'

Once they were seated, on the only available bench, he turned and gently took hold of her hand. 'Come on then, tell me a little bit about yourself and your family.'

'There's not a lot to tell really. I think you know most of it already. As you know I live with my Ma and Pa. I work as a burler and mender at Atkinson's Mill. My Pa is the local carrier for the mills. He goes all over the place doing his job.'

'Aye, I think I've probably seen him with his horse and cart.'

'That's more than likely.' Here Edith had to give a cynical laugh. 'He always wished I was a lad, you know, to carry on the business. He likes me to help with his horses. We've got a smallholding behind the house where he keeps some pigs and hens. Mind, he likes me to help with them as well. We're Methodist as you've probably gathered seeing we went to Chapel this morning. He's very strict about that, allows no drink in the house. Other than that I don't think there's a lot to tell because I've already told you about Elsie. Now then what have you to say about you and your family?'

'I work in a factory but at Morgan's foundry, not textiles but engineering. I've got a bit bigger family than yours. My eldest sister, Annie, is married to Harry and they live in one of those quaint cottages in the row at Denholme Clough. Didn't you say you had an aunt who lived there?'

'Aye, that's right my aunt Hilda lives there, but we don't see her often. Mind, there are a few young couples in the row so I'm not sure if I'll have seen your sister or not. I might have done.'

'Never mind, I'll take you to visit her sometime.'

Edith's heart gave a small leap for joy as it seemed that she was going to see more of him.

'Harry's got a smallholding at the back, he keeps a few hens. He works in the mill as a weaver but he's at Whitaker's Mill. Funnily enough Annie's a burler and mender but she's at Whitaker's as well so I don't suppose you know either of them through work. But at least you'll have something in common when you meet. I've also a younger brother, William, who's a real handful. He's still at school but he'll be leaving soon. Goodness knows what Ma and Pa will do with him then. My Pa's an upholsterer. That's about it for me.'

More subdued Edith asked, 'Haven't you forgotten somebody who used to be part of your family?'

'Oh! Of course there was Freddie. I know I did mention him before and that he'd died in the trenches. He was ever such a kind and gentle chap. You'd have liked him, everybody did.' Edith could hear the hint of sadness in his voice as he said this.

Looking rather rueful Edith spoke softly, 'I wish I came from a bigger family, or at least did have a brother then Pa wouldn't treat me as a lad. I miss Elsie so much for our chats.' Then brightening she added, 'Any roads I think I'd best be going now, I promised Ma I wouldn't be late in for tea.'

'Did she mind you coming out this afternoon with me?'

Feeling ashamed now that she had not told her mother about meeting him she stammered, 'Well, I wasn't sure if I'd be seeing you again so I didn't really say anything about us meeting.'

Seeing she was embarrassed he tried to put her at ease, 'Will you walk out with me steady? It'd please me very much if you would.'

'Oh, I'd like that,' she replied with small

butterflies of delight going through her body.

'How about going to Keighley Picture House next Saturday evening?'

'Aye, that'd be grand. I like the cinema but don't often have chance to go or anybody to go with.' The purpose built cinema had first opened its doors in 1913 so her mother and father had taken the two girls at that time. But since Elsie's death Edith had not been nor had her parents offered to go with her.

'Have I to meet you at the bus stop, by the Sunday School, for the five thirty bus to Keighley? That should get us there on time,' Alfred suggested.

'That'd suit me fine, I'll be there.'

'Come on then, if you've to get home I'll walk you part of the way there,' he said considerately aware she did not want her family to see her with him yet.

Edith knew she looked like the cat that had got the cream and there would be no way she would be able to keep it from her mother about Alfred. Opening the heavy back door she shouted, 'I'm home, Ma.'

'Had a good afternoon, love?' her mother's voice called back.

Here was her opening being handed to her on a plate, 'Yes, Ma. Actually I met a nice young man.'

Sarah looked keenly at her daughter as she

replied, 'Oh yes! What's his name then?'

'Alfred.'

'Alfred what?'

'Alfred Taylor.'

'Um, I don't think I've heard of an Alfred Taylor. Where does he live?'

'At Denholme Gate, he's a foundry man at Morgan's.'

'I knew it. You've not just met him today, have you?'

Looking as if butter would not melt in her mouth Edith asked, 'What do you mean, Ma?'

'I've seen that look in your eyes for the last few weeks.'

Now looking rather shamefaced Edith admitted, 'Well, today was the first time we met proper like. He took me to listen to the band in Foster Park. There's nothing wrong with that which could cause you and Pa to object.'

'Yes, well, I suppose, as you say your Pa can't disapprove of that. At least there'd be plenty of folk around to make sure it was proper like. But you still should have told us.'

'I'm sorry, Ma. I wanted to, but I wasn't sure if he was serious and would really turn up.'

Studying her daughter Sarah began to wonder what this chap was really like and felt the need to ask, 'Why should you think he wouldn't turn up? Any respectful man would keep his promise if he'd made a date.'

'No, Ma, you've got it all wrong what I'm saying. I didn't mean he wouldn't come; it was just silly doubts inside me. I knew he would really 'cause he's ever so kind and nice.'

'I suppose he's asked you to walk out with him steady?'

'Yes, he's taking me to The Picture House in Keighley next Saturday. That's all right with you isn't it?'

'Well if you've gone ahead and organised it, it'll have to be. But I think your Pa will want to see him for himself if you're going to meet him on a regular basis. We'd better sort something out, then when you see him next Saturday you can invite him here.'

She now panicked in case this would put him off, having to see her parents so soon in their relationship but she dare not admit this to her mother so she tried to sound as if it was just what she wanted. 'Yes Ma, thanks. That'll be great and I just know you'll like him.'

Sarah gave a sniff, 'We'll see won't we? Time will tell.'

As soon as Edith arrived at work the next day Agnes noticed the change in her and was quick to query. 'Well, lass, and what have you been up to this week-end?'

Edith was so full of herself she burst out, 'Oh Agnes! I've met a young man who wants to walk out with me.'

'Have you indeed! I must say he certainly seems to have done something special for you. There's a glow about you that I haven't seen for a while now. What's his name then?'

'Alfred.'

'H'm and where is he taking you for this first date?'

'We've already been out this Sunday to Foster Park to listen to the band. He's taking me to the picture house at Keighley next Saturday.' Then suddenly realising what she had not asked him, she put her hand to her mouth and exclaimed, 'I never thought to ask what we were going to see.'

Agnes laughed. 'I wouldn't worry too much about that. If I know owt you'll probably spend more time sneaking a look at him than the film. Anyway it's 'A Dog's Life' that is on at the moment.'

'What is?'

'The film that's on at the cinema next week, it's Charlie Chaplin in 'A Dog's Life'.

'Oh that sounds great! I like Charlie Chaplin, it should be good. But then as you

58

say I probably will be looking at Alfred most of the time.'

Trying to look serious Agnes frowned at her, 'Well enough of this frivolity, time to get on with some work.'

Edith was not sure how she worked through the rest of the week's toil, many a time instead of seeing the material in front of her she saw Alfred's cheerful and pleasant face. She felt relieved that there was no telling off forthcoming for poor work, so she could only presume that more by luck than management she had done her job to satisfaction. All the while she kept planning what to wear and wished now she'd had the foresight to make herself a new dress on the long evenings she had spent at home. Then, at least, she would have looked really smart. She did the best she could in the time available by buying a new collar for her best red, floral dress but decided, after all, she was being silly because it was herself he liked her for, not just what she was wearing. She would look as smart as anybody else. There just was not the money around to throw it around on clothing.

5

It was not a minute too soon when the day she was so longing for arrived. She was sure she would burst with excitement. Her mother had broken the news to her father that Edith was meeting a young man. To their surprise he had not said much at all about it, but at least he had not put any opposition in her way. As she got ready, her mother fussed over her making sure she looked well presented in her recently altered dress. Just as she was going out her father came in the door from work. Looking Edith up and down he grudgingly said, 'You look nice, but remember you're a well brought up young lady. I want no disgrace brought on this family.'

'I know, Pa, I'm not stupid.' She felt disappointed that he could not just for once have said that she looked nice without going on to chastise her.

Quickly her mother jumped in before an argument erupted between the two of them. 'Well off you go then, you don't want to be late otherwise you'll miss the bus.'

Still her father had to have the last word. 'Don't you forget what time the last bus home leaves Keighley. Make sure you're on it, other wise the door will be locked.'

'Of course I'll be on it, Pa. See you both later.'

Feeling relieved that she had escaped out of the house and away from the tension without too much of a fuss she rushed off to the bus stop. Only then did the neurotic doubts begin to flood in again about him being there. She should have known better. As she turned the corner she could see his distinctive stature stood in the front of the queue. Putting his hand up briefly, he gave a gentle wave to acknowledge he had seen her. Quickly, with excited steps, she moved forward to join him.

Soon they were sat together on the rattling, old and draughty bus, but none of this was noticed by the pair of them, as Edith looked at Alfred with adoration. She had no need to hide him away now; her mother and father knew she was meeting him. Despite her happiness a slight touch of sadness crept in that nobody had seen her out with Edward like this. Even though the years had gone by since his death, at times she still grieved for him. Coming out of her thoughts she felt Alfred take her small hand in his large, rough one, which by now she had realised, was not dirty as it looked, simply the oil from his job was embedded in them.

Turning towards him she gave a shy smile, 'Ma says she'd like you to come to tea next Saturday, so she and Pa can meet you.' Hoping she was not being too forward by inviting him home so soon, she felt the need to ask him, 'I hope you don't mind that I've told them all about us going out?'

'Of course not, that's fine by me. In any case I'd like to meet them.' Laughing he added, 'Don't worry, I'll be on my best behaviour.'

The evening turned out far better than Edith had dared hoped. She felt there was an instant affinity with him which made it feel as if they had already spent a lot longer than a few hours in each other's company. He was likable enough, if only she could stop the picture of Edward invading her mind. She knew she had to, that part of her life was over. His death had seen to that, yet at times she felt his presence very strongly as if he was close by calling her name.

She gave a slight jump as she heard a soft voice in her ear, 'You're not bored with the film are you? If you are we can leave and go for a walk before we get the bus back.'

'No. Why do you think that?'

'I dunno, but you seemed to be miles away, not seeing the screen at all.'

Edith heard a loud 'Shh' come from behind

them. Turning towards Alfred she gave a big grin and he put his finger on his lips mocking the person who had told them to be quiet. This small act seemed to bring them even closer together, and she gave him a big smile showing her understanding.

★   ★   ★

Just as she hoped would happen, her parents on their first meeting took to Alfred straight away. His manners were impeccable and could not be faulted. He chatted away constantly to her parents, without any inhibitions, thus making an excellent time for all. This broke down the final barrier with them and they had no objection to him formally walking out with Edith.

Neither Alfred nor Edith had much money to spare but their Saturday night treat was to visit the picture house at Keighley, known locally as the flea pit. Edith loved to see the films and as long as she was happy then Alfred was satisfied. Her father also allowed her to meet Alfred one night during the week and on Sunday afternoons. Other times he wanted her help in tending the horses when he had returned from his rounds. Being summer and the evenings warm, Edith and Alfred usually went for a walk when they met on a Wednesday evening. For some reason their footsteps seemed to lead them to the barn where they had first met. It did not take Edith long to realise that Alfred was a very passionate young man. She willingly joined in his kisses and caresses, but it did not take him many outings before he was trying to take things further. When he unbuttoned her blouse and put his hand on her breast, despite knowing it was wrong, she had not the will power to stop him as she felt tremors of fire go through her. Suddenly it was not Alfred with her but Edward. She moaned softly as his rough hand roamed more and more over her body. She came back to reality with a start as she felt him pull himself away from her and she heard his words of agony, 'I'm sorry, Edith, I was getting carried away. I meant you no harm.'

Not wanting to appear as if she was free and easy, yet not wanting to offend him, she was at a loss what to say. Besides which, the sensual part of her was deriving great enjoyment. Reality taking over she turned and gave him a gentle kiss on his lips. But instead of the desired effect, it ignited the flame in him again and before she knew where she was he was pushing her back on the ground and gently rolling on top of her. This time Edith's panic quickly took over and abruptly she gave him a push and with a hysterical laugh in her voice she bellowed in his ear, 'Stop that this minute. I'm a well brought up lass.'

Looking really shamefaced now, Alfred turned to her, 'I can't help myself, you just feel and smell so good. I do love you Edith.'

Looking at him in amazement she managed to stammer, 'What did you say?'

The full impact of what he had said hit Alfred, then looking at her gently with love shining in his eyes he said it again. 'I love you, Edith.'

So taken aback by what he had just realised, Alfred did not notice the slight hesitation in Edith's voice as she replied to him, 'I love you too.'

'You will marry me, won't you?' he queried.

'Is that to be taken as a proposal then?'

'Of course, what else could it be?'

'Well then, get down on your knees and ask me properly if you really mean it.'

With no more ado, and much to Edith's astonishment, he did indeed get down on his knees and say, 'Edith, I love you. I worship the ground you walk on. Will you please do me the honour of becoming my wife?'

This suddenly felt all wrong to Edith. It was not Alfred that she had wanted to say these words to her, but Edward. She was sensible enough to realise that Edward had gone away from her for good. All in all Alfred was a kind, generous man with a good sense of humour. What more could she want? She could do a lot worse than become his wife. Besides, she was realistic enough to realise there was little chance of her receiving another proposal of marriage. There were not the men around to meet in her village, most of them had perished in the war and most of those who had returned were already spoken for. Where else could she go to meet young eligible men? No, her parents liked him and she was sure he would make a good, reliable husband. Besides she was very fond of him herself.

Looking at him seriously she told him, 'I think you'd best ask my Pa first, if it's all right for us to get engaged. Don't you think so? You know what he's like; he's strict in everything being done as it should be. I can't see there being any problem though, after all, they both like you.'

'If that's the way you want it I'll ask him, don't worry. But it is you I want to marry.'

Inside Edith could feel mixed emotions, happiness that somebody wanted to marry her, yet a sadness that this was not the person she had really wanted to propose to her. What saddened her even more was the fact that she knew Alfred was a kind and generous person and she did not want to cause him any unhappiness by not being all he wanted in a wife. No, she would have to set her mind at it, this was her life from now onwards, one way or another Edward had to be put to the back of her mind. To show her appreciation and hopefully with love she put her hands at the side of his head and turned his lips to meet hers. Suddenly this small act started to move events out of hand again as Alfred took this as a signal that she was giving her all to him.

Edith felt bile rise in her stomach as panic built up. Pulling away from him with all her might and seeing the look of surprise on his face she quickly said, 'Enough for today. Don't you think you'd better go and see my Pa now if you're going to ask him? He doesn't like people visiting very late, and you want to catch him in good humour because you want his answer to be yes.'

Seeing the sense in this Alfred quickly jumped up and grabbed her hand, 'Come on then, what are you waiting for?' he challenged cheerfully, not taking any offence by her behaviour.

Like two young children they set off at a run, but finally Edith pulled up short, 'Stop, I've got a stitch.'

Alfred laughed at her, 'A likely tale, bet you're getting cold feet already.'

'No, I'm not. Honest.'

Looking at her gently he asked with concern in his voice, 'Are you really all right?'

Evading the question and answering as if she misunderstood, Edith said, 'Fine, it's going now. But let's walk the rest of the way, not run.'

'That's okay, by me. It gives me more chance to be on my own with you.'

As they were going at a slower pace Edith started to ask the questions that were flooding into her mind. 'But where will we live when we're married?'

'We'll have to try to save up, then I'll go and see Mr. Goodwin to see what he's available to rent. He owns lots of the small cottages in the village. We'll only need furniture and such like, so we won't need to save too much money.'

'Yes,' Edith said feeling a bit disappointed. She did not think she could face living in one of those tiny, damp and cold cottages after the standard of living with her parents. Still, she reassured herself, there was time enough to get a compromise sorted out which she would be more contented with.

Little did she know the main thing on Alfred's mind was he hoped it was not too long before they found a house and were married. He did not care where they lived as long as Edith became his. He did not think he could hold out much longer, every time he held her it set him on fire in his loins.

Pushing the creaking door open she shouted to her parents, warning them that she was not on her own. 'Hello, it's me. I've brought Alfred to see you.'

Her father looked up suspiciously from where he was wrestling with some book work for his business. Edith realised this was not his favourite task and never put him in good humour. Still, it was too late to go back out again as her father was already talking to them, 'Oh aye and what can we do for you this evening, young man?'

Not looking as confident as he previously had, Alfred stammered, 'Er, hmm, I've something to ask you.'

'Have you now. Well you'd both best sit down hadn't you? What do you say Ma?'

'Aye, I'll just put the kettle on then we'll have a brew. Won't be two shakes of a donkey's tail, then you can get on with what you've to say Alfred.'

How he wished he could get it all over this minute, so quickly he said at Mrs. Thompson's retreating back, 'It doesn't matter about tea, honest, I'm not bothered.'

'Get on with you, lad. It'll not take more than a few moments. Anyway, I bet Pa wants a cuppa. Whatever you've got to say can't be that important that it won't surely keep a short while longer.'

Knowing it would be churlish not to agree, Alfred said with his stomach churning, as if it would never take the tea into it, 'That'd be grand. Thanks ever so much.'

Edith gave him a small smile as much as to say, 'I'll be all right, don't worry.'

She felt her heart swell inside with pride for both her parents and Alfred. She did not think she had ever felt happier and more content than at this moment in time.

Whilst they sat having their tea her father started a conversation with Alfred discussing his job in the foundry. He did some of the carrying for the firm Alfred worked for.

Knowing the next day was a working day for them all Alfred did not want to outstay his welcome. He gave a cough and cleared his throat. With a stammer he came quickly to the point. 'Mr. Thompson, I've come tonight to ask you if I can have your daughter's hand in marriage.'

'What's that you say?'

'I want to marry Edith.'

'Oh aye and when do you propose to do that?'

'Well not just yet. We'll have to save some money for furniture then put our name down for a house in the village.'

Alfred could feel his heart pounding as he was sure his request was going to be turned down.

'I see,' Edith's father replied before pausing as if pondering. Finally he said, 'Hmm I can't see we've any objection to that. Can you, Ma?'

Alfred could not believe his ears at this reply, he had been so sure he was going to meet with a refusal.

Edith could see her mother was already bursting with happiness for her. 'No, I've none at all. Aye, lad, I'm fair pleased to welcome you into the family. Come on; drink your tea up to celebrate. Sorry we don't have anything stronger in the house.'

Pleased and rather bemused with how it had gone Alfred stood up, 'Thanks for the tea Mrs. Thompson, but it's time I was on my way now. It's a fair walk home and I don't want to keep Edith up too late when she's work tomorrow.'

'Aye, lad, you're right enough there. We'll have a really good chat about things next time you come.'

With this her parents bid him good night. Edith shyly said, 'I'll just see him to the gate.'

71

Her father gave a laugh, 'Don't you think he can find his way out then?'

Seeing her blushing face he tried to make quick amends. 'Don't be long. I'll be locking the door for the night in ten minutes.'

By, she thought, as she went through the door, her father was in good humour this night and for once treating her more like the young woman she was than the lad he had always wished for.

As soon as they were alone together she quickly grabbed Alfred's hand. 'I'm so happy this night. I wish it could just go on like this for ever and ever.'

'Aye, so do I, lass, but never fear, I'll always look after you. We'll be so happy together, you see.'

Edith had a sudden shiver as if someone had walked over her grave. Her thoughts quickly flew to Edward and she hoped his spirit was not getting cross with her because she was going to wed another bloke. Giving herself a mental shake she realised this was silly thinking.

'I'd best go in now; otherwise you never know with my Pa, he might really lock me out.'

'Aye do that, but I'll see you Saturday the same as usual? We'll sort out a time to go and buy you an engagement ring,' he added as he remembered she would need one.

'I can't wait, take care walking home.'

Now at every meeting their precious amount of time together seemed to go past too quickly for Edith. In the warm weather they walked on the heather moorland. Somehow Edith did not feel like being cooped up in a picture house with a lot of strange, uncommunicative people.

She became aware just how much of a passionate young man Alfred indeed was. She could feel his kisses were getting more and more out of control for him as these no longer satisfied his urges. She did not know whether it was good or bad but their walks still often led them to the old familiar barn.

Despite her lack of knowledge in such things Edith had begun to understand that Alfred was getting impatient for more from her than kisses and cuddles. This made her torn in her mind what to do. She had always regretted not letting Edward have his way, because look what had happened to him. But then sense would take over and she realised it was not the same thing at all. Alfred was not going back to any war only to work each day. Even though she loved Alfred in her own way, deep inside her, she still loved the image of Edward. He had been her first love and that memory would always stay with her. When

Alfred kissed her and she closed her eyes she would picture it was Edward again, loving and caressing her. She knew this was unfair on Alfred but as long as he never knew then what harm was she doing? After all she had promised herself to him and she would try her best to make him a good wife.

6

His firm lips were pressing so hard on hers that she could barely breathe. She could feel his calloused hands begin to move over her body, yet she felt powerless to stop them. Briefly he moved his mouth from hers to utter the words, 'Say you will, Edith, please. I can't wait any longer and, after all, we're to be wed soon.'

All the while his hands kept gently caressing her breasts until she felt her nipples go hard and firm. Suddenly one hand moved down her body gently caressing as it went until it reached the hem of her skirt. Once there it moved inside and slowly back up her leg. An inner voice was saying, 'Stop,' yet another voice argued, 'You did not let Edward have his way and look what happened.' Within her own body she could feel a heat as if a fire had ignited that sent sensual waves through her. She was powerless to stop what was happening, it was so enjoyable and making a feeling she had never experienced before that she wanted it to just go on and on. Gently his fingers probed her most sensitive area and her body started wriggling at the feeling of excitement it brought her. She could sense herself getting moister as his fingers gently started to move inside. She knew this was wrong but it was so exciting and she was beyond all reason.

Quietly Alfred begged her, 'Please let me love you properly, Edith. I won't hurt you I promise.'

By now Edith had lost all control and just moaned, 'Don't stop please,' and with this she gave a low sigh of pleasure. She felt Alfred's weight on her as he forced her legs gently apart and pushed his way into her. She gave a quick 'Ouch,' as he penetrated her but that pain was quickly forgotten as Alfred started to move gently up and down then becoming more forceful as his last inhibitions evaporated away. Now there was no pain, only pleasure for Edith. Alfred started to groan, 'Oh! Oh, this is beautiful.' At the same time Edith felt as if the world was exploding around her. Coming down to earth with a bang she wondered what she had done wrong as Alfred quickly leapt off her and moved away turning his back to her.

Anxiously she asked, 'Alfred, whatever's the matter? What have I done?'

'Just give me a minute, Edith.'

Suddenly she realised there was stickiness in between her legs and shouted to Alfred,

'What is it Alfred? What's happened?'

'Nothing, my love, only pleasure.'

'Then why did you move away like that?'

She could hear a funny noise coming from Alfred and see his shoulders shaking wondered what on earth had gone wrong. As he turned towards her she realised he was laughing, 'Come on, Edith, you're not telling me you're as naive as all that. I had to jump off quick; you didn't want me to give you a bairn, now did you?'

Realising the full impact of what he had said she saw how foolish she had been in her passion. She had never even given a thought to the consequences of her actions. It was a good job Alfred had but now she set about worrying, 'Are you sure I won't have a bairn?'

'No, of course not, why do you think I to move off you as quick as that? I'm not that foolish. Your father would skin me alive if I put you in the family way. Come here and give me a cuddle. Did you enjoy it as much as I did?'

'Aye, it was great, but I was so carried away I forgot all about the risk of having a bairn. It's a good job you kept some sense.'

'Only just I can tell you. Oh! I do love you Edith, and you were wonderful, all I expected and more.'

Deep down somewhere Edith knew she

had done this for the wrong reason. She knew she should not make Alfred into Edward but it was beyond her power to stop herself. It made her very sad that she could not love Alfred simply for himself. He was a good bloke and she knew that without a shadow of doubt.

His voice broke into her thoughts, 'You've gone very quiet. No regrets have you?'

'Now why should I?' Her guilty feeling at the thoughts she had been having made her turn to him and give him a large loving cuddle to try to make her words sound even more convincing.

He pulled away as another thought struck him, 'It wasn't too painful was it?'

'No, it was good so stop fretting.' She felt him relax in her arms but suddenly pulling away from him she jumped up, 'Come on, it's time for me to go home. I'd best not be late, you know how cross Pa gets if I am.'

'I realise that and we don't want to set him against us, I agree with you there. Nay, lass, I'd do nowt to hurt you intentionally, you know that. Come on then, I'll walk you home.'

Despite knowing it was wrong, the visits to the barn became a frequent thing for Edith and Alfred. Each time Edith knew she should have the will power to say, 'No,' yet all that kept nudging her memory was the fact she had said that to Edward and look what had happened. Any roads she enjoyed what they did, even if it were wrong. If she was really honest with herself, whether it was with Alfred or in her mind with Edward, it gave her real pleasure. At times she nearly burst out laughing thinking what a hussy she was becoming.

She had not really given any more thought to the possible consequences, only maybe that they had always to be careful not to be caught in the act by a passer by. Other than that she left it to Alfred because he had said he would take care of her and she put her trust in him to do just that.

Always having been a little bit irregular, she now gave no thought to the fact she had not come on for quite a while. When she started feeling queasy and not really just in the mornings, she thought she had either eaten something or caught a bug. The longer it lasted the more she decided it was something not agreeing with her. Maybe the water was not very good that they used to make the tea with at work. Not wanting to appear a weakling she did not like to ask the others if they felt like she did, she had not heard anybody complain they felt sick. Finally, having enough of feeling poorly she turned to

Agnes, one afternoon, when she felt particularly bad, 'I don't think that water's too clean that they use in the boiler for the tea. What do you think?'

Agnes turned round swiftly and looked keenly at her, 'Oh aye and why's that?'

'Well, each afternoon after I've had my drink of tea I feel queasy. How do you feel?'

'Fine and what other things have you noticed about yourself?'

'What do you mean what other things?'

'Like I said other things, besides the queasiness?'

'Um, well I get awful heartburn with it.'

'You do, do you? Look, I'll have to spell it out because I don't think you've a clue what I'm getting at. Have you missed? Are your breasts tender? In other words have you been having fun and games with that young fella of yours?'

'I don't know what you're getting at. So I'm late coming on but that's not unusual for me. I suppose now you've mentioned it and made me think, my breasts are a bit tender but there again they often are a few days before I start. I'd just really thought I'd happen been leaning over my work more than usual and that had made them tender.'

Suddenly feeling a shiver of fear going through her Edith moved closer to Agnes and whispered, 'Why, Agnes, what do you think ails me?'

Edith could not believe her ears when Agnes burst into hoots of laughter, 'What ails you? Nay lass, I wouldn't call it an ailment. Mind you, when your Ma and Pa find out something might ail you then.'

'Ssh Agnes, don't let them all hear, we're getting some funny looks as it is. If I've something wrong with me I don't want them all to hear and get to know.'

'Nay, lass, you've nowt wrong with you if you ask me. But I do think you're going to have a bairn.'

'No! I can't be that's impossible.'

'Look, I'm not trying to pry but are you really sure you can't be pregnant. After all it's only you who knows what you've been getting up to with that fella of yours.'

Blushing now and not really sure what to say at this Edith stammered, 'Well I didn't really mean I couldn't be, but Alfred promised he'd take care of everything so I wouldn't be.'

'Oh, you poor dear, you're not the first to be tricked like that.'

'No, that's unfair on Alfred, after all it does take two,' she said generously.

Then she suddenly realised the full impact of what they were discussing. 'Oh my God it can't be true? Tell me it can't.'

'We'll have less of that blasphemy, and yes, lass, it can and I think it is true.'

'Me Ma and Pa will kill me, they really will. Oh, what am I to do, Agnes?'

'Slow down, first things first. You'd best talk to your young man and see what he proposes to do. He'll stand by you, I take it?'

'I'm sure he will,' she replied weakly. Then with more conviction she added, 'Yes, he will.'

Try as she might her mind would not keep on her work. She felt sick inside but not only with the pregnancy but with the implications of what was going to happen. All she wanted was home time and her evening for meeting Alfred to come. Her main concern was if Agnes had guessed what was wrong with her, would her mother also be able to tell so easily? Her mother was certainly no fool. The quicker she could see Alfred and they sorted it all out the better it would be for all of them. Somehow or other she managed to behave as if everything was normal. If her mother thought anything was amiss she certainly did not give any hint or say anything.

As soon as Edith met Alfred, she lost all her self control of the last few days. Grabbing his hand she pulled him along, 'Quick, let's get out of here on to the open moors so we're not in earshot of anyone. I've something to tell you.'

'Slow down, Edith, what's all the hurry? In fact what on earth's the matter with you? You're not like your normal self at all.'

The anxiety she had kept bottled up for the last few days burst out of her, 'Oh just shut up and get a move on and do what I say.'

It had the desired effect on Alfred as he was lost for words; he had never seen her like this before. He did as he was bid and strode out to get to the openness of the moors.

As soon as they reached a place where Edith decided it was safe to speak she quickly stopped in her tracks and turned to Alfred. As he bumped into her she spoke sharply, 'I'm pregnant.'

With his mouth open Alfred gaped at her and finally stammered, 'What?'

'You heard me the first time. I'm pregnant, so what are we going to do about it?'

'Do about it?'

'What on earth's wrong with you? All you're doing is repeating what I'm saying.'

'Um, yes well give me a few minutes to take in all you've just said.'

Quickly Edith rushed on as if Alfred had never spoken, 'Mind, I don't know why I'm worrying about the future. I probably haven't one as I'm sure my Pa will kill me when he knows. So what's there to worry about?' The last part came out hysterically.

Now coming to his senses and realising Edith desperately needed his love and support Alfred caught her up and put his arms around her. 'There's only one thing to do. We'll bring the wedding forward and get wed as soon as we can. I've told you before, I love you. You didn't think I'd desert you now did you? After all it's my baby as well.'

'But we've not much money saved and any roads where will we live?'

'Stop fussing so; let's take it a step at a time. First thing is to cope with telling your Ma and Pa. I know they'll not be well pleased but we'll just have to sweet talk them around. But I'll tell you what, lass, I'm made up, I really am. I know it isn't the way we planned but don't worry I'll look after you and the bairn. Oh! I do love you so. Come here and let me give you a cuddle. I'll have to take extra special care of you now.'

Edith in need of as much reassurance as possible fell into his arms without any hesitation. Alfred quickly took this as a sign that Edith wanted more loving. She pulled away from him in great agitation, 'Here, what do you think you're doing?'

'Why loving you of course.'

'Don't you think there's been enough harm done?'

Alfred fell into a burst of laughter.

'What's so funny?'

'Think about it. Nothing can happen now whatever we do. You're already pregnant so we might as well make the most of this time.'

'I don't know, it all feels wrong now. I know you'll say that's silly but it didn't feel wrong before but it does now.'

'Just come here and give me a big cuddle then and don't worry I'll look after you whatever your parents have to say about it all.'

As she snuggled up to him he started to talk about the practicalities of what they would do. 'Can you get your Ma to invite me to tea on Sunday, and then I'll be there with you so you're not on your own when the news is broken to them.'

'My Pa might be that cross that he'll turn you out,' she added with real concern in her voice.

'Well, it's up to us to make him see sense and realise there's no point taking that attitude. After all, I'm going to wed you and the quicker we do it the less reason folk need to know why the wedding's been brought forward. Let's hope he accepts all that, and then maybe they'll let us live with them to start with. After all, there's plenty of room at your house.'

'Aye, you're right there and he might want to let us do that 'cause he'll not want to lose me looking after the horses,' Edith replied with a slight tinge of sadness in her voice.

But then she suddenly saw some humour in the situation. 'You never know, you might get roped into that job. I hope you're not afraid of the animals?'

'Course not. You know I'll help if needs be and he'll let me.'

Some of the panic started to go out of Edith as she realised here was somebody who was going to really look after her. She still could not help a slight twinge of regret that this was Alfred not Edward. But she knew from now on all that had to be locked in a separate compartment in her mind. This was it then. Alfred and this baby she was going to bear would have to be her new life from then on. There was nothing she could do about it. Destiny had taken a hand and the path seemed to be already mapped out for her.

7

Edith instinctively shrank back and she wished herself anywhere but here as her father exploded, 'What! Say that again.'

'I'm pregnant.'

'You stupid, stupid girl, how many times have we told you that kind of thing is for after you're wed?'

Hanging her head in shame and feeling petrified, Edith whispered, 'I know, but there's nowt I can do about it now. What's done is done.' She did not like to point out that neither of them had really explained the subject to her, so she laid some of the blame at their door.

'You can say that again.' Then looking keenly at Alfred her father asked of him, 'And what have you to say for yourself now, I ask you? We welcome you into our family and this is all the thanks we get. Shame and disgrace brought on us. How I'll be able to hold my head up in Chapel, I don't know.'

'I'm sorry; we never meant it to happen. But I've told Edith I'll stand by her. We'll just have to bring the wedding forward, that's all.'

'You say that's all as if it is as simple as

that. Haven't you any shame?' her father exploded, angered even further by this comment.

Seeing things were getting very difficult and not going the way they wanted at all, Alfred tried to respond in a manner so as not to get her father any more annoyed. 'Yes, Sir, I'm very ashamed with my behaviour, that I've abused your hand of friendship. But it can't be undone so we thought if we were married as soon as possible we could keep the real reason for the wedding being brought forward a secret. I know that won't right a wrong but it might make amends.'

Sniffing and looking cynical her father asked, 'Oh aye, and what do you propose to give as the reason for moving the wedding forward?'

Looking a bit confused by it all now Alfred had to confess, 'I don't really know, but I'm sure if we put our heads together we can come up with something. Then when the baby is born we'll just have to say it's come along early as some do.'

'Compounding one lie with another are we?' her father replied not happy at all by the actions Alfred proposed. It was against his principles to not tell the truth.

Her mother had kept quiet all the while but now she quickly butted in, 'He's right, you know it is the best way. We'll no doubt get a few knowing looks but nobody will say it outright what they think. Sometimes things have to be done the way we don't like.'

Her father gave a groan, 'That'll make no difference, as I said before I'll never be able to hold my head up in Chapel again. How will I be able to look the preacher and my friends in the eye? You've brought nowt but disgrace on our heads. You stupid girl what did you think you were at?' Lowering himself into a chair at the kitchen table with his head in his hands he continued. 'Well, your Ma and I have always tried to do right by you. I never thought I'd see a day like this. We don't have much in life. Some would say we were better off than most, but what we do have is our good name.'

Placing a hand on Joe's shoulder, as she came to stand behind him, Sarah said, 'Nay, lad, don't take on so. It's as big a shock to me as well you know. But just you think back to what we always used to say, that family comes first. Who else has she to turn to but us?'

Joe looked up at Sarah saying, 'I know, I know we've to stand by our lass.' Then giving a sigh he continued in a calmer voice, 'I suppose you're right, Ma, it is the only way.' Then he added sadly, 'She is the only family we have left,' and Edith knew her father was thinking about Elsie.

Wanting to throw her arms around him but knowing he did not like demonstrations of affection, Edith said with real gladness in her voice, 'Oh thanks, Pa, you'll not regret this, no you won't.'

Alfred taking his cue from Edith held out his hand to shake her father's to show they were still friends, 'Thank you Mr. Thompson, I'll take care of her always.'

'All right, let's not get carried away. But by God you better had, lad.' After an uneasy silence Joe continued, 'We'd best get on with discussing the arrangements if the wedding's to be soon.'

'Aye, I suppose first of all we'd best sort out where they're going to live. What do you say, Pa?' suggested her ma.

Now her father looked keenly at them. 'Too right we had. Now then the pair of you, have you any ideas on that score?'

Seeming a bit hesitant about putting the idea forward Edith said quietly, 'Well, we do have plenty of room here.'

'Oh, we do, do we?' answered her father.

'Yes, I was going to suggest that. I'd like to have Edith still here with us and then I'd be able to help when the bairn comes,' said her mother quickly before anybody else could reply. 'Is that all right with you, Pa?'

'Aye, I suppose so. Tha's turned my world upside down so you may as well make a proper job of it.' Laughing slightly he added, 'But I know it means the peace is going to be disturbed with a young one. Next you will be expecting me to push him out in his pram. Where will it all end?' Edith could tell these last words were not said unkindly but with some pride in them.

Then a thought struck Joe that he had automatically said 'him'. He hoped it would be a grandson because it was what the house needed, a lad in it. It would make a change from lasses about the place. Joe relished the thought that he could get used to a lad in the house. He was starting to warm to the idea of this grandson.

Just then Edith let out a sigh of relief that it had all gone better than she thought it was going at one point. She knew her father was not well pleased but at least he was letting them get wed. Wanting to show she really appreciated what he was doing she pushed her chair back; she put caution to the wind and rushed over to him wanting to give him a kiss and cuddle.

Not being a man to show his emotions, as soon as he realised what she was doing he pushed her away with a gruff, 'Enough of that now.'

Edith instantly felt deflated at his attitude, but she did know from the past that he often sounded more abrupt than he really was.

Her mother being well used to seeing him like this quickly changed tack, 'Now then, let's come up with some possible dates for this wedding and we'd best see the Minister as soon as we can to organise if he's available on any of the times we've chosen. I'll do a really nice spread here for you after the wedding service.' Giving a laugh she added, 'I've still got my wedding dress but it's no good offering you that, it would never reach the ground on you.'

Turning to Alfred, Edith said in a rather rueful voice, 'It's a pity it wouldn't do, I used to love to look at it when I was a little girl. It's a really beautiful dress.'

Her mother knew she was disappointed, 'Don't fret, we'll organise something. I'm sure between us we can sew an outfit as nice. We might even be able to use some of mine even if it's only things like the lace.' Sighing she added, 'Aye, my Ma and me sewed that dress between us for my wedding.'

'I could never let you spoil it by cutting bits off for me,' Edith said kindly feeling her mother felt sad because of the memories.

'Nay, lass, what does it matter? I won't be using it again and who else is there? Any roads there's not many folk still have theirs. Most people have usually already cut them up to make christening gowns for their own children.' Then a thought struck her, 'Or is that your plan for mine? Do you want to hang on to it for that?' Then rushing ahead of herself and not giving Edith chance to answer, 'The cake, I'd best get on with that otherwise it'll not be ready and at its best.'

Edith put out a restraining hand as she saw her mother already making a move. 'Not tonight though, Ma, there's enough time to start it tomorrow.'

Laughing at herself her mother had to admit she was running ahead of herself. 'Aye your right there, I'm getting carried away with myself.'

Edith heard her father give a sniff. 'They'll carry you away one of these days, you're right on that. Fuss, fuss that's all you do. You see what you've done now Edith - given her something else to fuss about. This is all we'll hear until the wedding.'

During all this discussion of arrangements Alfred had kept silent but now he felt he had to say his piece, 'I'd best tell my Ma and Pa before we say anything to other people. They'd be upset to hear about something so important from anybody other than myself.'

'Okay, lad, but make sure you do that soon.

We've not much time to waste before we need to get things organised,' conceded her father.

Once it was all agreed to their benefit, Alfred wanted to leap from his seat and throw his arms around Edith with joy, but knew better than to do that in front of her parents. He felt so proud of himself knowing he was going to be a father. Never mind the gossips, all that really mattered was he was going to wed the lass he loved. He was aware of one slight concern he had. He knew now he was taking on the responsibility of becoming a married man and was going to become a father then he would have to get his one vice in hand. There was no way he would have any spare cash to enjoy the odd flutter.

*   *   *

As soon as Edith told the girls at work, rather nervously, the news of her wedding she received the knowing looks and snide remarks just as she had expected to from them. Even Agnes challenged her in front of the others with a hint. 'Come on, what's the rush? I bet you're having a baby, you've got that glow about you.'

Edith felt really annoyed with her. She had thought her to be her friend and would have kept quiet about what they had already discussed in confidence. After all, it was Agnes who had helped her realise what was wrong with her in the first instance. Now she felt Agnes should hold her tongue but seeing she was not Edith played her at her own game. 'Come on Agnes, what do you take me for? It's the glow of a bride to be, of course I'm happy at that thought.'

Laughing Agnes continued, 'Time will tell and that's a fact. There'll be no hiding it in a few months for sure.'

A little shiver of fear went through Edith as she realised what Agnes said was true. She knew she would not be able to keep it hidden forever but perhaps she would be lucky and not show too quickly. Oh well! At least she would not be at work when she had the baby so she need not face their jibes about it not being an early baby as she would say.

All her spare time seemed to be taken up with organisation of the wedding. Her father did not say a lot but at least they had received his approval for it. Her mother was very fussy all the time. Edith wanted to scream and tell her to stop talking about it. Mind, she had been so kind she had even let then sort out, to their liking, what was going to be their bedroom after the wedding. Then Edith felt contrite at getting annoyed with her mother.

Before she knew where she was, her special

day was upon them. By some clever needlework her mother had created a lovely wedding gown for her. She had done this by partly using her own wedding dress and partly by adding bits and pieces that she could manage to get her hands on. Edith was thrilled by the final result and felt it would make Alfred really proud of her. There was no bulge showing yet so nobody could tell the real reason for the quickness of the wedding, even if they had their own thoughts about the haste there was no evidence as yet to prove their theory. Anyway with life so uncertain after the war people were still, at times, rather rash in their actions.

As the organist started to play Alfred knew Edith would commence her walk down the aisle on the arm of her father so he turned to get a good look at her. He could not stop his mouth from falling open as he stared at her in amazement. He had always thought her to be a pretty young woman but seeing her in her full finery she was beautiful. There was a special glow about her. As father and daughter reached the alter he moved forward with pride to stand at her side. He turned to her with a smile of sublime happiness on his face.

Neither was hardly conscious of the words they spoke; only knowing somehow or other they managed to say the right word in the right places.

Edith was happy, but there was a small part of her that held some regret that it was not Edward beside her. She felt slightly guilty at these thoughts as she knew she had found a good man in Alfred. Alfred felt deep feelings of pride that this beautiful young woman, at his side, was going to be his wife.

He felt her small hand get hold of his and was conscious of her face turning towards him and moving near his own for a kiss. He seemed unable to move as realisation suddenly hit him, he was a married man now with a bairn on the way. Suddenly he heard a voice, 'Well aren't you going to give your wife a kiss then?'

Quickly recovering himself he answered, 'Of course I am,' and gently put his lips on Edith's. That was enough to send warmth to his loins. His thoughts started to instantly run riot thinking about being on their own for the wedding night.

All too soon he felt her move away from him as the organ started up again and it was time for them to walk back up the aisle. After a few photos it was back to the house for food. As Edith's mother had promised, she had prepared an excellent spread for them. Alfred's mum had also helped her get it ready. He had known she would want to be involved and there was no controlling her when it came to occasions like this. His parents had barely made any comment about his rush to wed, but at least they had offered their support.

Altogether it was a happy day for the pair of them. Edith just wished the nagging doubt would leave her, whether she had really done the right thing. But there again in her heart she knew there had been no alternative for her, after all she was carrying Alfred's baby.

Much to their delight her father had even paid for them to have a honeymoon for a few days at Scarborough. Not that he had not added with his usual sting in the tail, 'Was it really necessary as they'd already put the cart before the horse.' But even so, they were both thankful he had given them a chance to have a few days on their own. So as soon as the meal was over, her mother sent her to get changed into her going away outfit. They had not much time to spare before they had to catch the bus into Bradford then the train from there to Scarborough.

Neither of them spoke much on the journey, being wrapped up in their own thoughts, after such an emotional day. But once they were in their room at the boarding house, Alfred grabbed hold of Edith and started to kiss her. Edith could tell his passion had been building up all day, she had somehow sensed it. She was equally as willing as she had that old feeling coursing through her veins.

All the while Alfred was thinking what a lucky man he was to have enchanted such a lovely lass and that she had consented to be his wife. He knew in the end there had been no choice for her but to set the wedding date. Still, they had been betrothed before that had happened. He felt a slight sadness that he did not want Edith to know; because he regretted that he had not been able to get their own home for them to start married life in. But as her mother had said, they did have plenty of room to spare in their house and they seemed all right even if her father was a bit strict. He was sure it would work out fine for them in the end and they would be happy.

But now he had her to himself for three whole days and he intended to enjoy every moment of that time. There did not seem much resistance from Edith, already he could sense she wanted to give herself to him again.

He was not wrong in this assumption, as soon as Edith felt his lips on hers again that familiar sensation ran through her body once more. At times she felt guilty as if she were being too forward for a well brought up lass, but she could not help herself. It was as if there was a smouldering fire within her which came to full life as soon as Alfred touched her.

The three days were spent making the most of each other's bodies rather than visiting any of Scarborough's attractions. What the landlady thought about them being in their room so much of the time neither cared, they were past bothering. All they knew was that their flesh wanted to be joined as much as possible.

If Alfred had known some of the thoughts in Edith's head he would have been disturbed and not truly satisfied. Her thoughts turned to Edward. Somehow the two men in her life had become intertwined and Edith was not sure whether it was Edward she still loved or Alfred feeling like Edward. But she was happy in the life she had chosen for herself whether destiny had taken a hand in it or not. One way or another she was confident life would move smoothly forward for her.

8

Edith had never really given a thought to what married life would be like, and more particularly whilst they were still living with her parents in their home. Somehow she had imagined things would simply go along as before with her mother looking after them all, only with Alfred as part of their life.

Much to her dismay, any newfound softness her father had seemed to show towards her before the wedding had totally vanished. In its place she found a hard, unrelenting person who made it difficult for her to relate to as her father. He acted as if he wanted to punish her, both for being pregnant before her wedding and for the fact she was not the lad he had always wanted. He made her work doubly hard helping him with his live stock. Whether it was her condition or state of mind, Edith did not know which, but the work seemed harder and heavier than ever.

She could see her mother giving her sympathetic looks but Edith knew she would not go as far as to cross her father on her behalf.

With great frustration it seemed as if her married life was not turning out at all like her high expectations. On her honeymoon she'd had so much pleasure during her love making sessions with Alfred. Now suddenly she felt so strange and shy if Alfred touched her. Every time they made love she was afraid her mother and father would hear the old, metal bedstead squeaking.

She could sense Alfred was getting exasperated with her. It did not seem to make any difference to him where they were and when they did it as long as he derived his own satisfaction. To give him his due, he never grumbled at her refusals but she could sense his disappointment in her behaviour. If they'd had time to go to the old barn and be on their own it might have helped things.

For himself Alfred was very worried. He could see what Edith's father was doing to her; but he knew he could not say anything because, after all, they were staying in the house by his charity towards them. It did not take Alfred long before he began to realise he had a problem dealing with money. It seemed to run through his fingers like water but he was trying his best to save to get them a home of their own away from her parents.

At times Edith forgot she was having a baby; her life was so taken up with everything else in it. But one day as she felt the pains grip her insides she soon enough realised what was happening to her and the fear set in. With a panic stricken look on her face she screamed, 'Ma, I think the baby's coming.'

Her mother was quick to see the dread and responded accordingly, 'Shhh, calm yourself. Don't fret yourself, lass, it'll be hours yet before the birth. It's only just started. There's no need for you to rush to bed yet awhile. Best to keep going, it'll help to make the pains easier.'

'Are you sure, Ma?'

'Of course I am, lass. Now haven't I helped at enough births?'

'I suppose so,' replied Edith but she had not a lot of faith in what her mother was saying at that moment. Already her insides felt as if they were being ripped apart. 'It'll not get much worse than this will it, Ma?'

'It will, lass. I'm sorry but there's nothing I can do about that. Just tell me when the pains come about every five minutes then we'll put you to bed. But I'm sure that'll be a while yet.'

Still uncertain what was really about to happen Edith felt the need to ask, 'But don't we need to send for the doctor now?'

Her mother gave a gentle laugh. 'Stop fretting so. I'll let no harm come to you.

Haven't I just said I've dealt with enough births before and after all this is very special, it's my first grandchild? Now let's consider if we've got everything ready that we'll need. You think about getting yourself organised. At least that might help take your mind off the pain.'

'Just as you say, Ma,' replied Edith not really caring what they did as long as it brought some ease to the agony.

But her mother was wrong. Whatever she did it hurt like nothing she had ever felt before. Edith felt certain there was something going wrong and she was about to die. Much to her dismay an involuntary loud groan came out at the next bout of pain.

Her mother ran quickly to her side, 'What's wrong, lass?'

'I think I'm dying, Ma.'

Her mother gave a small laugh at this much to Edith's disgust. 'You're not. It's only natural what you're feeling. We've all gone through the same when we've had a bairn.'

'Well, if it's like this every time I'm not having any more and that's a fact.'

Her mother gave her a sceptical look. 'We'll see, time will tell. Anyway I'm sorry lass, but it'll get worse before it gets better.'

'Oh, Ma don't say that,' Edith shouted in great agitation. She had not known pain could just go on and on like this, all the while increasing in intensity. If only Alfred would come home. In her panic she said these thoughts out aloud.

'What on earth are you thinking of? You know full well even if he was here he'd be sent out of the way. It's not respectful having the men folk around at a time like this. Anyway, I think it's time we got you to bed. It's all ready for you.'

'Whatever you say, Ma, you know best. The quicker I get this over the better.'

But it was not a short labour. It seemed to go on for ever before she proudly produced a lovely baby boy. She was so glad it was a boy; she felt she had given Alfred what he deserved. All her pain was quickly forgotten as she looked down at this little mite in her arms, already with a mass of black fluffy hair on his head. She could not believe how immediately she fell in love with the small new life. She soon realised this was what it actually meant being a mother. At last she felt so happy and was thinking of the pleasure of moving forward with this new family of hers.

What she had not bargained for, as the baby lay so peaceful in her arms for the first few minutes of his life, was that he could so quickly change into making so much noise and disturbance in their lives. Edith was quick to understand her father did not like all this noise. His impatience soon began to show once he was over the first joy of being a grandfather. She could not believe it when a few weeks after the birth of John, as they had decided to name the baby, that her father looked up at her one evening as they were all sitting quietly and told her, 'Well I think you're fit enough again to start helping me tomorrow. I still need help with the horses and other livestock.'

Edith could only open and shut her mouth in amazement at this and could see a look of shock on her mother's and Alfred's face. Her mother was the first to find her voice and said softly, 'Don't you think she's enough to do now looking after John?'

'Sarah, I'll thank you to mind your own business. She's a strong young lass, it'll not harm her to do a bit of work for their keep,' snapped her father.

Even Edith was taken aback when her mother ignored this comment and still persisted. 'But Alfred does give us money for their food.'

With a bellow her father looked straight at her mother, 'Sarah, that's enough, I'll hear no more from you.'

This time Edith could see her mother was silenced. There was no more to be done, somehow she had to manage and do as her father bid. Gently her mother touched her arm, 'Don't fret, lass. I'll look after John when you're out there helping.'

Edith just gave a watery smile, 'Thanks, Ma.'

At times Edith felt ashamed by her actions with Alfred so soon after John was born. He had only to touch her once they were in bed and she was sexually aroused. Lack of understanding made her feel she was being far too forward with her sexual appetite but her will power was not strong enough; once her body was aroused it seemed to have a mind of its own. Not that she heard any protest from Alfred, but she was frightened her mother and father would hear how often their bed squeaked. At least if they did hear they had the tact to give no indication, that much at least, she could be thankful for. She tried to be so careful about not getting pregnant again, because she most certainly did not fancy going through that pain ever again.

She had also heard when she had worked at the mill, some of the women's gossip saying that if you were breast feeding there was little chance of you getting caught.

This had stuck in her mind so she was totally taken aback when she fell pregnant again very quickly. She realised this was a hard way to learn not to take everything she heard from other woman as gospel but with a pinch of salt.

Her father was none too pleased when they broke the news, Edith could easily sense that. But it was a different matter with Alfred. He was over the moon and Edith had to admit he had already proved to be a very loving and caring father. But Edith did not know how much longer she could take it staying with her mother and father. She could not face living again as she had done during her first pregnancy. Helping her father with his livestock right until she gave birth was just too much for her. Already she knew this was what he expected if they continued to live there.

In the end she had to say as much to Alfred. 'You've got to do something about getting us out of here. It'll kill me I'm sure, if Pa keeps me working like this. Any roads, I want time to be with John not leaving him with Ma all the time to be caring for him. He's our bairn and it should be me who's looking after him. If I'm going to work like this here for nowt, I might as well go back out to work at the mill and earn money to help us get a home of our own.' As she finished her long speech she could feel the tears pricking the back of her eyes and start to run down her cheeks.

Alfred put his arm around her with quick reassurances, 'Don't take on so, I've some good news for you. I've managed to put enough to one side to buy some furniture and pay the first rent on a cottage. As luck would have it I've heard of one that's come empty on the edge of the moor. I know it's a bit isolated and bleak but it does mean there are not many takers. You know as well as I do that the ones in the village centre are already spoken for before they become empty. This being the case it can be ours if we want it. What do you say to that, lass?'

Edith gave a small jump for joy, 'We'll take it, owts better than having to stay here any longer. Eh, it'll be right grand having a home of our own.' With this Edith threw her arms around Alfred. She felt proud of him at this moment, that he had done all this for her.

Alfred felt a glow inside for this was an unusual show of affection outside the bedroom from Edith. At last he had managed to do something right that had made her really happy. He had always felt there was something he did not know about which was holding her back from him.

Pulling back from Alfred she asked, 'When can we move into it?'

'Whenever you want once I've settled it with the agent. I'll go tomorrow and confirm we want it, and then we'll break the news to your Ma and Pa. I don't know how they'll take the news. I think your Ma will be sorry to see us go, she's right fond of John. As far as your Pa goes, I don't think he was too happy at the thought of having two young ones here, but there again he'll miss your help around the place.'

'Aye, I think you're right there. But it will be good to have somewhere to call our own. We'll make it right grand.'

'I know that, lass, you're a born home maker. But wherever we are, as long as I'm with you, I'll be happy.'

'Get away with you, you soppy ha'ppeth.'

As they had expected her mother was disappointed when they said they were leaving. 'There's no need to move you knows as there's enough room here for all of us. I'll miss John being around.'

'I know, Ma, but we'd like to try living in a place of our own. Any roads it'll be noisier than this when there are two of them howling. You'll happen not be as keen to have them around then.'

'Oh I don't know. Sometimes it can be too quiet on your own. I'm sure it helps keep me young having little ones around.'

'I'll come and see you often, and you'll always be welcome to come and see us.'

'Aye, I'll probably have to do that. It's a fair trek with two bairns from the moors to here.'

Little did Edith know how her mother wanted to beg her to stay with them. Life was not easy at times with Joe, but at least having Edith and Alfred living with them had helped. Now she would have nobody to talk to in the day and it would not be much better on an evening. Joe was not much of a conversationalist at the best of times. On the other hand she could not bring herself to beg. Despite being of gentle nature it was beyond her to make such pleas.

Edith saw none of her mother's hurt as she was so wrapped up in her own happiness at having their own place at last. She could only think her mother would be relieved to be getting them all out from under her feet.

Her father reacted just as she had expected him to, giving the impression that he was glad to see the back of them and get the house back to peace and quiet. Edith knew her father was often tired when he came in from work because he worked long, hard hours but even so it would have been nice if he had made a show of being disappointed that they were going.

Some of Edith's happiness did evaporate

when she saw the house. It certainly was not what she had been used to at home. But still her mother and father had promised them some more furniture and Alfred's father being an upholsterer had said he would make them two fireside chairs. So Edith decided by the time they had their bits and pieces in then surely it would look different, more like their own home.

Alfred was apologetic when he saw the look of initial disappointment on her face, 'Sorry I couldn't get you anything better, lass, but I will in time, I promise.'

Feeling upset for his hurt she turned to reassure him, 'Nay, it'll be real grand being on our own. I'll soon have it looking spick and span, never fear.'

Now they had decided to move, even if it was not really Edith's choice of home, she could hardly contain her excitement. Her mother had sorted out odds and ends to give them, her excuse being it was high time she had a good clear out. 'I've always kept too much rubbish, now I've a good reason to get rid of some of it. After all, these things will now be put to good use.'

'Well they hardly look like rubbish to me and we're both very grateful for them.'

Her father had even offered the service of his horse and cart after chapel the following

Sunday. For him this was a real break in tradition as he did believe no work should be done on the Sabbath. Whilst her mother looked after John they'd had a trip to Keighley and with the bit of money Alfred had saved bought themselves a new bed and a rug. Then they had found a good quality kitchen table and chairs with a dresser to match in a second hand shop. After buying a few other odds and ends they were nearly broke again but when Alfred saw her excited face he decided it was worth every penny spent.

When her mother made her first visit to them, after they had moved and settled into their own home, she confirmed this fact. 'Aye, lass, you've made it look right grand and homely. She's done you proud here, Alfred.'

'I know that. She's not just a pretty face our Edith. She must take after her Ma.'

Laughing at Alfred her mother said, 'Enough of that flattery young man, it'll get you everywhere.'

Despite this light banter what neither Edith or her mother could bring themselves to say were the words that they missed each other's companionship and were lonely in their own way. Edith knew she had the baby to keep her company and would soon have another one, so her hands would be full. But it was not the same as having her mother to talk to most of the time. In other ways she did enjoy the evenings on her own with Alfred. It gave them chance to get to know each other properly. He was very different to her father, he did not ignore her on an evening to sit and read as her father often did with her mother. Alfred was a real chatterbox, and so good humoured sometimes Edith wished he would be a little quieter.

As far as her mother was concerned, she was just lonely. Suddenly there did not seem enough to occupy her in that large house of theirs. It was too big for the two of them and far too quiet. They rattled around in it. She was aware many of the people squashed into the small cottages on Denton Row in the village would be overjoyed to have so much space and peace but to Sarah there could be too much of a good thing.

9

Both Edith and her mother could not believe how quickly the years went by. Most of Edith's time was taken up by looking after her many children. Not meaning to, but it still happened; she had six children in eight years. It seemed of no undue concern to Alfred that they had such a large family; he spoilt each one of them, giving them his last halfpenny if need be.

Each birth became more difficult for Edith; the pain became no easier, if anything worse each time, contrary to what other women said it was like for them. After each child was born it took longer to recover and she seemed to have a never ending tiredness about her. What she would have done without the help her mother gave, she just did not know.

Every time she found out she was pregnant, Alfred promised they would move house. But despite the fact he was earning what was good money at that time, they still never seemed to have any spare, so the much desired move never came about. Edith just did not know what he did with all the money. She knew he had a very generous nature, perhaps too much so and he would certainly help anybody in dire circumstances. What he did not seem to understand, was that at times it was his family who were in need. They had a desperate shortage of space in their home.

How they managed to produce so many children amazed Edith because they certainly had no privacy. Sometimes Edith still fretted that there was something wrong with her; she enjoyed the sexual act between them and knew she was partly to blame for all the babies. She would get Alfred so carried away that the pair of them would forget all about taking care. As she moaned in delight, 'Now, now Alfred,' the fact they could be producing another child was the furthest thought from her mind.

Then she would find she was pregnant again and feel really disturbed and at her wits end. But it was too late by then. She could see what her mother and father thought about all these babies although they never condemned the pair of them. But still she could tell they were worried where it all would end, and when she thought about it, so was she.

After John there had been Martha, their kind and bonny little lass. It had pleased Edith to have a girl next. Alfred did not seem bothered what they had as long as they were healthy. Mind, he did seem to give special attention, at times, to Martha. When they had one of each Edith would have been quite happy to finish there. Martha was a good baby. In fact all her babies were good but for one. She had then produced two more boys in quick succession, George and Fred. She had actually not become pregnant as quickly the next time and had hoped that was it, but no such luck. Next was another girl, Ethel, who Edith was under no illusions about the fact she was rather a plain baby and then finally the trouble of the family arrived, Harry. From day one he seemed to be a problem. At first he demanded constant attention and as he grew older he somehow managed to get into more and more mischief than the rest of them put together. Edith had to admit it had been a very difficult delivery, the worst of all of them. So in honesty she was not surprised he caused so much trouble. After the birth the doctor called Alfred into the bedroom.

'I want to talk seriously to the pair of you. This has to stop,' he said bluntly.

Still a feeling bit bemused from the effort of it all Edith looked blank. 'Stop, what do you mean, doctor?'

'Keep having babies at this rate. In fact, you must stop having any more babies at all.'

Edith felt her colour changing to a brilliant red, she was so embarrassed the way he had said this. It seemed to have been in a leering way that made what they did to produce babies seem dirty. Maybe she was being over sensitive after going through a particularly difficult time. Then he seemed to go on in a kinder voice, 'I'm not condemning you for having children, that's your own business. It's just that Edith's had too many in such a short a time. Besides that she wasn't the best person to have a lot of babies in the first place, she's not overly strong herself. But this really must be the last. Do you understand what I'm telling you and the implications if you ignore me?'

Edith quickly said, 'Aye, of course I do doctor.'

Alfred looked shamefaced at the possible hurt he might have inflicted on the lass he loved so much. 'I don't want to do owt to hurt our lass, you know that doctor. Aye, I understand what you're saying and there'll be no more, rest assured.'

'Well, make sure you both do understand because if there's a next time it could really be the last time. I don't think I can be any clearer than that. We had a struggle this time, pulling them both through safely. Another time we might not be as lucky. Come and see me the pair of you once Edith's up and about if you need advice on how to make sure, but you must take precautions whatever you do, that's a certainty.'

After he had left Alfred looked apologetically at Edith, 'Sorry, lass, I never meant you any harm. But I do love our children, I like having them around me.'

'I know you do but he's right six is enough for anyone's book. I'd have been happy with two.'

'Aye, I don't know. I like them all around me but I suppose you're right we have enough. Well we'd best make the most of this little fella if he's to be the last.'

Edith often looked back afterwards and thought ruefully; maybe this was where they had gone wrong with him. Knowing he had to be the last one so there would be no more babies in the house and he would always be the youngest they spoilt him something rotten. Unfortunately, his behaviour reflected this.

Whatever reaction Alfred had shown to the doctor's words they had at least had the desired effect. Harry was the last baby. Now whenever they made love Alfred was careful that there were no mistakes. He took extra special care of her.

Edith knew in many ways she was a good

mother, her family were well cared for but in other ways she resented all these children to look after. She had not realised when she was at work in the mill, how much she would miss it until she was tied to the house looking after six youngsters.

She always made sure the children were well dressed. In fact, she had heard whispers that quite a few of the villagers thought them one of the best turned out families and wondered how she managed it. Thankfully she was a good needle woman and she had a lot of help from Alfred's sister, Anna. Poor Harry and Anna had not been blessed with a family and Edith thought it was a crying shame as she was so good with the children. When it became apparent that Edith was going to have a large family, on one of her frequent visits, Anna said, 'Edith, I hope you don't mind me saying this and I hope you won't take offence but as you've already guessed it looks like Harry and I won't be lucky in having any bairns. It hasn't happened so far for us and times running out fast for me. So I was wondering if you'd let me help you with your lot sometimes. I appreciate you have no difficulty making their clothes but your hands must be full and your time taken up looking after them all. So if you don't mind, I'd like to make some dresses for the girls. Harry and I would also like to have one or the other stay with us sometimes at a week-end. Then we'd take them out for the day on the Sunday after chapel.'

Edith was quite taken aback by this long speech, from such a quiet woman, so at first was lost for words. Anna could feel her stomach trembling wondering how Edith would react to her request. At last, much to her relief, Edith spoke in what seemed to be a friendly voice, 'I don't see any problems with that, well at least from our side.'

Anna looked at her sharply not quite comprehending what she was saying and implying.

Seeing her look of dismay Edith burst out laughing, 'No, I'm not saying you're not capable of looking after them. What I mean is you might soon get fed up with having them once you see what it really involves. They can be a handful; I'll tell you that for nowt.'

Anna let out a huge sigh of relief, 'Oh! Is that all? No, I don't think we'll get fed up of having them. We'd have never offered in the first place if we'd thought that. After all, we'll be handing them back, it's not like we're having them full time.'

'True enough, maybe you've got it right there. That could be the best way to have children.' Then seeing Anna's face become crestfallen she quickly added, 'I know it isn't really, but at times it seems a good idea. I don't mean to upset you, not after your kind and generous offer.'

'It's all right, most of the time I accept I'm not going to have a bairn but every now and then I feel I've let Harry down and that we've missed out. That's when it upsets me.'

This arrangement worked out to everybody's advantage and Anna and Harry tried not to show favouritism but it soon turned out Martha seemed to want to go with them the most often. When she became old enough to visit on her own, that's where she could more than likely be found.

All the children liked visiting their Grandpa Thompson even if he was a stern man. It was Big Mary, the pig that was the attraction. She was so tame the children could ride on her back. As soon as they arrived at their grandparents' house they would be quick to shout, 'Can we go and see Big Mary now?'

Maybe her father had mellowed with age or simply he liked being a grandpa more than he let on, but he would be quick to agree in taking them out to her. It was too much to ask of him to let his stern mask drop but he would call to the children, 'Come on then if you want a ride. Don't waste time as I've not a lot to spare.' But Edith knew wherever the pig was they would all be there pushing and shoving each other to see who could get the first ride.

In her heart of hearts Edith could not say she really loved Alfred as deeply as she felt she should, but they did settle down into a contented life together. He certainly was a kind, gentle husband and father and although he was not Methodist himself, like her father he did not touch the drink. No, she had no complaints on that score.

It was just his generosity that worried her at times. He never thought to put anything aside for a rainy day. If he saw somebody more in need than himself then he would not hesitate but help them. This caused more arguments and disagreements between them than anything else. When he was broke well before pay day Edith usually ended up snapping at him, 'Don't you think you should put your own family first. They do say you know, 'that charity begins at home'.'

Alfred turned to look at her with a sorrowful expression, 'I'm sorry, Edith, I didn't know I'd left you short.'

By saying it like this he made Edith feel guilty as if she was being mean and nasty. Then she would try to make amends by saying in a gentler voice, 'Well, make sure this is the last time. We'll manage this week and I suppose their need was greater than ours.'

Then he would feel even worse because he could not tell her the true reason for his shortage of money. Deep down Alfred knew that he was doing wrong and did not like it any more than Edith. Even though he felt guilty for his own actions there was no way he could stop, it was an addiction. Being the way he was Edith just presumed his money went on helping his mates and he never gave her any reason to believe otherwise. Not that he would see any of his own go short and he was sure they were not in want of anything. There was always a good meal on their table and the children always looked so clean and tidy. He knew Edith's mother slipped her some food and gave her things for the children, but there was no harm in that. He was not too proud to accept a bit of charity when he knew he threw money away himself. But he did know he had Edith to thank for how they managed; it was only because of her careful budgeting and housekeeping that they did it. He loved her so and put his conscious to rest by kidding himself one day his luck would be in and he could give her all she desired.

Edith had her own ambitions which she kept well hidden. She had a yearning to have some of the good things of life for herself. She knew she was a proud person and was not really sure where she had inherited this from, but at times she felt she deserved something more from life, better than she was getting. For some unknown reason she had the notion that she had been cut out for a better life. Maybe she had rushed too quickly into marriage with Alfred and should have waited to see if another proposal from a better source had come along. It was too late now, what was done was done and that was all there was to it. Then common sense would take over and she realised she could not have waited in any case, not when she had been pregnant with his bairn.

But it did not stop the resentment gnawing away inside, and worse still she knew she took some of this resentment out on her eldest daughter, Martha. It seemed beyond her power to stop herself, but nearly every Saturday she seemed to get a bad headache. She had to take herself off to bed and leave Martha to do the jobs and look after the young ones. As Martha became more capable she gave her more and more tasks to do. Deep down she knew it was not right and she was being hard on this young lass of theirs and for no good reason. Her conscience made her acknowledge, in her own way, that what she was doing was as bad as Alfred and his giving money away.

Sometimes Martha would find the courage to challenge an order, 'But, Ma must I? I want to go out and play with my friends. They do not have to help their Ma.'

Edith would lose patience and snap back, 'Just get on with it. I need your help with so many to look after. I'm not bothered what your friends have or haven't to do.'

Edith knew how she had felt when she'd had to help her father with the horses, but it seemed different to ask for Martha's help with such a large family. It all came back to Alfred not being sensible with his money in Edith's mind. If only he would save some for a rainy day, she was sure she would feel more content within herself then maybe she would not take it out so much on the children.

10

As soon as she saw his unhappy face she knew she had been right to feel unsettled about what he was up to. Taking a deep breath she almost shouted at him. 'Well, what's happened? I can tell something has, so there's no use denying it.'

'I wasn't going to deny anything. I've been laid off,' he replied abruptly.

'What do you mean laid off?' she asked with a sinking feeling in the pit of her stomach.

'Exactly what I've just said to you that Morgan's have no more orders.'

'But you've always been so busy there.'

'I've seen it coming. There's been less and less work of late. But I've said nowt to you because I didn't want to cause you unnecessary worry in case they started to be busy again. You never know from one day to the next as an order can suddenly come in. But it hasn't, so they've laid us off. They've said if more work does come in, they'll set some of us back on.'

Edith could feel her fear increasing for their future and felt cold all through her body. 'But what are we to do? What will we live on? Oh Alfred, why us?' she pleaded.

'Stop fretting so lass. I'll get straight on looking for another job, never fear. There must be something around. I'm not proud; I'll take any job that comes along.'

'Yes, but where? There's not another engineering firm on the doorstep.'

'Have you not been listening, I've already said I'll take whatever work I can, it doesn't have to be in engineering. I'll have to go further afield happen. Maybe to Keighley or Halifax or even Bradford, wherever - as long as I find work. I'm sure there must be work in one of those places.'

'Aye, but there'll be a few of you chasing the same jobs, cause you're not the only one laid off, I'll be bound.'

'True enough, but don't fret I'll get something.'

Her fear made all her resentment bubble to the surface and without intending to she snapped at him, 'Oh I do wish you'd taken notice of me and put something by each week, like I'd wanted to do, just for such an eventuality as this. We'll not manage long without your wage coming in and that's a fact. Maybe Ma will look after the young ones and I could try to get set on at the mill again. That'd be better than nothing.'

'We'll think about it but it is early days yet. Let's see what happens and how I get on finding a job first. Best not say anything to your Ma and Pa 'til we see what turns up. No need to worry them as well.'

'Aye, I suppose you're right there.'

Both of them were deeply concerned over the weekend. They could sense each other's unhappiness but were too upset and worried to broach the subject again. It was like they were afraid that if they voiced their thoughts it would make matters worse.

Edith was up extra early on the Monday morning and pushed Alfred quickly out of bed. She gave him a good breakfast and had a pack up ready. 'Here, you'd best take this with you. It's a meal to eat while you're looking for a job as there's no spare money for you to buy food out.'

'Thanks, lass, I'll be glad of it and that's a fact. I don't know what time I'll be back, it all depends on how I get on.'

'I know that. Go on get away with you and good luck.'

Edith barely managed to get her washing done that day; she was so agitated about whether Alfred was finding work out there or not. As soon as he came through the door and she took one look at his miserable face she knew what had happened. He had not found the work he was hoping for.

'All the firms seem to be in the same boat as Morgan's. They've no orders coming in. They're all just holding their heads above water and managing to keep on who they've employed with them now. There's certainly no room for new workers. I'll just have to try another town and maybe look at work that I don't need any skills in. It won't pay as much but less is better than nowt and beggars can't be choosers. Don't fret, lass, I'll find something.'

All Edith could feel thankful for, at this moment, was that she had already made all the children new outfits ready for Whitsuntide which would soon be upon them. They always had new outfits then, so she could not let them down this year. Besides which, if they were seen in their new clothes nobody would guess they had financial problems. Unbeknown to Alfred she had managed to put a bit of money by, so that would keep them going for a little while if she was very careful with it. Any roads he might come back the next day and say he had found another job. There must be people out there looking for somebody as hard working as Alfred. Aye, she was sure he would soon enough get a new job.

Events did not happen like that. Out he

would go each day with a cheery smile and stating, 'This could be the day Edith that I find work.'

But he would come home looking none too happy. 'Sorry, lass, there just wasn't anything going today.'

Once he had found there was nothing whatsoever in his own area of work he had dropped his sights considerably but still to no avail. There were just so many people in the same boat as them. Edith became more and more despondent where it was all going to end. They had not been able to keep the truth any longer from her mother and father. Any roads sooner or later, she was sure, one of the children would have let slip what had happened.

Her mother, knowing things must be hard for Edith with her brood, thankfully kept discreetly slipping Edith some food to help them. They always had plenty of provisions produced from the livestock, and her mother collected more eggs from the hens than she could use, so these were passed on to Edith under the pretext they were for the children. They came in useful for all of them.

Edith had always prided herself on her good table of food, now she had to learn the art of being thrifty with it. Everything had to be used until every ounce of goodness had been utilised so there was nothing left in it to eat. Six fast growing children were forever hungry and Edith became fed up of hearing them whining, 'What's to eat, Ma, I'm starving.'

Whatever she gave them did not seem to keep them full for two minutes. Even worse, they were no longer able to use the parlour on Sunday. There was not enough money to spare for coal to light that fire. It was essential that she kept the range going in the kitchen otherwise she could not cook what food there was. She started to put less food on her own plate; she knew the bairns needed it more than she did. But all this made her resent Alfred and the children. This was not the life he had promised her when he proposed. He had said he would always take care of her. Well, she most certainly did not call this being taken care of.

She knew she was hurting Alfred with her attitude but she could not stop herself venting her anger on him when each evening he walked through the door with that dejected look on his face. So again it was evident he had not found a job that day.

Edith was both so angry and worried that one particular evening as he came through the door she burst out. 'We can't go on much longer tha knows. There's barely any food left in the house. I've no more money to spare for bus fares. You'll just have to walk now when you go to look for jobs.'

'But I need to go further afield, if I'm going to find work. There's nowt going around here,' he beseeched.

She gave him a withering look and said no more but both were hiding their anger. Actions soon became louder than words and neither would bother speaking to the other on an evening unless it was really necessary.

As it soon became obvious that Alfred was not going to work each day they'd had to tell Edith's mother and father about him being made redundant, though they did not initially give the full details how much it was affecting them. Now at the end of her tether and feeling at her wits end she finally poured out all her feelings to her mother. 'I don't know what's going to happen to us, I really don't. I've had to stop paying the rent so, at least, I can still buy us food for the bairns. Without your help, giving us something, we'd not have lasted this long and my small savings are at an end.' With a sob she added, 'I can see all of us in the work house yet.'

'Nay, don't give up hope, lass. Something will turn up I'm sure.'

'I can't go on any longer.' This was all she

could say before she burst into great sobs racking her whole body.

'Don't take on so, lass, there must be some way we can help you get through this. I'll talk to your Pa.'

This had the desired effect of stopping the sobbing. 'No, Ma! You mustn't do that. Alfred wouldn't like it. I know he hardly ever looses his temper but all this is upsetting him so much he's real down with himself. He feels he's let us all down. I keep trying to tell him that's nonsense; it's not his fault Morgan's received no more orders. After all he's not the only one in the same boat. But he takes it so personally.' This was said with a slight exaggeration so she actually found the words stuck in her throat to admit this. She then carried on, 'It's just having six bairns does make it hard to make ends meet and particularly when they're growing so quickly and forever hungry.'

'I know all of that, but we've no shortage of food here so there's no reason for you not to have some. I'll give you as much as you need, you've only to say,' her mother told her kindly.

'But it's not just that. Now he has to walk all over the place looking for work his boots are starting to fall to pieces. We can't even afford the shoe leather to repair them.' Once again the tears came when she thought about this.

'Come on, stop it Edith, don't take on so. We'll sort something out one way or another, never fear. I'll put the kettle on and make you a nice brew and I've just cut into a fruit cake. Here, have a piece of this. We'll never get through it the two of us so you might as well take some home with you. I cooked a nice piece of ham yesterday so you can take some of that as well.'

Sarah was worried because one look at her daughter and it was obvious she was not getting enough to eat for herself, but giving the children most of what there was.

Still Edith protested, 'I can't take the food off your table.'

'Look, lass, if I want to give you it I can. I know we're not as well off as before. Your Pa lost his work carrying for Morgan's when their orders dropped off but we're still not doing too badly. The other mills keep him busy. Besides, we do have something put by for a rainy day. Your Pa only said one night last week how he was wondering how Alfred was getting on. But you know him; he'd never ask Alfred outright.'

'No and Alfred told me not to tell you or Pa. I suppose it's a man's thing, too much pride which needs to be forgotten at a time like this.'

A thought had just occurred to Edith but she was not sure how to ask so she just plunged straight in. 'You don't think Alfred could work with Pa, do you?'

'Nay, lass, he's worked on his own far too long to work with anybody else now. In any case I don't know that he's enough work to support two. It'd mean buying another horse and cart as well. But leave it with me and I'll happen put it to him.'

In her heart Edith thought her mother was only trying to be kind to her, she did not really believe her father would do anything like that for them. He was a great believer that people should stand on their own feet and that they had made their own bed so they must lie on it.

She also now realised she would have to tell Alfred that she had talked about their problem in depth with her mother in case her father was so annoyed he said something to him in anger. Normally Alfred understood, but at the moment, even he was not behaving like his usual good natured self. Edith could comprehend how he felt, all this had made him feel dejected and as if he were letting his family down. But he was not; Edith knew it really was not his fault, even if at times she did blame him. In her heart she knew he was a good bloke and she was lucky.

She plodded home wearily from her parents dragging the youngest children with her. Even they seemed to sense how she felt and moaned and whined all the time at the walking they had to do. Nowadays Edith knew her temper was on a short fuse but she could not help herself as she snapped, 'Oh! Stop it do, otherwise I'll tan all of your backsides.'

They were not used to their mother being so cross with them and fell into a sullen silence for the rest of the long trek home. This put Edith in a worse bad humour. As soon as she opened the door and saw Martha daydreaming, not getting the meal ready as she had been told, she pushed the door shut with one almighty shove that sent a resounding crash through the house, 'Wake up girl. What do you think you're playing at? It's hard enough to find the money to buy the food without you daydreaming and not getting it ready.'

Despite being so gentle natured even Martha was at her wits end with all this rowing, her lip trembled, 'I'm sorry, Ma. I'm tired after school and I seem to have so much to do for you.'

'Oh you do, do you madam? Well what do

you think I've to do for all of you, I ask you? I suppose you think I've nothing to do. Well let me tell you young lady I get tired as well. Never thought of that I suppose? To be honest not only do I get tired with all the work, I'm sick and tired of all of your attitudes.'

Martha, knowing better than to say any more, turned to get the potatoes ready but in her agitation knocked some to the floor. 'You stupid girl,' her mother roared. 'Leave them, I'll see to them now. You're more a hindrance than a help.'

Martha ran out of the house with tears streaming down her face as she thought of the injustice of it all. She did her best; after all she was not grown up like her mother yet. What did she expect of her? Little did Martha know her father had seen her rush out, as he came down the path on his way home, and stood looking after her with a puzzled expression.

As soon as he walked in the house he questioned Edith, 'Well, what's wrong with Martha?'

'How do I know, a paddy most probably at having to help me.'

'Come on, Edith, admit it, you're hard on the lass at times. Because that's all she is, a young girl, yet you expect so much of her.'

'How do you know what it's like? You don't have six children to look after all the time,' she screamed back at him.

Alfred held his hands up in resignation, knowing Edith was going to have the last word. He knew better than to argue with her when she was in this kind of mood.

'Any roads there is something I want to tell you,' Edith continued in a much calmer voice, as if the heated discussion of the last few minutes had never been.

Alfred felt a shiver of fear go through him as he hoped to goodness she was not going to say she was pregnant again. They had been careful and not only could they not afford another mouth to feed, it was Edith's health that Alfred was really frightened for.

'Oh yes, come on spit it out, you'd best tell me and put me out of my misery.'

'It's my Ma.'

Now Alfred was at a total loss what this was all about, 'Your Ma?'

'Aye, I was upset when I was there today and I think I said more than I should have about how we are coping or should I say not coping.'

Alfred let out a sigh of relief; this was not as bad as he thought even if it was bad enough. 'Is that it?'

'It's enough isn't it?'

But Alfred did not react how Edith had expected, 'Come here you daft thing, it doesn't matter if you've talked to her. After all, she's your mother and what are they there for? Don't fret, no harm's been done I'm sure.'

'Yes but she says she's going to talk to Pa and you know what he's like.'

'Look, it doesn't matter. He might say a few harsh words giving his opinion on how we're coping with the situation, but that's all he can do. Now that's not too bad is it?'

'No,' Edith said hesitantly, because even though she was a grown woman, with children of her own, she still had a hidden fear of her father. Somehow at times he still seemed to dominate her life and when he was around made her feel like a child who had to do the right thing to please him instead of the grown woman she was. Of course, she knew deep down it was Alfred not her father whose opinion of her should matter. Wanting to have the last word on the subject she added, 'But you know what he can be like, he can be so harsh.'

'H'm,' was all Alfred said. He knew it was pointless saying any more, but if truth be known, he knew exactly what Edith meant, but he was not going to tell her so and upset her even more.

11

When her mother and father had made an unexpected visit that evening Edith had to eat her words at what her father had to say to them both. Thinking she must have somehow misheard she asked him, 'Repeat what you've just said again, please.'

Giving her a rather disdainful look, her father impatiently said once more. 'I've a pair of cottages in the village that I've owned for quite a while coming empty soon. I've been renting them out. One came empty the other week; the husband found a job further afield so the whole family's moved. Now the same thing has happened to the family in the adjoining one so they're leaving at the end of next week. You can have the pair of cottages then we'll get them knocked through so there will be plenty of room for all your brood.'

'But I think it'll be too much rent for us to afford for the pair,' she said sadly giving a cynical laugh. 'Nay, we can't even afford the rent on the one we've got now.' At the same time she was thinking it was also unfair that two blokes had found work, whilst her hard working Alfred had found nothing.

Her father bellowed at her, 'Girl! Don't you understand anything I've been saying? I mean I'm giving them to you. They'll be yours so there'll be no rent to pay. They'll belong to you. Now have I made myself clear enough?'

Still looking at her father blankly Edith repeated, 'Giving them to us? But I didn't even know you had any, let alone renting them out.'

'I've had them for a while now but that's no concern of yours. I don't need to tell you all my business.' Then in a kinder voice he added, 'You're no fool, lass. You must realise one day all I have will go to you. Who else is there to inherit? You might as well have some of it now as wait for me to die. Your Ma and I have enough to see our days out.' Once more taking on his usual stern approach he continued, 'After all, they're my grandchildren and I want them well looked after. It'd do my reputation no good if I was seen to be letting them starve.'

'Oh Pa you've shocked me! I can't believe it. That's wonderful isn't it Alfred?' Inside she was wondering if it was all a dream and she would soon wake up to the cold light of day.

'Eh, it's grand. I can't thank you enough,' added Alfred feeling beside himself with happiness that his wife was happy again.

'Yes, well, it should help you. At least

whatever takes place in the future you'll not want for a roof over your heads and with no rent to pay that'll make a big difference in what you need to earn in order to keep all that tribe of yours. Now won't it lad?'

'It will indeed.'

Edith was wondering if this was really the father she thought she knew who had done this for them. This man she had always thought of as rather hard and unkind. He was not showing that hardness to them now; there could not have been a kinder approach than this.

Her mother looked at her smiling. 'Now then, Edith, no more need for that long face you've been wearing of late. I told you I'd talk to your Pa and I have.'

'Thanks, Ma. I don't know what to say. You've both got me at a loss for words.'

Alfred gave a laugh, 'Well, that makes a change.'

Her father happily joined in with him, 'I'll agree there.' Before Edith could chastise them both for saying this her father went on, 'Now, here's the last bit.'

Edith exclaimed, 'There's more!'

'Aye, I've run my own business too long on my own to take a partner so what I propose to do is give Alfred fifty pounds to set up on his own. It's up to him how he uses it and what business he chooses to go into. It's not a lot of money but I'm sure, Alfred, you've got enough about you to make something of yourself with that.'

'Oh I will that, never fear. Aye, I'll think of something and get it going and look after this daughter of yours well enough again,' he said with real delight in his voice.

Edith's eyes started to fill with water, but this time not tears of worry and sadness but tears of joy.

'I just can't believe we're to get out of this mess,' she said incredulously.

Clearing his throat her father looked at her, 'I realise it isn't Alfred's fault Morgan's ran out of work and, as I said before, one day it'll be all yours so you might as well benefit now. I couldn't stand by and see my grand bairns starve, now could I?'

'No, Pa, but I still can't believe all you've said. It feels as if I'm dreaming and I'll wake up to the reality of where to get our next meal from and how to sort out about the rent money.'

'No you won't. I've seen your landlord and paid off the rent arrears. I've also paid your rent up 'til the end of next month. So that should give you time to do what needs to be done in your new home. Also each week I'll give you ten bob to help you feed the bairns, that's 'til you're back on your feet. You're family, all the family we've got and I believe in looking after your own.' Then he looked hard at Alfred, 'Just make sure this nightmare doesn't come back again for our lass.'

'I will, have no fear of that and I'd like to add my sincere thanks. I can't begin to tell you how much I appreciate all you're doing for us.'

After discussing it further her parents took their leave. Edith threw herself into Alfred's arms, 'I just can't believe it. You'd have never thought it of my Pa, would you?'

'I've to admit I wouldn't. This doesn't seem like him at all. But still you know the saying, don't look a gift horse in the mouth.'

'What'll you do with the money? What line of business do you fancy?'

'I don't rightly know at the moment. I'm that taken aback that I can't think straight and I've never given it a thought as I'd always presumed I'd go back in a foundry somewhere. I'll think on it. I'm sure something will come to me but my minds too flummoxed at the moment to think straight.'

'Aye, I know what you mean. I don't know whether I'm coming or going I feel so excited, particularly after the last few months we've had.'

Finally they both managed to settle

themselves to sleep knowing the next few weeks were going to be hectic if they were going to pack up and move house. A brood of six had somehow accumulated a lot of things. Then Alfred would have to get his business going, he could not put it off for very long if he was going to be earning again. They needed that money if they were going to buy food enough for them all. She did not want to see the fifty pounds swallowed up in living costs and not used for what her father intended.

Edith suddenly felt something digging into her side just as she had finally slipped into asleep. 'I've got it. I know what I'll do with that money.'

At first she thought she was dreaming but as the voice became louder and the nudging harder she realised it was really Alfred trying to awaken her.

Mumbling as she tried to open her eyes, 'What time is it?'

'Never mind the time; I've thought what I'll do to set up in business. I just had to tell you, I couldn't wait until morning now I've sorted it out in my mind.'

'Come on tell me then I can go back to sleep.'

'You might sound bit more enthusiastic,' Alfred said in a hurt voice, but he still carried on. 'Anyway, what I've decided is I'll get a horse and cart. In fact Fred told me the other day about a rig out he knows is up for sale cheap. Then I'll stock up with groceries and possibly fruit and vegetables including any other odds and ends that people want delivering and I'll go around with my cart. I'm sure your Pa will let me stable the horse in one of his spare stables.'

'M'm sounds all right but do you think you'll make enough from that for us to live on?'

'I don't know but there's only one way to find out and that's to try it. Anyway I don't want it to stop there, when we've got it going well we can always expand. Any roads as I see it people always have to eat. I know if they're short of money they don't buy as much but there are still a lot of the villagers employed at the mill and have the money coming in to buy decent food.'

'Can I go back to sleep now?' queried Edith without asking any further questions.

Alfred felt disappointed that she did not want to talk more about it but he could not really say so, 'Aye if you want to. I don't think I can now my mind's too busy planning it all out.'

Alfred kept up this activity in both mind and body for the next few weeks as he rushed around in a frenzy. Luckily he did manage to get the horse and cart he had heard about so when the time came to move house they used that to move their belongings.

When Edith first saw the houses she did not know what to really think of her father's offer. They were both filthy; up to them her little cottage on the moors looked a palace. She could see there would be plenty of room between the two houses as there were four bedrooms and she gave a silent chuckle as she thought about the two kitchens. That was nonsense. To her she could not see how they would make the two houses into one. She said as much to Alfred. 'How on earth does Pa think we'll make a home out of these two places? Does he expect one part of the family to live in one house and the rest in the other?'

'Of course not so don't worry your pretty head about it. I'll sort it all out. It'll not be too hard a job to make something of them. After all, they're a side by side pair and there's certainly the space in them to do something. Being how they're at the end of the terrace will make the job easier, never fret lass.'

She had to concede he had a point. 'I suppose so. It's just they look so cold and uninviting up to our little cottage.'

'Aye, but remember how that looked the

first time we saw it and look what you've done with it. I'll never forget your face when you saw that, utter disbelief that you were going to live somewhere in that state. After all, when you think about it, all the work we've done in it has only been for the landlord's benefit at the end of the day. At least these will belong to us, so anything we do will be for our own good.'

'Yes,' exclaimed Edith beginning to feel panic building up inside at the task ahead. 'But it took a lot of hard work to get the cottage as it is and then I hadn't all the children to look after. Besides we've no money to spare for the work.'

'Look, stop fretting I'll sort it out somehow or other. Remember what you always tell me, 'as one door closes another opens'.'

He was not far wrong in what he said there because her father called to have a quiet word with him when Edith was not around. He did not beat around the bush as he said, 'I realise you need money to do these up a bit and as they've been my responsibility and they have deteriorated into this state whilst they were, here's a little bit to help you with the work. If you put the labour in yourself you should manage with that.'

'I don't know what to say. Edith will be ever so fussed.'

'Let's just keep this between our two selves. It doesn't always do for the women folk to know everything. I'm sure you can think of a way to explain how you've managed to get what you need. I'll leave that up to you.'

Still in shock from the amazement of all that was happening Alfred could only just find the words to thank him.

The children made a lot of protest about moving. Edith had known they would, because they loved the freedom they had to play and roam on the moors which was right outside their own doorstep. She did point out to them that they would have a lot more space at the new place which would give them much better sleeping arrangements. But they were having none of this and whatever she said did nothing to appease them. She became fed up of hearing one or another voice behind her, 'Oh Ma! Must we really move? We're all happy here. Anyway, Ma, it would save you a lot of work if we didn't move.'

At times Edith would lose her temper, 'Don't you understand? I don't mind that work. I want a better house for us. 'Sides it'll be our own place, we can do what we like with no landlord breathing down our neck and no threat of being thrown out. How much longer do you think we'd have been able to stay here and not pay any rent? You'd all have been in the workhouse, that's for sure if your Grandpa Thompson hadn't stepped in to help.'

Still she knew they were not totally convinced as she continued to hear the moans, 'Oh, Ma, we like the moors but I suppose we'll have to make the best of it.'

When Edith told Alfred how they were, he just laughed, 'Ignore them, lass, they'll soon find something there they like as well if not better. You know what kids are like. Any roads it's you that matters, you'll have a home all of your own to be really proud of.'

⋆   ⋆   ⋆

It suddenly struck Edith that she had not really looked at her eldest daughter, Martha, for a good while. As she looked intently at her it struck Edith what a pretty lass she was becoming. She was tall already for her age and looked as if she would leave her mother and her well behind in height. She had beautiful auburn hair that had a natural wave. But most of all it was her eyes that caught people's attention. They were a deep brown and had a look of perpetual surprise about them. Aye, the eyes were really her most redeeming feature. But it was not only her looks; she was so good natured as well. She had made no protest at moving, instead she did all she could to help get packed and certainly helped bring some of the younger children in line. Tears pricked Edith's eyes as she realised how like her own dead sister, Elsie, she had become. Aye, a bonny girl she was turning out to be but, thankfully, she was far more robust than Elsie had been.

At times she felt sorry she was so hard on the lass, but at other times it was as if something was burning up inside her and she could not help it. It was like an inner resentment that festered there. She knew Alfred was aware how she treated this girl. He had only to look at her, as much as to say leave it but would say nowt because he did not want to make it harder for the lass. Then at other times he could no longer hold his tongue and had to say, 'Leave her alone, Edith. She's only a young girl. You don't want her to feel like you did when your Pa made you work so hard.'

She knew Alfred was right in what he said but try as she might she still carried on. It went far deeper than that, it was as if it were a way to vent her hidden anger and resentment for what life had brought her.

It was not a moment too soon when Alfred at last started his deliveries. Until they moved into the new house he could not get fully going; he could not make it to all the houses he wanted to. Early morning, twice weekly, he would get to the market to buy his provisions and then go back down into the village with his deliveries. With his easy going way he soon charmed his customers and they were more than willing to buy from him with further requests coming for items he did not stock. So the next time he went to buy provisions he would come back loaded up with even more things than the last time.

Edith felt slightly envious of his success and soon had her own thoughts how she could help. She had already made plans in her mind what she wanted to do herself once they had moved. She decided she was probably happier than she had been for a long time. At least they were getting themselves organised and making some sort of decent life for the family now.

12

Once they were settled into their new home and there was plenty of room, as Edith had anticipated, she decided the time was right for her to outline her plans to Alfred.

He was startled by what she told him. 'You intend to what?' he snapped.

'I've just said, the spare lounge would make a nice little shop. I'll run that in the day whilst you make your deliveries to the more remote areas.'

'What do you propose to sell in your shop?' he asked with disbelief at what he was hearing.

'All different sorts of provisions that people need. I thought that you'll be able to get stock for here when you go to the wholesalers for yours. I suppose reps will also call and get things delivered for me as well so maybe I could order stock for you that way. So as I see it, it will help both of us. As I see how things go I will sell anything else that there's a demand for and people need. I hope to sell a wide variety of goods to attract the customers in.'

He accepted her point on that but brought

another objection up. 'I don't want my customers coming here instead of buying off me as that would be pointless.'

'I've given that a lot of thought as well and as I see it your customers would find it difficult to get here. Besides which, you can travel to customers much further afield with your cart than would come here.'

'That's all well and good but to buy stock costs money, as you full well know. So how do you propose to overcome that little obstacle?'

'Don't worry, it's all sorted out. Ma's going to lend me what I need and I'll pay her some back each week. She's not in a rush to get it back.'

'My, my you have been busy but I don't like the sound of you borrowing money from your Ma. Don't you think your parents have already done enough for us?'

'Yes, but it's only a loan this time, it's not as if she's giving me the money. Anyway I'd already thought I'd pay her back a little more than she lends me so she won't have lost out on it either. Ma's more than happy to lend me the money. Let's be honest Alfred, the money you earn from the round isn't really enough to keep all of us, with all the things we need. The youngest will soon need some new shoes. It's one thing or another that needs buying with our tribe. No, I think it's a good idea. I'm really excited about it. Besides in the school holidays and evenings the eldest are old enough to help out.'

Edith still felt disappointed at the lack of enthusiasm he was showing and more so as he added, 'Well it'd been nice if you'd let me think of other ways to earn extra money. After all I'm the man of the house, the bread winner. But now you've thought of it I've to admit there is a possibility it could work. But I don't like the idea of the children being brought into it. I've asked you before to let them enjoy their childhood whilst they can. They grow up soon enough; don't make this time for them all work as well. Let them play and behave as children do.'

'I will, don't worry. It'll all work out fine,' she said confidently.

Despite his reservations about the idea, Edith soon won him around as she usually did. It only took their Sunday afternoon of fun and games. When Edith wanted something she knew how to get around him by being extra generous with her favours. It had become their practice to send the children to Sunday school in the afternoon, supervised by the eldest two, John and Martha. There was a special building erected in the village in 1838 for that purpose, very near to the village centre.

For some reason, once the children were out of the house Edith could find it easier to mellow towards Alfred's attentions. The children would not have been gone long before his arms were around her pulling her towards him. He would start gently kissing her, then caressing, all the while leading her towards the bedroom. Edith always fell for this show of affection and offered no resistance. In fact, to Alfred's delight she was very amenable to being adventurous in what they did. Alfred was fully aware that she used this to manipulate things to her own advantage and when she wanted something particular from him she was even more submissive. But this suited both of them; Alfred was sexually satisfied, whilst Edith derived pleasure herself yet at the same time getting her own way on other things. If this was the way she wanted to use sex to get what she wanted then Alfred was more than willing to go along with it.

After a particularly enjoyable time in bed Edith propped herself up on one arm and looked down at Alfred, 'Well, have you given any more thought to my idea?'

Not wanting to appear too agreeable at giving way and liking to play her at her own game, Alfred asked with tongue in cheek, 'Now why would I want to do that?'

'Because you know it's an excellent plan and you said yourself you wanted to make a go of being in your own business.'

'Aye, but then would it be my own business if you ran the shop your way?'

'Course it would. I'd not be able to do it without your help, now would I?'

'I suppose not, but let's be serious about it for a minute. It will mean a lot of hard work for you on top of looking after the bairns.'

'I am being serious about the whole thing and I realise all that. It'll not just be hard work for me but all of us. We'll all need to pull our fair share of weight as I've said before. But I'm certainly not afraid of hard work, I'm well used to it,' she said the last part rather sadly

'H'm,' Alfred looked at her laughing again, 'I hope you're not implying I'm afraid of hard work.'

'Course not, but I'm just pointing out it'll be more than just taking your cart around if I do open a shop.'

'Come here and give me a kiss if that's what you really want to do. You'll have to do a bit more hard work on me.'

Looking at him Edith asked, 'Do you mean you'll let me set it up?'

'Course I do. Have I ever refused you anything?'

Edith bent over him and gave him a big kiss and cuddle, 'Oh I do love you Alfred.' When she felt like this she really convinced herself she meant it.

These were the moments Alfred treasured. He felt for a few minutes, at least, he had her true love but then she would somehow go back into herself.

★ ★ ★

Once he had made his mind up to get the shop set up for Edith there was no holding him back. He soon had the room completed, and then went on to make a counter and shelves. Even the children become involved in what he was doing and wanted to help in any way they could. Edith was certain this was really the right thing for them to do to boost their income.

Meanwhile, being a small village, word of what they were planning soon spread around and before they knew it people were knocking on the window as they went past asking, 'Will it be open before very long?'

Alfred, keeping as cheerful as ever, would laugh, 'I'm working as fast as I can at it. Never fear, as soon as the doors open for trade you'll know. We'll look forward to seeing you in here buying our goods.' Most of the villagers were getting to know Alfred with his horse and cart, so were used to his banter. They would simply laugh back, 'Be off with you,' with good humour.

Being even more encouraged by this reaction to the news of the shop opening Edith was making enquiries where it was best to buy her stock. She knew Alfred would have to go to the fruit and vegetable market on a regular basis for her. But he did call at various other wholesalers to stock his cart. No, she wanted to sell more than he carried around. There would have to be sweets for the children and all variety of groceries and food stuff giving more choice than Alfred could carry. She even wondered whether to have wool and such like in, but she realised maybe she should walk before she ran.

Much to their delight the shop became an instant success, just as she had hoped. They were open long hours, from early morning and did not close until late at night. Then often there would still be a knock on the door. Edith or one of the others would shout, 'We're closed now, you should have come earlier, but we'll be back open first thing in the morning.'

Usually a pathetic voice would reply, 'But we've run out of . . . ,' and this would be some silly thing, 'and I need some now.'

Wanting to keep her good reputation for helpfulness, Edith would more often than not fall soft and open the door to serve them with whatever it was they wanted. As requests came for different varieties of items, if Edith could see a real demand, then she would start to sell it. In no time at all, for the first time in all their years of marriage she was actually saving money on a regular basis.

Even Alfred's cart proved as popular as ever. One evening he returned home and told her he had something to discuss with her once they were on their own. Edith was not sure whether this was good or bad but was impatient to hear what he had to say, 'Can't you talk to me now?'

'No, I want you to be able to listen fully to what I've to say, without being nagged by one or other of the children.'

'All right then, but I hope it's worth waiting for.'

'Of course, would I say anything that wasn't?' Alfred laughed. His insides felt knotted up as he was excited and yet keyed up by what he wanted to discuss and Edith's possible reaction.

Edith heaved a sigh of relief when the last one of the children was in bed. It seemed to take forever getting them there and tonight, it was worse than ever because she was impatient to hear what Alfred had to say.

As soon as she was back in the kitchen with Alfred she could contain herself no longer, 'Come on then, spit it out what you've to say. At last you've got my undivided attention.'

Suddenly Alfred felt at a loss for words and found it difficult how to start. Edith grew even more impatient, 'Come on, for goodness sake get on with what you want to tell me. It can't be that bad.' Then as an after thought added with worry in her voice, 'Is it?'

This brought Alfred's confidence back and he laughed now, 'No, of course not. No, it's just an idea that's all. Well, you know we've been managing to put a bit by lately. I've been looking at how things are going and it seems to me everything is moving forward to using motorised vehicles. Horse drawn is going out of date. I think we should get a wagon. It'd be a lot quicker for me to go to the market and suppliers in Bradford. With a wagon, your things would be here a lot earlier and I could carry more stock in one load. I've worked out figures and it'd pay for itself in no time. We'd have no horse to feed and it'd save me having to go back and forth to your Pa's all the time to stable the horse.'

Here Edith interrupted his flow, 'My, my you have been busy. I don't know though. I'm not sure about all this advancement. Pa's done well enough with his horse and cart. He's not changed, even though some other carriers have and he's still doing all right.'

'I've talked with him about it and he says if he were younger he would have to think about moving forward himself because those with motor vehicles are getting some of his trade. In fact, he was saying to me he's wondering if it's time he retired. He's feeling his age a bit now.'

'That'll be the day when he retires! Seeing is believing with him. I don't know what to say about you getting a motor vehicle. It feels nice and safe to have something saved, it makes me feel a lot happier. Will it take all our savings to buy a wagon?'

'If I'm truthful I've got to say it most probably will. I've looked around and I know they do cost a fair bit. But we'll soon save back up again, even quicker than before when I can earn more money. It's a pity but I'll get next to nowt for the horse and cart as they're becoming more or less obsolete, nobody wants them now. Still I can have a go and try to sell them to help recover some of the money I spend on a wagon.'

'How long would it take you to find one and get it?'

Here Alfred gave a small cough, 'Actually I've seen one I rather fancy over Halifax way.'

'You have, have you? Obviously you've already been looking and really made your mind up to get one whatever I think.'

'Now don't say that, I haven't just arrived home with one. I'm listening to what you're saying.'

Edith interrupted him here as another thought came to her, 'But you can't even drive.'

Here he did look a bit shame faced, 'Well actually I can. Fred Yates has been giving me lessons in his van.'

'By, you are the sly one aren't you? Well there's not much left for me to say. If you think it's for the best you'd better go and get one. Just make sure you're right. I don't want to have no money coming in ever again.'

'I will, don't worry on that score. Right, I'll get on with it as soon as I can; now we've made the decision to get one.'

As good as his word, a few days later he arrived home with the wagon. Edith still did not feel too happy about this form of transport when she saw it. It was so big and moved much quicker than the horse and cart. The children were overjoyed with it. The eldest of them wanted to know when they would be old enough to have a go at driving it and the young ones wanted to be given a ride in it instantly. They knew they would get their own way with their father. 'Come on then, jump in. Some of you'll have to go in the back, there's not room for you all in the cab. The young ones better come in the cab with me, that'll be safer. Do you want to come with us, Edith?'

'No, I'll give it a miss this time. Besides I'm in the middle of cooking tea, I can't just leave it. Mind, one of them had better stay to look after the shop for me. Martha will you do it? We can't just shut shop to suit your Pa. After all, we're going to need all the money we can get now he's spent what we had saved.'

'Oh come on Edith, just the once won't hurt. It'll only take a few minutes.'

As usual Martha was willing to fall in with her mother's wishes for the sake of peace, 'Yes, Ma, I'll stay behind. I'm not that bothered about going.'

But one look at her crestfallen face and Alfred knew she was. He could see the look of disappointment there. He always had a soft spot for her because Edith seemed to be so hard on this first daughter of theirs. 'Come on, Edith, surely this once won't hurt shutting the shop for a few minutes,' he reiterated.

'Of course it will. What do you think folk will say if they try the door and it's locked when we're usually open? Have sense, Alfred.

165

They'll soon stop coming if they think they can't depend on us.'

'All right you've made your point,' then turning to Martha he said in a gentler voice, 'I'll find time to take you out tomorrow. Is that all right with you, lass?'

'Yes Pa thanks.' She rushed to her father and gave him a big hug and kiss, looking cheered up once more.

John shouted out in good humour, 'Stop it, you soppy thing. We're all sat here waiting to go. There'll not be time before tea if we don't get off now.'

Edith was now back in good humour as she had won her own way once more, 'Go on away with you then, and that's the shop bell Martha.'

* * *

In no time at all Edith had to acknowledge Alfred had been right in his planning ahead. The wagon was much better than a horse drawn vehicle. He could bring more stock back for the shop in one go and could go much further a field for his deliveries. All in all life was, at last, beginning to look pretty good for them all.

They had a nice home now. Thanks to her father they even had money to spare. Edith

166

decided maybe it was the right time to think about having that much longed for holiday. But then she realised they could not do that. There would be nobody to look after the shop and they most certainly could not shut the door for a few days.

As if reading her mind, her mother suddenly said to her one day whilst on one of her regular visits, 'How about Pa and me looking after the shop for a week and you and Alfred take the children away for a real holiday?'

At first Edith was lost for words. Finally she managed, 'Oh, Ma! I don't know what to say. I'd only been thinking to myself I fancied doing that, but the shop was the problem. But even if you do look after it what about the fruit and vegetables we pick up at market. How'll you get around that problem?'

'Your Pa has already said he'd use his cart to pick up anything we need. As soon as I mentioned my idea of a holiday, he started thinking about it. You know he wouldn't get rid of the horse, when he retired couldn't bear to part with him after all his faithful service. He said George could earn his keep again. So all you need to do is decide where you want to go, get booked, then packed and on your way.'

Edith was so taken aback she repeated

herself, 'I don't know what to say.'

'There's nowt to say. Just look at it this way. You're doing your Pa a favour.'

Now Edith was well and truly puzzled, 'How's that?'

'Your Pa's lost with himself since he gave up work so he's actually excited at the thought of having something to do, even if it's only for a short time. So there's nowt else to say, just tell Alfred and then get yourself sorted out.'

'Oh, Ma, I don't know what I'd do without the pair of you. You do know how much I appreciate all your help? I know I don't always tell you but it does mean so much to Alfred and me all you both do for us.'

'Get away with you. We know well enough, there's no need for words. After all your Pa's said often enough you're the only family we have.'

Even after all the years that had now passed, Edith detected a hint of sadness in her mother's voice and knew she was thinking of Elsie. Putting an arm around her mother and drawing her close Edith spoke in a soothing voice, 'I know, Ma. I know.'

13

Looking back years later Edith realised that she probably had some of the best times of her life during that period. At that time she loved Alfred as deeply as she ever would, not that she ever completely gave up the yearning for Edward. In her imagination he had grown into an exceptional person who, had he lived, would have given her a life of bliss. Alfred could never match up to these images.

Yet unbeknown to Edith there was a man called Edward living in Scotland who had never given a second thought to that girl in the barn who had shunned his amorous responses.

Edward had not perished as Edith had believed. Instead he had been captured and became a prisoner of war. Due to a head injury received in combat, prior to his capture, he had lost his memory of most of his life, and spent his time in the prison camp not knowing who he was. It was only when he was reunited with his mother and she began to recollect to him details of his life showing him photographs and taking him visits to places he had known did the memory slowly return including all of his last leave. But he had no interest in contacting Edith. He never gave her a second thought as his life had moved on from that.

He had been lucky to secure a job at a local family firm and in no time he had befriended the owner's daughter rather well. They had soon become more than friends and finally Edward proposed marriage. He was in love with her as much as he was capable of but he also had an eye open for one day progressing in the firm, if indeed not owning it. His wife to be was an only child and there were no other close relatives to inherit.

Edward married Mary and they produced two children — a boy and a girl. Edward felt quite indifferent to his children and left it to his wife to give all the love and attention they needed. Edward was far more concerned with bettering himself and getting all the things he desired out of life.

Edith had not realised on their last meeting she had actually seen the start of his selfishness developing by his only desiring her to satisfy his own needs, not having a care how Edith felt. As he grew older so his selfishness also grew. If she had been fortunate enough to meet up with him again she would not have given him a second glance. The good looks of his youth had soon vanished as he lost most of his hair at an early age, and with an indulgence for good food he quickly became rather stout, making him seem much shorter than he really was.

But his wish was fulfilled as he became the head of the firm on the death of his father in law and he walked around with a smug self satisfied expression on his face. He was so wrapped up in his own self importance that nobody else mattered. Little did he realise his wife and children had no love or respect for him. He was in fact a very sad person with one love in life — money.

★ ★ ★

As it turned out one thing was for certain for Alfred and Edith, it was worth spending the money on the holiday, if only for the look of delight on the children's faces when they arrived at Blackpool. In the past they'd had the odd outing to Scarborough, but in their eyes Blackpool was a different place altogether. Alfred was in his element being able to give his undivided attention, for a whole week to the children he loved so much.

Once or twice on an evening he did say to Edith, when they were on their own, 'I hope the business is running all right.'

Edith laughed at this comment as she was

usually the worrier, 'Stop fretting, do you think my Pa and Ma would let any harm come to it? They'll manage, don't you fret. After all, it's only a week which is no time at all. You might as well get resigned to this way of life because I could get used to having holidays. If things carry on as they have been, we might be able to manage to get away again most years.'

Alfred was rather no-committal, 'Maybe, we'll just have to wait and see how things go and how your parents have actually managed. Remember, to have any more holidays we are dependant upon their goodwill.' This was rather an unusual comment for him as he was usually the one who let ideas and fancies run away with him. Still Edith was not concerned as she knew she had a year to work on him, which was long enough to get him around to her way of thinking.

Alfred and Edith were like a couple of children themselves when they were on the beach. They crammed everything they possibly could into the week. Daytime was spent on the beach, with the children playing in the sea and sand whilst the youngest had donkey rides.

Alfred laughed, 'I'd like a ride as well.'

Edith laughed back, 'I wish you could, it would be well worth the money to see the sight you'd make on the back of a donkey.'

At night there were plenty of tram rides to the Pleasure Beach or Blackpool Tower. Even Edith yielded to Alfred's demands that they join the children on some of the rides. By the time the week was at an end there were still many things they had intended to see but the time had run out. Edith did not think she could ever remember laughing so much in her life. Because all of them enjoyed it so much the children soon started on at Alfred telling him they wanted a holiday again next year.

As with all good things all too soon it was at an end. Later Edith was to decide it was after that holiday when things started to change. It was not in a way that she could really put her finger on, but still she could sense a difference.

Alfred had not needed to worry about the shop whilst they were away enjoying themselves. All was well. In fact he decided it had run so smoothly that most customers had not even noticed they were not there. Edith quickly understood her father had been in his element working again and being at the helm, not that it was in his nature to ever admit it. Even her mother had enjoyed her time in the shop and she had liked the gossiping and company of the customers. Although she had wanted companionship from Joe for long enough, now he was retired she found it a bit too much him being under her feet most of the day. He was like a lost soul with no job of work to do. He had been used to working hard and long hours and being constantly busy. Luckily he still had his smallholding which gave him an interest but not enough to keep his mind occupied all the time. Suddenly he felt like a spare part. Even though he had never taken to the idea of a motor wagon instead of his horse drawn cart, yet once he was retired he went out and bought himself a small motor car and learnt how to drive, so the pair of them could get around more easily.

It was a real treat for her mother, although Edith had to laugh each time she saw her in it, at the look of terror on her face. She was always convinced some harm would befall them before they reached their destination. These were the good parts of Edith's life but deep down she still felt something was going wrong somewhere but could not put her finger on it.

She could not understand how suddenly when she checked her stock that Alfred had brought her, it would often be a little short, yet all the time before it had been spot on. At first she just presumed the supplier had been out of stock with some of the items but in the end she had to acknowledge this was happening on far too regular a basis for it to be really the case. Yet when she challenged Alfred he was very glib with his excuses then would look hurt when she seemed unconvinced and demand of her, 'Don't you trust me, your husband? Do you think I'd cheat you?'

Not wanting to cause a rift between them Edith would just shrug her shoulders and say, 'Of course not, I'm only concerned where my stock is. I want the shop to work well for us. We can't do with loosing things.'

'It will be all right, stop fussing so.'

But it still gnawed at her because she knew everything was not as it should be. At other times things would seem to be going as they should, then she would think all her worries were a figment of her imagination. But something else would happen to set that unrest off again. Common sense told her she was not seeing all the money Alfred was earning from his round. She decided he must be keeping some for himself, for some unknown reason, which she had to admit was not unreasonable as he did not ask for much. The only problem was he would then ask her for money to buy stock saying he was short. But on being challenged he would simply blame it on bad debts. Somehow all this did not ring true to Edith but she just did not know what else she could do other than challenge him with it. If he denied it how else could she prove it? She just had to accept his excuse as to what was really happening. So all the while she felt she was taking one step forward and two back.

Alfred was trying his best not to let Edith see that he was upset himself. But what had started as an odd flutter seemed to have become an addiction with him.

Even the children began to notice something amiss. Martha often helped out in the shop after school and at week-ends and began to comment on the lack of stock being put back into the shop. She said to her mother, 'I thought I told you we'd run out of liquorice last week? You said Pa was going to get more in but he's been to the wholesalers and not brought any back.'

Edith was fed up with trying to think of excuses. Often it was easier to say, 'I know he's been but they were out of supplies there as well.'

Martha knew better than to say any more but she would look at her mother as much as to say pull the other one.

On top of that Edith had to pay the money she owed to her mother back at a slower rate than she had intended. Somehow or other there always seemed to be a call on her money so she would have to apologise to her mother and tell her that was all she could afford at the moment. Not that her mother minded, she knew that, because in fact she had actually said to Edith, 'You don't need to pay me back at all you know, I've told you enough times. After all, what I have will be yours one day in any case, so what does it matter that you have some of it whilst I'm still here.'

But Edith would have none of it. 'But we agreed, Ma and it's only right I stick to that agreement, it was a business deal after all. That's what I'm supposed to be running so it must pay its way properly and I must pay all debts off.'

Resigned, her mother gave in for the moment but she felt she had to have the final word and said in exasperation, 'Have it your own way, you will in any case whatever I say. Just like your Pa you are in that sense, too stubborn for your own good at times.'

But in the privacy of her home Sarah did voice her concerns to her husband. 'Joe, I don't like what's going on at Edith's shop. There's something not right, I can tell. I just can't seem to put my finger on it and she'll not say a word wrong against Alfred.'

'Leave it, Sarah, it's not for you to interfere and you can do nowt about it. It'll all sort itself out in its own good time, I'm sure.'

Meanwhile back at her daughter's home things were going from bad to worse. On one particular evening Martha called to her mother, 'Is Pa home yet?'

'No love why?'

'Have you seen the time? He's usually in well before now.'

'Good grief is it that late? I've been that busy I never noticed the time,' exclaimed Edith. She had not realised it was so late and no Alfred home. 'He must be having a busy day. I expect he'll be in any minute now, you mark my words.'

Now it had been brought to her attention, Edith herself was listening for his usual cheery whistle that could usually be heard as he came down the road. Thinking out aloud she said to no-one in particular, 'I wonder if I should send George or Fred to your Grandpa's to see if he's called there and forgotten the time with chatting. Mind, I've never known him to do it 'til this time even though he can talk the hind leg off a donkey.'

She was surprised to get a reply when Martha called out, 'I think you'd best do that, it' so unlike him to be as late as this. I hope he's all right.'

'Course he is, why shouldn't he be? I've already told you he'll have had a busy day and no doubt he'll have a good reason for being late,' she said with more confidence than she felt.

But Martha still persisted, 'Do you want me to get Fred or George in so you can send them to Grandpa's to see?'

'All right, if you really want to do that. Aye, it might be best to remind him to get a move on if he's stuck there telling the tale.'

Edith could feel an uneasiness that she did not want to mention to Martha. It was as if some sixth sense told her there was something wrong.

'Oh Fred, be a good lad and nip to your Grandpa's and see if your Pa's there. It'll not take you long if you go on your bike.'

'Oh, Ma must I?' he whined.

'Yes, go on. Quicker you go and quicker you'll be back here. Any roads, if he's there you can have a lift back in the wagon with him.'

This was enough of a bribe to get him on his way.

With still no sign of Alfred, Edith decided that was where he must be, but it seemed no time before Fred was back and on his own.

'Didn't you get a lift back with your Pa?'

'He wasn't there; they've not seen him all day.'

'He wasn't there?' she asked amazed.

'That's what I said.'

'Who do you think you're talking to young man?'

'Sorry, Ma, can I go out and play again now?' he asked, totally unconcerned about his father's whereabouts.

'Off you go then, but don't go too far as it'll soon be time to come in.'

As she was still pondering what to do Martha ran in, 'I can hear his wagon coming up the road now.'

Edith looked keenly at her daughter, 'Are you sure it's him?'

'Yes, Ma, I'd know it's engine sound anywhere.'

'Oh well at least he's coming home now, better late than never. He must have been delayed.'

'Do you want me to go and get the lads in for bed?'

'Aye, you do that for me. You're a good girl. Thanks love.'

This amazed Martha getting such praise from her mother, because it was a very rare thing indeed.

Edith felt relieved once she knew he was on his way home, but could now feel the anger building up inside that she had been so worried about him. But the words of reprimand she had intended to say to him, as he came through the door, never left her lips. Instead she shrieked, 'My God, what's happened to you?' as she saw his bruised and battered face.

'I was knocked out.'

'Knocked out!'

'Aye somebody waved me down, said they needed help, then the next thing I knew I was coming around with my head feeling as if it'd been hit by a sledge hammer.'

'When was this? Have you reported it to the police yet?'

'It was this morning, as I was on my way to the wholesalers, and no, I haven't been to the police, there didn't seem much point. They'll never catch them. They'll be well out of the way by now who ever it was that did this to me.'

'But you should have come home instead of carrying on to the wholesalers and doing your round,' Edith shouted in anguish.

Alfred looked rather shamefaced now, 'I didn't go to the wholesalers, and I haven't done any work today.'

'Well, what have you been doing if you haven't done that and you haven't been to the police?' Edith was now beginning to lose sympathy and instead felt angry with him.

'They took all my money.'

'All of it! Do you mean my money that I'd given you as well, to pay my bills at the wholesalers?'

'Yes everything.'

'But that still doesn't explain where you've been.'

'I don't rightly know I just seem to have wandered around. I couldn't face coming home and telling you. I knew you'd be so angry.'

'Why, am I so fearsome?' she asked puzzled and hurt by this comment.

But before he could answer, the full impact hit Edith and she let out a sob, 'But how can I pay for the things I've had now? I've no more money. I gave it all to you so you could settle my accounts and get me the other things I wanted.'

'I know, lass, we'll think of something. Maybe your Ma will lend you some more money.'

This made Edith see red. 'I wouldn't dream of asking her, she's done enough for us as it is. They both have. Besides I still haven't paid back all that money I borrowed before to get started. As things look now it seems unlikely that I'll ever be able to repay it. Oh, what have you done to us Alfred?'

Looking at her really shamefaced now he

moaned, 'It wasn't my fault, I've explained it all to you.'

By now Edith could feel the doubts nagging in her mind. She knew other money had gone missing; it all seemed rather too convenient that this had happened to him now. But, after all, he was her husband so she had to stand by him whatever.

She still felt she needed to ask him, so she could maybe help him in some way, if she could get to the bottom of things. Looking keenly at him she asked, 'What is going on Alfred?'

'I don't know what you mean; I've told you what happened.'

She had to admit he did look as if he had been attacked, but something just was not adding up and she could not fathom it out. She knew there was no point in questioning him further as she was not going to get anything out of him at this time.

Changing the subject she asked him, 'Do you want your dinner now?'

'I'll try some although I'm not that hungry. We'll work something out don't fret, lass,' he said unconvincingly.

For the moment Edith had to be happy with that but she was filled with dread about what was now happening in her life and where it was going to end.

183

14

Edith decided after much soul searching it was best to work on the theory that they had overcome the worst. He had told her about the money and somehow or another she had to sort out how she could re-stock the shop. That must surely be all there was. There could be no other reason than he stated. Maybe the way around this entire problem was not to have as many lines on the shelves. As things sold, happen she could get more in once again. All these thoughts whirled around in her head, but in the end she decided to think on it no more, because she was sure when she was least expecting it a solution would come to her.

But it all did not end there as she had thought. Alfred losing that money was just the start of it. Suddenly wholesalers were refusing to supply her. She would order the goods but they would never arrive and when she questioned them she would receive some vague excuse.

Then the representatives started to call. When the first one arrived, Mr. Harrison, from Wilson's she greeted him with a smile on her face, 'Oh I'm real glad you've come. We're getting ever so low on sweet stocks. I keep ordering various things but they never come and I can't get to the bottom of why they're not sending the items I order. Maybe now you're here I can get the shelves stocked again.'

'I hope so Mrs. Taylor, that's why I'm here.'

'So you knew of the problem I'm having getting the goods to come through?'

'I am aware of the reason and that's why I've called. I hope we can get sorted out to our mutual satisfaction,' he said in a rather cool voice.

'What is it then? Have they taken on some new packers who are getting the orders confused?'

'No, Mrs. Taylor, there's no problem at our end; orders are going out as usual. The problem is from your end.'

'I'm sorry, you've lost me. I've filled the order forms in as usual. I can't think what else you can mean.'

'Can't you, Mrs. Taylor? There's the small matter of settling your account. It's three months overdue.'

Edith gave a small nervous laugh, 'Now I know you've made a mistake. My account is fully up to date. My husband brought the money in himself.'

185

'I'm afraid not, as I've just said we haven't had any payment for the last three months. It's not the first occasion it's been late, but then it's usually arrived so we haven't said anything before.'

'But you should never have had it late. I've always sent it exactly on time. I repeat there must be some mistake, we must be talking about different accounts.' Edith felt she was pleading with him to agree with her.

'We're not. Look at these, they are the amounts you owe for the last few months?' he said showing her a page with figures on it.

'Just let me get my book to see I agree with you.'

Going into the back Edith shouted, 'Martha, come and mind the shop a while. I've a little bit of business to deal with.'

'Come through Mr. Harrison, it'll be a bit quieter here and we'll look at my book. Can I offer you a cup of tea?'

'No thanks, I would rather concentrate on this and get the matter settled.'

'See, these are my invoices and what I owe.' Edith peered at Mr. Harrison's figures, 'Aye, I agree with you on the amounts. But I do know my husband brought the cash in himself. Are you sure you haven't credited the money to somebody else's account?'

'Have you kept the receipts he was given? If

you say he came in with cash, he'll have been given one.'

'Aye, I should have, these are all my receipts for the last year.' Edith picked up a batch of receipts fastened together and quickly started to go through them. She suddenly exclaimed, 'Oh look here's one of yours!'

'Yes, it is our receipt but I agree that's paid, that isn't one of the bills in dispute.'

'Here's another.'

'No, not that either.'

'I don't know what could have happened, there doesn't seem to be any recent receipts here. I bet Alfred still has them in his jacket pocket. Aye, that'll be it. I usually have to remind him to hand them over. He's out now so I can't look any further for them because he'll have his jacket with him. Will you leave it with me to get the receipts off him?'

'I'll only leave it until the day after tomorrow, Thursday. It's getting quite a pressing matter, because it's no small amount outstanding and we need our money in to pay our bills, you know.'

'I realise that but I've already said it's paid, just give me chance to prove it.'

'I'll be back on Thursday. Good day for now.'

'Oh yes, good-bye,' replied Edith in a state

of amazement at his abrupt manner as the odd times she had seen him before he had seemed so friendly.

If truth be known Edith did not feel as confident as she sounded that everything was all right, as she had told him. Something did not seem to ring quite true. But one way or another she was going to get to the bottom of this, she had never been as embarrassed in all her life.

She went back into the shop looking rather white faced and Martha asked, 'Are you all right, Ma? You don't look at all well. You haven't a bad head have you?'

Not wanting to tell Martha the truth she put her hand on her forehead, 'Aye, I've just the beginnings of one. If you're all right here, I'll go and lie down for half an hour, then it'll happen clear.'

'I'm fine, off you go. Take as long as you like,' replied Martha in a concerned voice.

But Edith did not sleep. She tossed and turned as thoughts went around and around in her head. She did not like what she was thinking. She was impatient for Alfred to come home so she could give him what for, causing her all this worry even if he had only mislaid the receipts.

Meanwhile Martha served in the shop with her own thoughts and worries. She was sure it was more than a headache that her mother had. That man who had been with her had somehow seemed to upset her and he had rushed out of the shop looking none too happy. No doubt her father was involved. Martha loved her father deeply but she was aware that sometimes he did things that upset her mother. It always seemed to be related to money.

Edith lay fretting about what she was going to say to Alfred. She felt conflicting emotions; anger at what he kept doing and at the same time fear. Where it was all going to end and what was going to become of them? She kept thrashing about in her mind, first going one way then another but finding no answers.

Sleep was the furthest thing from her mind, but it must have come to her because the next thing she heard was Alfred's anxious voice at the side of her. At first she was at a loss where she was and what had happened as she heard the words, 'Martha says you've one of your bad heads. Is there anything I can do for you?'

Reality soon came back to her and before she could stop herself the words came rushing out, 'I think you've already done enough, don't you?'

Looking blankly at her and not comprehending what she meant he stuttered in panic, 'I don't know what you're talking about.'

'Well try this. Let me have the receipts for the bills I gave you the money for, to take into Wilson's so you could pay them for me.'

Blustering now as realisation began to dawn upon him what she was on about, he replied, 'I gave you them, didn't I?'

'No, you didn't and you know full well you didn't,' shouted Edith as she started to loose control of her temper.

'Sssh, don't shout, you'll only make your head worse.'

'I haven't got a bad head. I just needed to be on my own after the shock I'd received.'

'Shock, what shock?'

Really getting angry now at his reluctance to admit what she was saying she snapped at him, 'You not paying Wilson's accounts for the last three months even though I gave you the money to do so. Then other accounts have been paid late despite me giving you the money to pay them on time.'

'I was going to pay them - honestly. Anyway how do you know I haven't paid them?' he queried as this thought struck him.

'I had a visitor, Mr. Harrison. He'd called for the money we owed. The money I thought we had paid. They won't supply us again until that overdue money is paid in full. I felt a right fool contradicting him and saying you would have been in with it and the mistake was on their side.'

Not really knowing what to say, he asked with fear in his voice, 'What did you tell him?'

'Ah, getting through to you, am I? Well, don't worry I got us off lightly for the moment. I said you must have paid but mislaid the receipts.'

With a look of relief Alfred let out a sigh, 'That's all right then.'

'No, it isn't. He's coming in the day after tomorrow either for the receipts to show we've paid or for the money.'

Feeling really worried because he could not see a way out of this one Alfred put his head in his hands. 'Oh my God! What are we going to do?' Then cheering a little bit as another thought struck him, he asked, 'Have you some money put by? If so you can pay him on account to keep them happy?'

Edith snapped back at him, 'You know I haven't.' Then sarcastically she added for good measure, 'You had all I possessed stolen, if you remember. Come on, you might as well tell me the truth, what's happening with the money? Where has it really gone?'

'I told you it was stolen.'

'But what happened to the money that should have been paid to Wilson's?'

His answer came out glib enough, 'I'd just never got around to taking it in, so that was also on me when I was knocked out, and that was stolen as well.'

'Come on, Alfred, you can do better than that. What do you take me for, a fool?'

'I'm not staying here to have you doubt me, I told you what happened,' he replied with an unusual show of anger. With this Alfred rushed from the room and slammed the door behind him.

Edith called after him, 'That's right, run away as soon as there is something you don't want to face. What am I supposed to do about Mr. Harrison on Thursday? What do I tell him? Because I know for a fact he'll never believe your excuse, just like I don't.'

But she might as well have saved her breath, there was no reply. Her question had fallen on deaf ears. The next thing she heard was the wagon engine start up and knew he was getting himself out of the way somewhere.

Martha rushed into the room, 'Are you all right, Ma? I saw Pa rush out and thought he was happen going for a doctor for you. You haven't taken a turn for the worse?'

'Nay, lass, no doctor will cure this. I don't know where your Pa's gone and that's a fact. You'd best go down to the shop before we have what stock we've left pinched.'

'It's all right John's minding it for me. Come on, Ma, what is the matter? I can tell there is something.'

'I suppose you might as well know. You'll know soon enough. I think I'll have to let the shop go.'

'Let the shop go! You can't do that,' pleaded Martha.

'I don't think I'll have any choice in the matter. You know your Pa was knocked out and robbed,' here Edith could not stop herself adding, 'Or so he says.'

'Ma, don't be like that,' Martha replied feeling someone had to defend her father in his absence.

'Do you want me to tell you or not?' Edith snapped.

'Sorry, Ma, go on I'm listening.'

'Well, not only did he have on him the money I gave him that day, but apparently all the money I'd been giving him of recent months to pay Wilson's. They won't supply us again until they're paid and I've no way of doing that.' Then another thought came to her, 'Oh my goodness, I wonder who else he hasn't paid? They're not the only ones who haven't sent things I've ordered and I gave him money to pay them as well.'

'Ma, don't go on so. I'm sure he'll have paid the others,' Martha replied in her father's defence but was beginning to doubt the words herself.

'I'm not so sure about that anymore.'

'Surely there's some way you can work it out?' she said confidently as her mother always seemed so capable of sorting any problem out the family had.

'Well, I can't think of any way. In any case trade has not been as good in the shop since Mrs. Baker opened up just down the road. As it is she's taken some of our custom, so I've had to work harder than ever to attract customers back to us. Then other people have had the idea of delivery rounds, now with these horseless carts, so your Pa's not been doing so well.' Now Edith went into deep despair. 'We'll starve, I just know we will before your Pa's finished. This isn't what he promised me when we were wed.'

Martha went over to her mother and put her arms around her. Never had she felt as close as at this moment and she began to understand the reason for some of her mother's actions in the past. 'I'll help, in fact we all will. We'll do whatever we can to help. Have I to see what we've all saved in pocket money? Would that be of help to you?'

'Nay, lass, that'd only be like drop in the ocean. But thanks, that's real kind of you and if I do need it I'll ask.'

★ ★ ★

Alfred, once he was in his wagon just drove and drove. Finally when he found himself in an isolated spot on the moors he stopped. He was not quite sure what he had intended when he had driven here, maybe just to drive on and on until he was out of their lives. But he knew he could not do that, he loved them all too much. He put his head down on the steering wheel as sobs racked his body. If only he could stop this obsession of his - gambling. The trouble was the more he lost, the more he gambled in the hope that he would recover it. Sometimes he did have good runs of luck, which was how in the past he had managed to pay some off the accounts. Be it they were paid late, he had at least managed to pay the bills Edith had given him the money for. It was just a case of robbing Peter to pay Paul. But then it had all gone wrong. These last few months all he'd had was bad luck. The worse it became, the more he carried on in the hope he would get some back, if not all of it. But it had not happened, and now he had lost all the money. Never in his life had he imagined he would have to inflict wounds on himself to make credence to his story he told Edith.

There was no way he could tell Edith this,

his resolve was strong in that. This was always going to be his secret. Thinking how strong Edith was, he was sure she would find a way to put things right. For his part he would have to turn over a new leaf and try his best. No more gambling for him.

He jumped as a voice spoke at his side, 'You all right, mate?'

He looked up quickly to see a farmer looking at him, through the open side window, with a concerned expression upon his face.

He said the first thing that sprung to mind as he did not want him to know the truth. 'Aye, just had a funny turn, so I thought I'd stop a few minutes.'

Looking in at him really concerned now he asked, 'Anything I can do for you mate?'

'No, I feel a bit better now. I'll just give it a few minutes more then I'll be on my way.'

'Are you sure?'

'Yes, really I'm fine again.'

'I'll get on then, take care now.' With this he turned and whistled for his dog then went on his way.

Alfred knew he could not put off going home for ever. Finally, he decided he was ready to face Edith. He would have to take her wrath, but there was no way he would admit to any other way of losing the money, than being robbed. He felt better now as he convinced himself Edith would sort the matter out one way or another and things would be fine between them once more.

15

Although Edith was furious with Alfred she was also worried that he might have been pushed far enough to have gone and done something stupid after he had rushed out of the house. She did not know which to fret about the most, the missing money or Alfred.

Martha kept trying to console her mother, as she could sense her desperation. Alfred was not the only one who wanted a way out. At that moment Edith felt as if there was no way forward for her, she could not see any future for the family.

Finally, after a time of pacing the house in anxiety her mind was set at rest about Alfred because he came despondently back home. She had become so worried that, despite her resolution to stay calm, when he did walk through the door she burst out in anger, 'Well, are you going to tell me the truth now? I think I deserve that much.'

'I've already told you Edith, I was robbed. I've no more to say on the matter apart from I'll always make sure any money you give me in future will be safe. It won't happen again. I promise.'

'Don't make me laugh. Letting you have money to pay bills for me in the future.' Sarcastically as another thought struck her she added, 'Anyway what future, I ask you?'

'Our future and, of course, the children's,' Alfred said hoping it was true.

'Well I don't feel there is anything in front of us. There isn't a future.'

'Of course there is. We'll get through all this and I'll make sure nowt like this happens again.'

'Promises, that's all you're good at, empty promises.'

'No, listen, I do really mean it this time,' he pleaded.

Still Edith was not really listening to what he was saying; she was so beside herself with anger and worry. 'I've had enough for one day; my mind won't take any more. I'm off to bed, tomorrow's another day. I might be able to think clearer then.'

'That sounds like a good idea,' said Alfred, now feeling he had been forgiven and life would go on as it always did. But Edith was panicking as she'd had a sudden thought, maybe there was another woman and he had been spending the money on her. If he said it would not happen again this signified to her that if it was another woman then he had finished this relationship. She had never even given a thought about what it could be he was hiding. The last thing she would ever have thought of was gambling. It would not have entered her head.

The next day did not dawn much better and it was with trepidation she put the open sign on the shop door. She was right to be worried because another representative came through the door looking none too pleased. He had much the same comments to make to her as Mr. Harrison. Their firm had not been paid either and they would not supply any more goods until they were. Knowing there was no way she could pay the full amount Edith decided the best way was to try to be honest and say her husband had been robbed. She then offered to pay a small amount each month until the debt was paid off. In the end she offered all who came for money this solution in a hope to settle all outstanding debts. She was not even sure where she would get the money from but it was the only answer to the problem she could think of.

What she did know was by doing this it was the end of the shop. There was no way she was going to be able to pay the promised money and buy more stock. All she could hope for was to sell what she had, and that would make inroads into paying some of the debts, then they might as well have the shop back as a living room. How they would manage after that she had no idea. She hoped this time Alfred could come up with a solution, considering it was him who had brought about the mess in the first place.

Martha was upset. Even though her mother appeared hard at times she still loved her and did not like to see her hurt like this. So when she was so unhappy Martha felt as if she was suffering the same pain and sadness. Much to her annoyance her sister, Ethel, seemed to float through life with nothing really touching her. She moved about as if in a perpetual dream. Martha decided her mother had given up with her and simply let her get on with life in her own haphazard way.

At times Martha felt amazed and a bit annoyed that Ethel seemed to get out of doing so much, just by her attitude and approach to things. In another way Martha realised this was a compliment from her mother to herself in that she trusted her so much to do what she asked of her. As for the lads, her mother was of the old fashioned belief that household tasks were not a boy's job. Sometimes they had to help out in the shop; they enjoyed that. It gave them opportunity to help themselves to sweets, if nothing else. If her mother was serving on she made them pay for the things from the shop, just like the customers. They took any opportunity they could, behind her back, to help themselves to what they fancied. Harry was the worst; he seemed to have no conscience about anything he did. His behaviour did not improve with age; even her mother was often at her wits end with him. He always seemed to be involved in one escapade or another, usually causing trouble for someone.

Martha kept looking at her mother's unhappy face and in the end she felt the need to talk to her. 'Ma, is there anything I can do to help? I'm old enough now for you to talk things through with me.'

Even she had sense enough to see what was really happening, that her mother was having trouble with the shop, so it was obvious they were suffering repercussions from her father being robbed, just as her mother had predicted there might be.

'Nay, lass, there's nowt anybody can do. I don't know how we're going to manage once the shop's shut for good and that's a fact,' she replied with a sob in her voice.

'You've made your mind up then, you're definitely shutting the shop?'

'Aye, I'll have to lass, it's a case of needs must. I just haven't the money to keep it going any longer. The fewer goods I can replace then the less profit the shop makes. It's all a vicious circle.'

'Maybe Pa can get a job instead of his round. There might be more jobs around now than when he was looking last time.'

'Maybe, who knows? I do think he has been looking on the quiet. He's said nowt to me but I'm sure he has. Obviously he's had no success otherwise he'd have said something.'

Martha did not really know what else to say to help her mother so only added, 'I'll soon be leaving school and getting a job. You can have my wages if it'll help you.'

'I'll have to lass, but they'll not go so far as to feed us all.' Then brightening her mother asked, 'Any thoughts what you want to do? Are you going to try at the mill?'

'Most probably,' she replied, then looking proud she added, 'After all, that's what you did.' Martha was not particularly demonstrative after being rebuked so often by her mother but now she put her arms around her and immediately her mother responded, 'You're a good lass. Aye, we'll see if we can get you in the burling and mending. Would you like that?'

Martha's face lit up at that thought. 'Oh, Ma, I hope you can. I'd love to work there.'

'Well don't get too excited, we'll have to see, but I still do know one or two folks there and your Grandpa does, so you never know what we'll be able to do. Then there's the mill your Aunt Annie and Uncle Harry work at. They might be able to put in a good word for you there. Yes, I'm sure we'll sort something out. At least that'll be two of you out to work, only four left to go then.' Her mother gave a small bitter laugh at this thought. 'I don't think the rest of them are going to be as easy to sort out. I'm glad John's secured an apprenticeship as a mechanic. He loves tinkering with engines. At least he should always enjoy his job and when he's trained I'm sure he'll have something worthwhile as more and more people seem to be getting these motor vehicles.'

'That's right, Ma. I mean even Grandpa relented and bought one.'

'Aye, but your Grandma's still scared to death of the thing. Anyway enough chit chat, I'd best get on with tea. Go and watch the shop for me love, although I don't think you'll be that busy. The door bell hasn't rung all this time you've been in here.'

Fewer and fewer people were coming in as word passed around the shop was to close and often there were not the items on the shelves that they wanted. All thoughts of the times Edith had opened her door to them after closing time was forgotten as they now went to the new shop in the village that offered them more choice. Martha liked it much better when she was busy than stood idly around with only her own thoughts. But tonight she was glad she had chance to think because she wanted to consider if there was any way she could help her mother and father.

In the end she decided there was only one solution. She would have to talk to her Grandma Thompson. She always knew what to do for the best. She loved her Grandma Taylor as well, but somehow she could never discuss really important things with her. If she tried to, Grandma Taylor would listen for so long then suddenly her mind would flit to something else and the discussion they had started would never be finished. Besides which, they only just managed to live on the money they had so there could be no financial assistance from that direction.

No, she would go and see Grandma Thompson as soon as she could, then once she shared her worries she was sure she would feel much better. Now she had decided on a plan of action she did not mind hearing the shop bell ring to indicate a customer was coming in at last.

'Hello Mrs. Williams, how can I help?' she said cheerfully.

As Edith was getting the tea she heard the shop bell and gave a sigh of relief as at least Martha now had one customer to relieve her boredom. She knew how lonely it was in the shop on her own and how fed up the young ones became when they had no customers, but she had still to have the shop open whilst she had goods on the shelves in the hope of selling it off. Not that she was doing very well on that score, the shop was not bringing much money in now and Alfred was not doing very well with his round. In fact, hardly any better than the shop was. There were too many of them competing for the same customers and, after all, people had only so much money to spend. No, it looked as if the wagon would have to be sold soon if they were going to manage to keep their heads above water and pay off some, if not all, of their debts.

It was a good job they had no rent to pay, at least the money went further, but even if they sold the wagon that money would run out soon enough. What they would do then Edith just did not know. So whilst Martha was worrying how to help her parents, Edith was also worrying how she was going to look after all her brood once more. But as Martha came to the decision she would ask her grandma's advice, Edith came to the opposite decision — that one way or another she must manage, or at least Alfred and her must sort this out without involving her parents. They had been help enough in the past; she could not expect them to do any more for them. They had already given them the means to have a new start when they had moved here. If it had not worked out, then it was nobody's fault but their own, so they would have to get themselves out of this mess.

She knew it would be difficult to keep it from her father and mother because they were nobody's fools. Her father was like a sniffer dog; once he had the bit between his teeth he kept on until he found the truth. But they did know she was having competition from Mrs. Barker's shop so maybe they would accept that as the reason she was loosing customers. She was trying her best to keep them out of the shop because it was now very noticeable that she was short of stock. But now they had this motor car her mother and father were often known to arrive at any time unannounced to see them. They seemed to love to go for little jaunts around even if her mother was still frightened of going in the car. Her mother was happier than she had been for a long time, at last she had more companionship from Joe and he talked to her now if only to give her a detailed description of the sights they were visiting.

Edith just hoped and prayed that Alfred would come up with another job or some way of earning their keep before things became desperate. Then she could justify closing the shop to her parents by saying they were better off by Alfred's new job so there was no need for her to have to run the shop and try to bring up six children. Aye, that all sounded very plausible to her. All she needed now was for Alfred to get his finger out and find himself a job.

As soon as she heard the back door open and realised it was Alfred she quickly turned to him before he had even shut the door and put her thoughts into words, 'You'll have to sell the wagon you know.' This came out a bit sharper than she had intended.

Alfred looked at her in amazement, 'Pardon, what are you on about?'

'Sorry, you just received the tale end of my thoughts. I'll start at the beginning telling you what I mean.'

So she went on to recount what she had been pondering on prior to him arriving home.

Finally Alfred gasped, 'But sell the wagon? Surely it's best to keep it, and then I can get around looking for work. Anyway, failing all else I might be able to use it to set up another kind of business.'

Now Edith began to feel once more she was banging her head against a brick wall, he always seemed to have his head in the clouds. 'Alfred, setting up in any business costs money, which we haven't got as you full well know. Whatever you plan for us costs and we just can't afford it. So you can forget that idea. No, the wagon will have to go and you'll have to find work one way or another.'

Knowing he was beaten and that she was right in what she said, he conceded, 'Whatever you say. But you'll have to make your mind up if you want me to go on selling from the wagon or to start job seeking as from now on. I can't do both things. Once I stop going to an area, on my particular day, the other chaps will have their foot in the door to take over my customers before I know where I am.'

'You're barely breaking even now. It'll soon be costing us for you to go around your existing customers.'

'All right, then I'd best call this the last week. As I go around I'll put feelers out for any jobs that are going. If nothing turns up then I'll go job hunting next week. We can surely manage another week or two without selling the wagon, can't we? It'll give me the means to get around more firms in a day to look for work.'

'I suppose so, I'll try my best. I think we probably need to have one final big sales promotion to get rid of the rest of the stuff in the shop. That'll give us a little bit more money and buy us some time. But I did want to pay some off what we owe. I suppose that'll just have to wait until we've managed to get ourselves on an even keel again.' With a sigh she added, 'If we ever do.'

'Thanks, lass, I knew you'd understand.'

Edith had thoughts of her own, 'Aye I understand only too well. This looks like how my life is always destined to be, pulling us out of one mess or another.' It also worried her how, if Alfred did find a job, they would be able to live and pay off the money owed even with the sale of the wagon.

16

It was easier than Martha imagined it would be to get to see her grandma. As she left for school one morning she said to her mother, 'Is it all right if I call to see Grandma Thompson after school today?'

'Aye, I don't see why not. Ethel can help me for once. Just mind you're not late in for tea,' she replied seeing nothing untoward in this.

'Thanks, Ma, I won't be late.'

As luck would have it when she arrived at her grandma's she found her sat quietly in front of the fire, all on her own.

'Hello, Grandma.'

Her grandma looked up in surprise, 'This is an unexpected visit. Is there any special reason?'

'No, I thought I'd just come and see you. Ethel's helping Ma with the shop for once. Where's Grandpa?'

'He's taken Nell for a walk, and then he's probably going to stop and see to the hens on his way back. So he'll be a while yet. Did you want to see him?'

'No, I just wondered where he was that was

all.' Then knowing time was short before she would have to go home she admitted. 'Actually it was you I wanted to have a word with, so it's good we're on our own.'

'Oh yes! What could this be about Martha?' replied her grandma, not surprised by this at all, thinking she might have met a young lad.

Martha paused before saying, 'Ma and Pa actually.'

'What about them? They're both all right aren't they?' Sarah asked with panic in her voice.

Martha quickly reassured her, 'They're not poorly if that's what you mean. No, Pa was robbed of his money a few weeks ago. Well, actually he'd Ma's money on him as well, to pay all the accounts for the things she'd bought for the shop. Now she can't pay all the bills, but I think she's managed to come to an arrangement with the suppliers. That's not what's worrying me but I don't know if you've noticed that Ma is not re-ordering for the shop. In fact, she's selling everything off so she says and she's going to make the shop back into our front room. Mrs. Baker opening, you know at the other end of the village, that's not helped either. Then she says Pa's to sell the wagon, because he's not doing too well with that either, not now other people have come up with the same idea of delivery rounds. They keep rowing, Ma telling Pa he's to get himself sorted out and find a job. Then I know she cries when she's on her own, because I've heard her. She's that worried how we'll manage again.' Then looking proud Martha added, 'But I've told her when I leave school in summer I'll get a job in the mills then she can have my wages to help her out. I'd like to be a burler and mender like Ma was. Of course, John doesn't earn much, but I know he gives it all to Ma and she gives him spending money back. So I don't think it'd be too bad do you? With my help they might just manage.'

'Well, I do think it'd take more than what you and John will earn to feed all your tribe. But it will be a help that's for sure, although it's a while yet till summer. Then I don't want to dash your hopes but it's not always that easy to get the job you want. There has to be vacancies you know, for you to be taken on. But don't fret yourself, lass, they'll sort themselves out. It'll all come right in the wash, I'm sure.'

'I suppose you're right, but I do feel better for being able to talk to you. You won't let on to them that I have, will you? They might not be too pleased me discussing their problems.'

Laughing her grandma looked at her, 'You

should know by now I can keep my mouth shut.'

'Thanks, Grandma. I'd best be on my way home now. I promised Ma I wouldn't be in late for tea.'

'I'm glad you came here and felt you could talk to me. Anytime at all lass you feel the need, I'm always here. Take care now and come again soon. Get those brothers of yours to call and see me.'

'I'll try, but you know what they're like. 'Bye now.'

When Joe came back in Sarah quickly said to him, 'I've had a visitor.'

'Oh aye, and who might that have been?'

'Martha.'

'Martha! What ever did she want?'

'Now, Joe why have they to want something? She might have just called to see me.'

'But she didn't, did she? Let me hazard a guess. I bet it was about her parents.'

'How do you know that?'

'Ah, a little bird told me.'

'Come on be serious, how do you know?'

'I've got eyes in my head, haven't I? I can see what's going on, besides I still hear the gossip tha knows when I go into Bradford and such like. So what had she to say for herself?'

'Well, I promised I'd say nowt, but I don't suppose it matters talking to you. I know it'll go no further. She said Alfred was robbed a few weeks back of all their money.'

'So I've heard tell, although by all accounts it was a bit of a rum do.'

'How do you mean? You never said nowt to me.'

'I didn't want to worry you and I was hoping it'd all sort itself out in the wash.'

'Well, it hasn't. Edith's giving up the shop and she's told Alfred to sell the wagon because he's not doing too well on that either.'

'I see, and what does she propose they live on, air?'

'By all accounts she's told Alfred to get himself a job. Bless her though, Martha I mean. Do you know what she said to me?'

'Now how would I know seeing as how I wasn't here?' Joe said impatiently.

'She said she'd get a job in summer, when she leaves school and give her Ma all her wages, then that together with John's bit of money coming in, would look after them all. I pointed out it wouldn't be enough for all that lot. She wants to be a burler and mender just like Edith was. Do you think you could help her get a job in that line, when it's time? You still do have some contacts don't you?'

'Maybe, but that's a while away yet, plenty of time for that when we need to. Let's concentrate on the more important matter of her Ma and Pa. Funnily enough I've already been giving it some thought because as I said I was aware of some of what was going on but wasn't sure if they'd appreciate my help. Besides you know me, I don't like to interfere where I'm not wanted. But by coincidence whilst I was in Bradford yesterday I saw Willie Lambert. Do you remember him?'

'Hasn't he a coal business?'

'Aye, that's him. Well, he was saying he was looking out for another delivery man, because he's that busy and is finding it difficult to keep up to all the orders. But he was hoping to find somebody with their own wagon so he hadn't to outlay on another himself. Then he'd pay their wages and the running of the vehicle. I thought about Alfred straight away but I didn't say owt because I just wasn't sure if that was what he needed. Now, by what you say, I know all this seems just right up his street. I'd best go and see him after tea and tell him then he can go and see Willie tomorrow before the job goes. Mind, I don't think it'll go that quick. There'll not be that many around with a wagon belonging to them.'

'You'll have to be careful how you tell him

because Martha didn't want them to know she'd been talking to me.'

'That's all right because I can just say I bumped into Willie and heard about this job. I'll say I thought he might be interested with having the wagon. No, there's no need to bring Martha into it at all. Now be quick and get my tea because I want to get up there as soon as I can.'

'I will but one last thing. Where does Willie want the coal delivering? Is it around here?'

'No, that's the one drawback; it's the Odsal area of Bradford. But still Alfred has his wagon so he can travel, it'll make no odds. Anyway let's see if he's interested first, then they'll have to sort themselves out about that.'

★ ★ ★

'This is a surprise, Pa, I wasn't expecting you. To what do we owe the honour?' Edith said at being taken by surprise at the visit.

'It's Alfred I've come to see. Is he about?

'Aye, he's just watching the shop for me. Do you want to see him now?'

'More like the pair of you really. Can one of the children attend to the shop for you?'

'Aye, I'll just get George or Fred in. I won't be long. Help yourself to a cup of tea. It's a fresh pot.'

To Joe it seemed to take Edith for ever to get them all organised before he could get on to what he had to say. He was impatient to tell them now he had made his mind up. When they were both finally seated he plunged straight in, 'I saw Willie Lambert in Bradford yesterday. I don't think you'll know who I mean, Edith?'

Edith had to admit she did not and wondered why her father felt the need to tell her this.

'Don't look so puzzled lass. I haven't lost my marbles yet. There's a reason for telling you. He just happened to mention, in passing, that he was looking for another delivery man. He's a coal merchant. But what he really wants is somebody with their own wagon so he doesn't have to buy another one yet himself. He'll pay a wage and running expenses. It's not to replace somebody who's left, he's just that busy and his rounds have grown he feels the need to expand further. So I thought of you Alfred. Now what have you to say to that?'

Alfred looked indignantly at his pa-in-law, 'Why should I need that job?'

'I just thought I'd tell you. You might earn more on that job than your round that's all. No harm in telling you and if you're not interested it doesn't matter.'

Knowing he had sounded rather sharp Alfred admitted, 'I didn't say that. I suppose there'd be no harm in talking to this Willie and getting more details.'

'No none at all, look I'll jot his address down if you like.'

'Yes do that.'

'Have you a pen and paper then?'

All this time Edith had looked mesmerised by what was going on. It seemed as if her father had helped them out of a mess once again.

She did not think Alfred suspected anything, he had taken it at face value as her father had told it. It was a good job because he still had some pride left and she was sure if he had suspected her father was purposely helping them once again he would have more than likely refused to do anything about it. But she did wonder how her father knew they needed help. Mind, he had always been astute and that was a fact.

Aye, her mother seemed to be right on what she said, 'When one door shuts another opens.' So far it appeared to work like that for them.

'I'll get on home now then,' her father was saying, 'Before it gets dark. You know how your Ma worries.'

'Thanks for coming and telling me. I'll get

myself there tomorrow to see him,' said Alfred as he saw her father out.

When he came back in Edith exclaimed, 'That's a turn up for the books. What a piece of good luck, it looks as if it might be turning our way at last. Let's hope you get the job.'

But Alfred was not as enthusiastic, 'We'll see, we'll see. What your Pa didn't say was where the round was exactly. As his business is in Bradford it's sure to be there. You do realise it may mean another house move?'

Edith's face fell at this thought. It would be such an upheaval with their family, besides it would mean moving even further away from her parents. She would see them even less then. But she could not really say owt to Alfred because he needed this job and they could hardly look a gift horse in the mouth.

★   ★   ★

As soon as Alfred introduced himself to Willie and explained he was Joe Thompson's son-in-law, the job was as good as his. It was organised that as soon as he had wound up all his other affairs he would start his round. Knowing how much Edith wanted to stay put, he decided he would travel to work each day from where they lived now. That was the least he could do for her after all the grief he had caused.

Although this was what Edith had wanted him to do she was not really sure this was the best way to live. But she decided to leave it be at the moment as enough change had already gone on in their lives and she did not feel able to cope with any more at the moment.

Alfred was certain her father had a hand in getting him this job, but he was not going to let on to Edith and have words with her about it. After all, why upset the apple cart when things were going well for them once more? He had done enough harm without intending to. When they had married he had promised her so many things, but none of them seemed to have materialised. Somehow whatever he did, and it was always with the best intentions, it seemed to hurt the ones he loved the most. Now, he had a chance to start all over again and make good all his wrongs. This time he was determined to make it work out and supply a really good life for Edith. She deserved it. After all, looking after their brood of six was no easy task. He had been lucky there; he had picked a good one when he had picked Edith. He loved her no less now this day than when they were married. Not that he was really looking forward to being a coal delivery man. It would be a dirty and heavy job. It was something he had never imagined himself doing. But he gave a silent laugh, after all beggars cannot be choosers, and there certainly seemed to be somebody up there looking after him. Each time he had been at his wits end something seemed to turn up. Maybe Mr. Micawber, was not so silly after all.

Now it was up to him to make a go at this opportunity he had once more been offered. Alfred had enough sense to realise he could not keep going through life like this; opportunities would not keep on forever coming his way. No, this time he really had to make it work and definitely no more gambling.

17

Edith soon began to realise it was not really very practical them still living at Denholme and Alfred having to travel every day into Bradford. It made it a long day for him and she often felt concerned by the look of exhaustion on his face. In fact, at times, it was more than she would have thought a man of his age should be showing and feeling. Still, it was hard work lugging all those bags of coal and he was so busy he was fair run off his feet rushing from one delivery to another. Not only that, it was costly for the fuel to travel back and forth. Although Willie Lambert had agreed to pay the running costs of the wagon, he had told Alfred that he thought in all fairness it was Alfred's own responsibility to pay for the expense of getting to and from work. After all, his other blokes had to fork out for it themselves.

Willie, in the privacy of his own home, had said as much to his wife, 'I think he should be thankful I've given him a job. If he hadn't been Joe's son-in-law I might not have, who knows? Aye, he's a willing enough worker but between our two selves, I've heard this loss of money of his was a rum business. Not all he tried to make it seem to his family. Mind, he's proving a good salesman, I can't fault him there. He's such a likable nature he has the women eating out of his hand.' Here Willie paused and gave a quiet laugh, 'Do you know he's even got some of them to buy extra, telling them it'll likely be going up in price soon, so they might as well get extra stock in now while it's cheaper. Aye, I like his initiative; I've to say that. Cheeky young bugger, he is, telling them that. But who am I to grumble if he's selling the extra coal?'

'Aye it does sound as if you've got a right one there. I don't think I'd like to be in his wife's shoes. He sounds far too forward with the other woman by all accounts. No, not to my liking at all,' responded his wife.

'Now that's what's so surprising. He's good at wooing them to buy extra coal, but he's actually very much a family man. He thinks the world of all his kids, would do owt for them. I think that's half his problem, he'd help anybody in more need than himself. You know my motto, charity begins at home and with all that tribe of his that's certainly where it needs to start.'

'True, I'm glad we've only the two and both of them have grown up with no problems. However, much as he cares for his wife, I'm glad you don't talk to other women like that. At least I trust that you don't.' Amy gave Willie a tender look of admiration. Even after all these years of marriage he could still turn her heart over. Aye, she was lucky she had found a good one here. He had looked after her and the children very well; she had never wanted for anything and not once had she seen his eyes stray to look at other women. As far as he was concerned they just did not seem to exist.

★ ★ ★

At the same time Edith was full of praise for Alfred in her own mind. He seemed to be making a right good go of this opportunity he had been given, once again. She felt very proud of him at last. Now it was her turn to do something for him as most of their debts were now cleared with his efforts and the last of the shop stock selling. She had made her mind up so that was it and now seemed as good a time as any to do what she had to do. Martha was due to leave school in the summer, so if they could move by then, they could happen get her a mill job near their new home which would be far better than having to move jobs when she was only just settled in to one. John was a bit of a problem because he was an indentured apprentice mechanic; it made it a lot harder to find another firm to take him on. Besides that, he was well settled where he was so she was reluctant to move him. Still, she was sure something would turn up on that score.

As for Ethel, she would be glad to get her away from Denholme. Different as chalk and cheese she and Martha were. As young as she was Ethel was already chasing the lads. She had been seen far too often with that half cousin, Eddy, and by all accounts they were always disappearing behind the cycle sheds at school. No, no good would come of that. It was best if they could get her away from him. This was the ideal opportunity. Eddy came from a rough lot; Edith did not like that side of Alfred's family at all. They always sent shivers up and down her spine when she met them.

As for the rest of them, they would move school easily enough. There would be a few grumbles but they would soon settle once they had made new friends. They were popular lads and made friends easily. It was just her parents she would be sorry to be further away from. But she was sure they would understand and, after all, Alfred was her man so that was who she had to consider the most. Happen she could get them to have a telephone put in, and then if there was any emergency they could ring Alfred's work to get a message to her. They were getting older now and she worried about them. She had only just begun to realise the full implications of their age. She supposed it would be the same for their kids, in their eyes you are always their mother and father and they just do not realise things move on. One day, sadly, you become old without realising it yourself.

Edith gave a great sigh as she thought about this. Time moves on for everybody and she could not believe where her own time was going. She was so far removed from the young lass who had been courted by Edward.

Maybe this was going to be her next phase, moving away from Denholme. Already she felt a bit more contented in her mind the way things were going. Aye, she would tell Alfred that night what she had decided.

★   ★   ★

When Edith recounted her thoughts to Alfred she was quite surprised to see a relieved expression spread across his face. He walked up to the mantelpiece without saying a word and picked the pipe up he had recently taken to smoking. Not lighting it but just moving it around in his hands, Edith getting to a point

227

where she was going to ask him if he was going to put any baccy in his pipe so he could smoke it, he finally said, 'I'm glad you've brought the subject up. I've been thinking on it for a while myself. It would be easier for me if we moved but I didn't like to suggest it as I know you like it here.' Then looking a little sad he added, 'I realise I've not done all I promised you, when we were wed, so I hardly liked to ask you to do one more thing for me. For once I want to do things for you. But if you feel you're able to move then it's as good a time as any now to make the effort.'

'Well, I'd not have brought it up if I'd not thought so,' replied Edith a bit sharper than she intended.

'I know, lass.' Suddenly his face brightened as another thought struck him, 'Maybe John could stay with your Ma and Pa in the week and come home at week-ends. That'd kill two birds with one stone, so to speak. He'd not have to change jobs and you'd know he was there to keep an eye on your Ma and Pa for you. I know how you worry about them.'

Edith was a bit more reluctant at this proposal than Alfred had expected her to be. He had thought she would jump at this idea, but she had reservations and soon aired them. 'You've to remember Ma is getting older and looking after a growing lad takes a lot of doing. It's extra cooking and all his washing. Mind, I could make him bring his overalls home at the week-ends so I'd do those for him. They're big, heavy things to do and I don't want Ma straining herself doing them.' Grudgingly she added, 'I suppose maybe it would work. But then they'd all have to agree but there's no harm in suggesting it, they can only say no.'

They decided they would outline their proposals to the family before they put any of it into action. It was a surprising response they had from them all. Instead of the opposition they had expected to encounter, they all embraced the idea.

John only made the comment that he did not want to move firms with doing his apprenticeship but if he had to travel to work then he would. Alfred put forward his idea about staying at his grandparents, if they were in agreement with the idea. He quickly told them he thought this an excellent plan.

Martha was not bothered where she started work; one mill was much like another, as long as she learnt the burling and mending. Anyway, as she saw it there would probably be more openings if they moved. After all, there were far more mills in the town than the few in Denholme.

Ethel laughed silently to herself. She knew

what they thought, that they were getting her away from Eddy. But that did not bother her; she only used him to amuse herself whilst there was nobody else more interesting. No, at one of those town schools there should be a lot more lads that she could have fun and games with. Aye and there would happen not be as many nosy parkers to report to her parents all they saw. Yes, she decided this seemed a very good idea to her and she told her mother and father so in no uncertain terms.

Edith was amazed by her agreeing so readily and was deeply suspicious of this, but there was nothing she could do about it but just keep a sharp eye on her.

The younger lads were not bothered where they attended school. To them school was as bad wherever they went. But they did remember back how right their mother had been about the last move, and how soon they had settled in so they were not too bothered where they lived as long as they were with the rest of the family. It was all one big adventure to them.

Now it only left Alfred's and Edith's parents to be told. Not that Alfred's parents would be upset; they did not see that much of them as it were. No, it was her parents she was more concerned about.

The more she thought about telling them the more out of proportion the whole thing became. Despite being married all these years and having her own family she always felt she had to account to her father for what she did or at least now, what the family did. Alfred laughed at her, but not unkindly because he could understand some of these feelings. Her father had a very strong personality and even though he was a man of few words, he put his opinion very forcibly across. He was a knowledgeable man with a lot of contacts and more often than not his thoughts and ideas were right. But at the same time Alfred did wish Edith did not feel such a strong need to justify herself to her father. She should realise it was herself and her husband and family that mattered. But it had become such a habit Alfred knew he was not going to change it now.

'Look, I can see you're restless to get your Ma and Pa told now we've made our minds up, why don't you go and see them tonight. I'll stay here and see to the family.'

'Oh, would you? I'd like to do that, get them told. I don't want one of the kids going to see them and spilling the beans before I've told them. I won't be long. I'll just get my things then I'll be off.'

'Don't rush; take as long as you need.'

'Thanks, I will.'

Arriving unexpectedly at her parent's house on an evening, her father was too astute to know it was not for no particular purpose.

'Well, young lady, and to what do we owe this pleasure?'

Edith gave an inward smile at still being called a young lady by her father, despite the fact she was a mother of six.

'Nay let her get in Joe before you start asking questions. Come on sit yourself down. Do you want a brew? The kettle's just boiled.'

'Aye, I wouldn't mind Ma, if it's no trouble.'

'So how's everybody?' enquired her father innocently.

'They are all fine.'

'Um, all's well is it?'

'Yes, thanks.'

Well at least he had ascertained there were no problems there.

'No, it's just Alfred and I have been having a little talk, in fact all the family have, and we've come to a decision.'

'Oh aye, and what might that be?' asked her father impatiently.

'We've decided it would be better for Alfred if we moved nearer to his work.'

'Is that all? Have you only just realised it? I

could have told you months ago,' said her father, rather deflated that it was not something more interesting.

'I know, but what about you and Ma?'

'What about us? We're all right here thanks.'

Laughing with relief Edith said, 'No, I didn't mean that you'd to move as well. It's just we don't like moving further away from you.'

Her mother hearing this, as she came back in with the tea, quickly tried to reassure her, 'Nay, lass, it's your life and you must do what's best for your man and your family. We'll be all right and it's not so far in that car of ours.'

'No I suppose not, and we thought you could get a telephone installed then you could always contact us through Alfred's work if there was any emergency.'

Her father looked indignantly at her now, 'Oh! So you're organising our life and spending our money as well.'

'No, it's not like that at all. I'm only trying to suggest what's best for all of us.'

'Well, we'll see. I'll think on it.'

'What about John?' asked her mother in a concerned voice. 'He's going to have a long way to travel to work.'

Both women looked in amazement as Joe

interrupted, 'He can come and stay here.'

Edith looked at him, 'Now who is the one organising things?'

'It's up to you, it was only a suggestion,' he sniffed indignantly.

'And it is a very good one too, Pa. I was only teasing; you're not organising us really. No, we'd wondered ourselves if there'd be any possibility of you letting him stay here. He can come back home to us at week-ends and bring all his washing back. I'll still see to that for him.'

'Get away with you, lass. His lot will just go in with ours, it'll be no trouble,' responded her mother.

'No, Ma that I must insist on as you've enough with your own. 'Sides his overalls are that heavy when they're wet. No, I must do them at least.'

'Hm, it'll be a nice bit of company on an evening,' her father added cheerfully.

Looking hurt at this remark Sarah asked, 'Don't you call me company then?'

'Away with you, you know what I mean. We can talk man's talk.' Laughing he added, 'Anyway I might get my car serviced on the cheap. He'll soon be well enough trained to do that for me.'

'You're always the crafty one. Still, it'll be nice to have a young 'un around,' added her mother smiling. 'I always think it keeps you active being around young ones.'

'Have you seen a place that's taken your fancy then?' her father asked changing the subject.

'No, we've not even started looking yet. We thought it best to talk it through first. I'm sure we'll find somewhere easily.'

'But you'll have yours to sell, you know.'

'I know, Pa, but I'm sure it will easily.'

'Well look, lass, if you see one you really want and you've not sold yours, let me know and we'll find a way of helping you financially so you can get it rather than miss it.'

'Thanks very much, but hopefully that won't be necessary,' Edith agreed knowing it was not wise to argue with her father.

'Well if it is, don't forget what I've said,' he said still having the last word.

Edith went home feeling very happy at how well it had all gone. At least for once they all seemed in agreement which she took as a good omen for their future.

18

Things worked out far better than Edith had dared to hope. She decided it all must have been meant to be, the way it fell into place so neatly.

They quickly found a place they fell in love with at Wibsey. It was a rather odd looking stone built house that had been tacked on to a row of cottages, yet it looked as if it should have been there all on its own. Inside it was equally as strange, you had to go up steps and down steps into various rooms. But it was the landing window that Edith loved the most. It was massive, made up of all different coloured bits of glass. Alfred was equally as taken with it. To approach the house you had to go down a small track that went from the main road through the village. Instead of leading to the front as would be expected, this lead to the back of the house so the front only overlooked fields. It was ideal, close to the village, which would soon become part of the town of Bradford, yet feeling as if they were still living in the country. The price was right, and then the added bonus was that it was also only a few minutes from Alfred's work.

Edith thought with trepidation she was going to have to talk to her father about sorting their money out in order to buy it due to the lack of interest in their own house. Then out of the blue there was a knock at the door and two rather timid people were standing on the doorstep looking scared to death. The woman spoke first, 'We don't like to disturb you but we've just found out your house is for sale and we wondered if we could look at it now. We're so excited; we've always fancied it if it came on the market.'

Edith was in a bit of a quandary here, she was not sure if they were genuine or simply two people not quite right in their minds. But she did want to sell the house. Besides Martha and John were in, so she decided she should be safe enough. 'Aye, come on in, you'll have to excuse the mess. I'm forever tidying it up after the young uns.'

'Oh, that doesn't matter; we just didn't want it to sell to somebody else so we got here as quick as we could with no thought of ringing beforehand.'

Maybe she should not have told them but it slipped out before she thought, 'Oh I don't think there's any chance of that. There's been nobody else to look at it as yet.'

The woman looked at the man. 'I am surprised. I thought it would have been snapped up as soon as it came available.'

'Well it appears not. Do you mind if I ask your names? Mine's Mrs Taylor.'

The young woman giggled. 'How silly, I forgot to say. We're Mr and Mrs Metcalfe.'

'Fine, now I know who I am talking to. Best come this way.' As she led them around the house she asked, 'Are you from these parts?'

Mr Metcalfe, who had stayed very quiet so far, now spoke. 'We're from Keighley, but my Aunt Millicent lived down the road. We used to come regular like to see her, and every time we went past here I said to Maggie, that place over there, meaning here, would make a grand butcher's shop.'

Edith was rather taken aback at this comment. 'Butcher's?'

'Aye, that's what I am you see, by trade that is. But at present I work for somebody else in Keighley. Never thought I'd get out of there and have a chance of setting up my own place. Mind you, it's always been our dream.'

He looked shyly at his wife who said, 'Go on Bert, and tell Mrs Taylor, it doesn't matter.'

Edith began to wonder what was coming next.

'Aye, we've been very lucky. My Aunt Millicent passed away recently.' Then suddenly he looked even more embarrassed at what he had said, 'I don't mean that was lucky. No, not at all, that was very sad. We were very upset weren't we Maggie? Both of us are still very sorry to have lost Aunt Millicent as we thought a great deal of her. A lovely lady she was, the best aunt one could wish for.'

Feeling she had to say something here Edith butted in, 'Yes, I did know her, a very gentle old lady she was.'

'Oh she was,' jumped in Maggie. 'Carry on Bert, tell the rest.'

'Well you see, as you probably know, she'd no other family so she left all she had to us. The big surprise was she'd a tidy sum saved. So now we feel we can have the shop we have always wanted. But with her dying we've not been coming to the village recently so that's why we nearly missed this being up for sale and this is the place we've had our heart set on all along. It would make all my dreams come true getting this. Anyway another relative, on my wife's side who lives nearby, knew we'd our eyes on it, if it was ever available, so they sent a message to us quick like. As I said good job they did and we got here otherwise we'd have been so upset if we'd missed it. So would Aunt Millicent.'

'Yes, um, well that has been lucky for you. Anyway shall I show you the rest of the house? You might not want to buy it once you've seen it all.'

'Oh we will, we will. We've already decided,' chirped Maggie.

'Aye, but sometimes when you come in a house it's not always what you think and then you're disappointed. As you probably know it was originally two houses. Mind if I say so myself, Alfred did a grand job in altering it into one. Oh, Alfred's my husband. We had this room here as a shop for a time. We only shut it recently.'

'Aye, that's when we saw it, as a shop so we thought it'd be ideal for our purpose as well.'

'I'll finish showing you the rest of the accommodation. Anything else you want to know ask me as we go around. I've not had much practice at doing this, I've to confess.'

'We'll ask if there is something we think we need to know. But I can't think on anything, can you Maggie?'

'No.'

As soon as they had finished looking Maggie turned to her husband, 'Well then?'

He now looked at Edith, 'We'll have it. How soon can we move in?'

'But you haven't even asked how much it is?' gasped Edith.

'Oh aye, silly me of course we need to know the price. I'm that made up about finding it for sale that I forgot about that.'

This was the point that Edith was sure they would find they could not afford it but said kindly, 'Look sit down whilst I put the kettle on, then we'll talk it through over a cup of tea.'

'Fine, fine,' he replied a tad impatiently.

Edith still could not believe it when she told them how much they were asking for the house and the couple did not even blink an eye, just accepted it with no haggling. They seemed more concerned with when they could move in than what it was costing them. It was obvious they had no clue how to go about buying the house. In the end Edith, with her limited knowledge of the process, pointed them in the right direction. She told them they needed to give a solicitor the details and he would then see to it for them.

'That's no problem, we can use the one who's been dealing with the will, can't we Maggie? He seemed a nice enough bloke.'

After Edith gave them the details of their own solicitor they finally took their leave, in a state of great excitement. As soon as they had gone out of the door Edith wanted to shake herself, she felt as if she was just waking up from a dream.

Martha popped her head around the door, 'I take it they weren't interested?'

'Now why do you think that?' Before Martha could answer she carried on and burst out with, 'You're wrong, they're buying it.'

'Come off it, Ma, you're teasing me. Any roads, they'd not be able to afford it.'

'Well, you've just learnt a valuable lesson there, young lady. You should never judge by appearances.'

Martha looked at her mother with open mouthed amazement, 'You really are serious, and they do want it and can afford it.'

'That's right. Eh, I can't wait for your Pa to come in; he'll never believe it either. Not them buying it, 'cause he's not seen them, but that I've sold it so easily.'

Martha now had a perplexed look on her face, 'But how can they afford it?'

'Don't be so nosy young lady.' Looking at her daughter's hurt expression Edith laughed. 'I'll tell you, it is no mystery. They've been left a nice amount of money from an aunt who passed away recently.'

'Oh I see, but what interests them about this house? I'd have thought a young couple would have fancied something different.'

Then not wanting to hurt her mother's feelings as if she was implying she did not like the house she added, 'What I meant was this is more of a family house being the size it is. They'll rattle around in it just the two of them.'

'Well, it may surprise you to know it's this particular house they've had their eye on. He's a butcher you see and they want to start their own business. So they'll use the front room as I did for the shop. Now does that answer all your questions?'

'I think so.' Then another thought came to her, 'When will we move? What if I haven't finished school when we do?'

'Look, let's take it a step at a time, but as to your last question I'm sure your Grandma will let you stay with them for a week or two if needs be, but I don't imagine we will be moving for at least six weeks, whatever happens and that's all the time you have left at school. You might have actually finished by the time we do move, let's see how it goes.'

'Eh, but I'm so pleased for you, in fact for all of us. At least now I'll be able to look for a job when I do leave school, near our new home.'

'That's right. Now let me get on with things, your Pa will soon be in for his tea. I'm surprised the rest of them haven't been clambering for theirs already.'

'They have, whilst you were showing the people upstairs, but I gave them bread and dripping and told them to go away until you called them back. Cheeky monkeys, they nearly came up to have a look at the couple but I sent them away with a flea in their ear.'

'Thanks love; I don't know what I'd do without your help.'

Now Martha's day was well and truly made. It was not often she received such compliments from her mother.

Edith could not contain herself any longer, as soon as she heard the door open she rushed up to Alfred, 'You'll never guess what?'

'You've burnt the tea.'

'Oh you! No, I've done it.'

'Done what woman?' he asked looking perplexed and slightly worried.

'Sold the house,' she replied impatiently wanting go get on with the tale.

'Ah, come on woman, you're pulling my leg. We've not had anybody to look at it.'

'Now that's where you're wrong, I've had a couple look at it this afternoon.'

'But they never made their minds up that quickly.'

'They have an all. They want to buy it.'

'Oh aye, but how much for, not the asking price I bet?'

'Wrong again, at the price we're asking.'

'I don't believe it, you're having me on. It doesn't happen just like that.'

'Well it has.'

'Aye, but they'll need to borrow money, so it'll happen not go through in any case, if they don't get the money.'

'That's where you're wrong again. They have the money; they don't need to borrow it.'

'Now I know this is a set up.'

'Honest, Alfred, it's not. You remember Millicent Lund; she was one of your customers, well she passed away recently. It turns out it was the man's aunt and she's left all she had to this couple who came here.'

'Aye, but that won't buy this. I used to feel sorry for her that she was short of money. I'd slip her extra bits of food in with her order.'

'Well maybe that's how she managed to have so much saved. No, she had a nice nest egg that none of them knew about and the nephew's inherited it all.'

'Well I never.'

Edith laughed, 'I hope you're a bit more careful in future who you give extra to. Don't be deceived by looks and the hard luck story. You can never really tell what people have.'

'Don't worry I won't, not after this. It's fair

been a shock.' Then realising it was all true what Edith had been telling him, before she knew where she was Edith was off her feet and being spun around.

'Oh, this is great. At last Edith things seem to be going our way. We can get that house you liked now. I know how happy that will make you.'

'Put me down you great lump.'

'But I'm so happy. Come on let's see you smile now.'

'I'm pleased, honest. It's just they're all biting the table leg, as it is for their tea.'

'Let them for once, it'll do no harm to see that you're not always at their beck and call. Make a pot of tea and let's have a few minutes peace and quiet and talk about it all.'

'Before you sit down anywhere you'd best get those clothes off. Look at me now; I've coal dust all over my clothes. Get yourself cleaned up then I'll give you five minutes to sit and discuss things with you.'

Without outwardly showing it, Edith was just as pleased and excited as Alfred. At last it looked as if they were going to be having a good carry on and more settled life from then on. But Alfred did know it also depended on him keeping to his resolve not to gamble any more. This decision was proving very difficult to abide by but he was just managing to do it.

19

Edith was not far wrong in her thoughts. The move went well and by the summer of 1937 they were settled and contented in their new home. Martha found a job, in the burling and mending department at Parker's Mill only a bus ride away from home. Once she started the work she loved it and would recount many a tale to her mother, which would make her mother think ruefully of her days in the mill. John soon settled into his routine staying with his grandparents in the week and coming home at weekends.

The rest of them settled into nearby new schools as if they had never been anywhere else. Ethel still caused the odd worry because of her behaviour with the lads, but Edith decided she would grow out of it in no time. She could understand that it was all part of growing up.

Edith was happier than she had ever been and thought nothing could disturb her new-found peace. But once again she was wrong. This time it was an outside influence. Much to her dismay the rumbles of unrest that were spreading across Europe that there could be another war became stronger. Edith remembered, with trepidation, only too well the last war and all the fear, misery and heartache. She would look at her four sons young faces and feel a worry that made her sick. She could not bear the thought that they would more than likely have to fight and put their lives at risk.

On the one hand the threat of war seemed so real, particularly when gas masks were issued but yet it seemed to recede when they listened to Chamberlain on September 27th, 1938 in his radio message. He told the people of the nation in his broadcast, 'How horrible, fantastic, incredible it is that we are digging trenches and trying on our gas masks here because of a quarrel in a faraway country between people of whom we know nothing.'

Alfred knowing of the deep worry gnawing inside Edith did his best to reassure her. When two days after that broadcast Chamberlain flew to Munich to have discussions with Hitler, Daladier and Mussolini, Alfred assured her this proved all would be well, in a bid to calm her fears if not eradicate them.

'Look, lass, Chamberlain knows what war is about and how many lives can be lost. I'm sure he wants it no more than you. Isn't he away now trying to resolve it?'

Begrudgingly she admitted, 'I suppose so,

but I just can't forget the fear of the last war. It brings all the terror back to me.'

'Well don't let it, lass. It may never happen, so don't worry about something that isn't here yet. Come here; let me give you a hug.'

'Thanks, Alfred, for all your understanding.'

'What for? It's not me that'll stop the war, though I'd like to, if only to see a smile back on your face.'

'No, silly, just being you and understanding how I'm feeling.'

Edith's reaction to a possible war gave Alfred a few qualms about what was going on in her head. She had not lost any close family last time so how could she possibly know what it was like. Yet he was perceptive enough to realise this anxiety must come from a root somewhere.

Edith felt even more reassured when on his return to London Chamberlain made another broadcast with reassuring words for the British people. 'There has come back from Germany to Downing Street, peace with honour,' he told the nation. 'I believe it is peace in our time.'

This feeling of contentment was short lived as the rumblings became stronger and stronger once again, that there really was going to be another war. It was her sons who would go, that was all she could think. She did not really consider the bombs and the effects they could have on the civilians that they could actually kill.

Edith became more and more sullen and abrupt with everyone in her agitation at what could happen. In the end it was nearly a sense of relief to Alfred when war was finally declared. At last he knew where he was with her and how she would behave. He understood she would do anything to protect her sons, although it was a shame she had never managed to show all this love by actions and words in the past.

Before they knew where they were, a year had gone past since Chamberlain's words of reassurance. Alfred's family was no different to any other British home as at 11.15 a.m. on September 3rd 1939 they all clustered anxiously around their wireless set, on that sunny Sunday morning, to listen to the broadcast of the Prime Minister, Neville Chamberlain. 'This morning the British Ambassador in Berlin handed the German government a final note stating that unless it was heard from them by 11 o'clock that they were prepared at once to withdraw their troops from Poland, a state of war would exist between us. I have to tell you now that no such undertaking has been received, and that consequently, this country, is at war with Germany.'

Edith turned to John, looking pleased with herself, 'Well, lad, you'll be safe enough being a mechanic, they'll not want you to fight and be put in danger. Surely they'll need experienced mechanics for repairs to vehicles and such like. Yes, lad, we'll be keeping you safely here with us.'

The rest of the family just looked at their mother in open mouthed amazement at such a statement, fully convinced all the strain of the last few months of wondering if there was going to be a war had finally unhinged her.

John looked calmly at his mother and said in a gentle voice, 'Ma, you must realise Hitler is like disease within Europe and must be removed before peace can be achieved. Whatever I have to do to help with that process I'll do. It has to be done for all of our futures.'

His mother stared at him in open mouthed amazement at such a strong statement, and then quickly jumped up, so fast the chair clattered to the floor as she ran from the room. Alfred could see the tears already forming on her face. Martha made as if to follow her, but Alfred gently laid his hand on her arm motioning her to stay where she was, 'I'll go and see to her, lass. Just you leave it for the moment.'

Edith felt as if she was living in a nightmare, she could only see blackness ahead of her. She just could not explain the feelings but they made her so unhappy and disturbed. It was like she was waiting in the calm before the storm. Whatever any of the family said, it did nothing to ease the fear within herself. She soon found she became good at putting a mask of false cheerfulness on her face but Alfred saw through this although he did not let on to her. Despite his outward show of calmness he was equally disturbed in his own way. But his worry was different; it was Edith that was causing it. He still loved her right enough, but she had changed so much. At times he wondered if she was really going a little bit mad. Little did he know Edith often asked herself the same question.

Just like everybody else she did all she was told. She went out quick enough to buy the black material needed to make the black out curtains, and with the help of Martha made them and fixed them to all the windows. She was short tempered enough to tell any of them off who did not draw them properly.

Martha was soon home with the tale of how the glass roofs in the weaving shed had been covered with tar to stop the lights showing outside. Now artificial lighting had to be on all during the day. Not that it had any great effect on Martha because in her job in the burling and mending they had always needed the lights all the time to help them see the material properly for all its flaws.

Edith could not believe her ears when Alfred came home with his news. 'Seeing as I'm too old to go fight in this war I've volunteered to be an air raid warden.'

At first Edith thought this was some kind of joke, 'Oh aye, and what might that involve doing?'

'Don't you laugh; somebody has to do the job. If the bombs drop here it'll be a very important task. I've to help deal with any bomb incidents in this area. You'd all better listen to this carefully; another duty is to check the black out precautions. So we'd best make sure ours are all right and set a good example if I'm to say owt to those who are breaking the rules. Can't be telling them off if we haven't done it right here, now can I?'

Harry said in a very subdued voice for him, that set Alfred wondering if he was already up to something, 'No, Pa.'

Nobody really took Alfred seriously about the blackouts, but they soon started to when they read in the local newspaper the reports, which were in most evenings, of some unfortunate citizen who had allowed a chink of light to escape into the night and that they had been consequently fined or cautioned.

Then to make things worse, before petrol was rationed and whilst vehicles were still in constant use, car lights were banned. Edith then changed her source of worry to thinking of Alfred in his wagon as there were so many accidents being reported. Luckily the government finally relented on this and agreed that dim, hooded lights could be used. This brought her a margin of relief on one count.

Each of the family seemed to change; Martha started to complain she had nowhere to go now when she went out with her friends. Many of the cinemas and theatres were closed, although as time moved on slowly one after another opened their doors again.

It became a family ritual to all crowd around the wireless set for the 9 o'clock news from the BBC to hear about the latest developments in the war. Alfred tried to stop this because he could see Edith becoming more and more despondent. There was no good news and she would just ring her hands in despair. 'Oh! Where is it going to end? What will happen to us all? I hope your job is safe Alfred. I couldn't go through it again having no money coming in. I just couldn't.'

Alfred once more did his best to reassure her, 'Don't fret, lass. People still need to heat their home whatever's happening in the world and they need coal to do that.'

'I know but so many are unemployed, more now than ever, there'll be a shortage of money, so they'll have to cut down on coal.'

Alfred knew what she had said was true enough because unemployment had risen sharply as many major projects, particularly in the building trade, had been abandoned. But there again, already a lot of the other men from his firm had gone to war so there was a shortage of delivery men in his area of work.

'I know that but I'm sure the government will soon create employment. They're going to want things made for the military. They'll need extra people then, you can be sure about that. Besides, as more of the young lads volunteer, there'll be more work left for us old 'uns,' said Alfred with a laugh trying to reassure her.

Unfortunately it did not have the desired effect as she gasped, 'Oh don't say that. What about John?'

Alfred was quick to realise he had once again said the wrong thing and quickly tried to make amends, 'Haven't I gone through it all with you before. He'll be all right. I'm sure there'll be no need for him to join up, not with his job he should have a reserved occupation.'

'Aye, happen you're right. I'm just being a silly, protective mother,' she had to concede.

The whole family heaved a sigh of relief, that at least for a short while their mother was back to her old self. But it did not seem like that to Edith. She could still only feel that blackness, with no way forward. Even her parents could not get to see her so often. Her father was not keen to drive at night; even now he had been allowed some limited lights on his car. Edith was glad of this because they were getting older and she worried about them. They had always been an important part of her life; they were there when she needed them. In fact they were there all the time for her, whether she consciously realised it or not. No, this life frightened Edith tremendously for the welfare of all her family young and old alike.

20

John was the first to give them one of their biggest shocks. No sooner had they sat down to tea, on one of his weekend's at home, than he said in a voice that instantly alerted them all to the fact something was not quite right. 'Ma and Pa, I've something to say to you both.' Here he started choking and coughing, then still red in the face he continued. 'In fact to all of you not just Ma and Pa. I've joined up today; I'll be leaving you a week on Monday.'

Alfred heard a loud clatter as Edith dropped her knife and fork on her plate, 'You've what? Tell me I heard wrong,' she begged.

'Sorry, Ma, that's what I said. I've joined up.'

Before Alfred could say anything Edith started screaming, 'No, no, not you. You'd no need to go, you know that. Why, oh why did you go and do it you silly young fool?'

'Ma, listen to me, please.'

By now Alfred had reached Edith and was holding her tight to him as great sobs racked her body. 'Ssh, lass, let's listen to what the lad has to say. Come on now, just listen for a minute.'

John looked at his father gratefully. 'Thanks, Pa. I'm sorry I've hurt you both but I just had to join up. It was something inside me that wouldn't let me stay here and watch all my friends have a go and me being left here all nice and cosy and safe and sound. Besides, I told you before Hitler's got to be stopped, if there's to be any future for any of us. My belief in that is too strong for me not to do my part.'

Edith gave a hysterical laugh. 'It would have been no joke staying here. You'd have been just as brave. Anyway you could have become an air raid warden like your Pa, if you really wanted to do something useful for the war effort. We don't know what'll happen when the predicted bombs start dropping here, but one thing at least you can take shelter from them. There's no shame in staying at home and doing a job that's needed. You go in tomorrow and tell them you've changed your mind and want to stay at home after all.'

'Sorry, Ma, I won't do that. It's Sunday and they are not open but in any case it doesn't work like that. Once you've enlisted, that's it there's no turning back.'

Edith screamed even louder, 'Oh you foolish boy. Haven't you the sense you were born with?'

Quietly Martha moved over to John as she could see her mother's reaction to his news and the response she gave was hurting him deeply. Touching his shoulder gently she tried to reassure him. 'I understand, John, I do. If I'd been a lad I'm sure I'd have done the same thing.'

'Thanks, Martha,' replied John with a sad expression on his face.

Inside John felt as if he was crying. He did not want to have to do this to his parents but he wished they would understand how he felt and see it from his point of view. Alfred sensing the deep feelings his son was going through, as well as those emotions of his wife, wanted to take the hurt away from both of them.

'Look, the pair of you, there's not much time left if the lad goes on Monday. You don't want to fall out with each other at a time like this, now do you? Edith just listen to John's point of view and try to understand how he sees it. John, I can only say I wish you'd discussed it with us before you went and joined up. But I do understand how you feel, I really do. I'm sure once your Ma gets over the shock she'll understand your feelings too. Now come on the pair of you, let's make the most of the time we have left before we're parted.'

Alfred could feel Edith slowly relaxing and

calming down in his arms and felt proud of her when she looked at this first born lad of theirs and said, 'I suppose what is done is done and I am proud of you, John, you know that. It's just I love all my children and want no harm to come to any of you. What mother does? Aye, lad, we'd best make sure you're well set up when you go. Tomorrow we'll talk more, you tell me what you need and I'll get the things ready for you.'

John stood up and joined his father and mother. Putting his arms around his mother he drew her close to him. 'Thanks, Ma. I'll take care you never fear. I've so much to live for with such a loving family like this. But I do want there to be a future for me so one day I can bring a family into the world and know they'll be safe and have a happy family life like we've all had.'

Martha could feel tears pricking her eyes at the brave words this brother of hers was saying. Even Harry, who had usually far too much to say for himself, was silenced.

The days flew by and before they all knew it, the time had come for them to take their parting of this loved member of the family. Edith packed him up with everything she could think of that he would need and more besides. Plenty of extra warm socks and underwear were packed. She believed the army would not feed him, so as much food as she could convince him to take was put in his luggage. John had visions when he arrived at the army camp that he would be laughed at by the others. Little did he realise that most mothers were the same. So in the end, when he did arrive at the barrack's with all the other new recruits, all of them in his dormitory had a laugh at each other, not at him but about the lengths most of their various mother's had gone to in what they had sent with them to camp.

As he parted from his family, he began to have doubts in his own beliefs and suddenly wondered if his mother had been right all along and he should have stayed put. But then looking at his young brother's faces he knew he was doing what was best for them all. He had to help make the future world a better place.

Edith clung to him, 'You look after yourself. Don't do anything silly. No heroics, winning fancy medals is not important. The most important thing is to bring yourself back here safely to all of us.'

'Aye, lad, your Ma's right there. There's really nowt I can add to that apart from say the same, take care, John. Just do what you have to, but most importantly look after yourself,' Alfred added.

'I will, don't fret. Haven't I said before I've a lot to come back for?'

Martha felt no need for words, she grabbed hold of him and gave him a big hug, 'Bye John, see you soon.'

After he had left it felt as if a dark cloud had descended on the house. Nobody really knew what to say to each other. Edith did the only thing she knew to try to keep the fears at bay and that was work and work. She seemed in a mad frenzy as she rushed here and there. None of them knew where they were as the house was turned up side down for a Spring clean, even though it did not really need it as it was perfectly clean to begin with.

As he had promised, John wrote as often as he could, and whilst he was still in England, Edith felt reasonably secure in this knowledge. But when he wrote to say he was being posted to France the blackness descended once more on her. All the old fears were back. She felt she was forever watching for the telegraph boy.

Alfred was kept busy with his duty as air raid warden, not that there had been any raids over Bradford but at least he felt he was doing his part checking the blackout. He still listened to the news and read the papers trying to visualize where his son was and what was happening to him. Somehow Edith seemed to switch off from this. It was as if she thought that if she did not discuss it with the family then he would be safe. Harry being Harry was fascinated by what could be happening to his big brother and would put his foot in it by asking insensitive questions, 'Do you think John's shot many Germans yet, Pa?'

Edith looked at this youngest son of hers with a puzzled frown because he seemed to be getting pleasure from any gory details he could. 'Do be quiet. You've no idea what you're saying you silly boy.'

'But, Ma, I want to know what happens ready for when I join up.'

Here Alfred could not stop himself laughing. 'How long do you think this war is going to last or do you think they'll take you as a young lad?'

'But, Pa, I hope it lasts long enough for me to join up and have a go at them.'

Now his mother angrily butted in, 'Enough of that! It's enough with one of my boys out there fighting. Anyway, it might be over soon then we'll have our John back home safe and sound with us. I most certainly don't want any more of my boys going to war and being in danger.' Little did she know how true those words really were.

Only the very next day, as Edith was

cleaning the windows outside, she saw the telegram boy approaching. She nearly fell off the stool with fright and shock, then quickly realised he could be going to their neighbours. But he did not; he stopped in front of Edith and muttered looking embarrassed, 'Mrs. Taylor?'

'Yes, that's me.'

Looking apologetic now, it suddenly struck Edith how young this lad was who had to do this traumatic job. He held out his hand to give her something. 'I've this for you.'

As the telegram was held out to her, Edith felt as if the world was suddenly swimming around and the ground was coming up to meet her. Seeing her white face the lad quickly asked, 'Are you all right, Missis? Do you want me to get someone to see to you?'

Recovering herself slightly and wanting to know what was in the telegram she quickly grabbed it out of the lad's hand whilst trying to reassure him. 'No, I'm all right now, lad. You get on your way, I'm sure you've other people to deliver to.'

'Thanks, Missis, if you're sure?' the lad said feeling relieved to be on his way. He had seen these sad faces so often of late that he felt sick with it.

'Yes, bye,' Edith managed to mumble.

Taking herself inside, Edith sat at the kitchen table and for long enough she just looked at the telegram in front of her without actually opening it. One part of her wanted to read it, another part wanted to wait until Alfred or Martha came home from work.

Finally she plucked up the courage and after turning it over a couple of times to check it was really addressed to her family she opened it. The words swam in front of her eyes as she read them, 'We are sorry to inform you that Private John Taylor has been killed in action.'

She heard a voice scream, 'No, no,' then realised it had come from herself. Finally great sobs racked her body and this was how Alfred found her when he came in from work. Gently taking the telegram out of her clutched hand he read what it said. He wanted to join Edith in the sobs and he felt his own screams of denial go through his head. Aye, he knew it was bad in Dunkirk and he had listened to the news but somehow inside he had been convinced John would be safe and sound and in no time turning up on the doorstep on leave.

He had read over three hundred thousand men had been moved in the six days, that had seemed an awful lot of people to him, it was hard to believe that some had not made it.

Alfred did not know how to help Edith in her grief as she was totally oblivious to anything he did or said and was more than relieved when he heard Martha's voice ask anxiously, as if she already feared the worst, 'What is it? What's happened?'

Alfred held the telegram out to her, 'It's our John, and he's dead.'

Silently she took it off her father and read it then finally she asked in a stiff voice as if trying to hold back the tears, 'What have you told the others?'

Alfred then realised it was unusually quiet in the house. 'Edith where are the rest of them?'

But she just looked blankly at both of them for a few minutes then mumbled, 'How do I know? I haven't seen hide or hare of them.'

Realising what had more likely than not happened Martha put her thoughts into words. 'The young uns probably rushed in, dumped their things and went back out to play and never saw Ma sat here. George and Fred more than likely went to their friend's house straight after school. I'd best go and round them all up. They'll have to be told this sad news.'

'Thanks, love,' replied Alfred once again amazed at their eldest daughter. He knew she had been attached very deeply to John and how she must be hurting inside.

Alfred broke the news to the others as gently as he could but he knew they did not really understand the full implications. To them their brother was still away but one day he would come home. It would only be when that day never came that it would really hit them what had happened. In no time they were clambering to go back out to play as if life just carried on. Then it made Alfred realise it did. One more death in this horrific war made not the slightest difference to anybody except his family.

Edith made them all wear a black band on their arm as a mark of respect. But having no body to bury seemed very strange. The minister of the chapel, where Edith's mother and father still attended, agreed to say a few words. They all went along to the service, but when John was mentioned like this with no actual funeral service he was only one of the many sons already lost. Theirs was only the grief that other families had already gone through, some more than once. Edith was so locked in her own distress that she barely noticed how her parents seemed to visibly shrink at the news of their first born grandson's death. Whilst John had lived with them he had become such an important part of their lives.

21

When John had gone to fight in the war Edith had always believed if anything like this was to happen to him she would die herself. But it was not like that at all. It was as if her body had some inner sense that it had to survive for the rest of her family. She did feel dead inside; even if she was still alive and functioning and somehow she managed to look after them as she had always done. Once they were out of the house she would sit many an hour looking into space just thinking of that lad of hers. Her parents came to see her as often as they could, but they were getting older and her mother was not in the best of health. John's death had also had a great impact on them and for the first time ever Edith had seen her father moved to tears. She had been incapable of offering him any comfort that deep was her own grief and her mother quietly sobbed as she rocked her self back and forth, 'Not this again, not our Edith to suffer the loss of a child before her time.'

Edith was sitting in a trance like state, her thoughts going back over those moments, when a loud knock came at the door. She gave a visible jump of shock at being brought back to the present in such an abrupt manner. This propelled her to rush towards the door in the hope it was John home on leave, and as she glimpsed the uniform once she started to open the door, she felt a great joy go through her. Those silly officials had got it wrong after all - he was not dead. Then as her mind woke up to reality she understood it could not be John. Pulling the door open wide she felt the familiar sadness come back as full comprehension dawned on her that this really was not her lad at all but some stranger.

'Mrs. Taylor?' he asked apprehensively.

'Yes.'

'My name's Sid Johnson. I was a friend of your John's and sadly was there when he was killed. I thought I'd come and see you as soon as I could to tell you what happened. Those telegrams they send don't tell you details and are impersonal.' Then he looked worried as a thought struck him, 'You did get the telegram?'

'Oh aye, we received it all right. Look, you'd best come in. We don't want the local gossips having a field day.' All different kinds of thoughts and emotions were rapidly going through her mind.

Realising the poor lad looked weary and had probably had a hard time of it himself she gently asked, 'Have you been to your home yet?'

'No, I wanted to come straight here to see you.'

'Well thanks that was really kind of you. Just you rest yourself a few minutes whilst I put the kettle on.'

'Thanks, that'd be very welcome. I seem to have been travelling forever, then most of the way I'd to stand; the train was so crammed full.'

As she made the tea Edith's mind went through so many emotions. She had so wanted to hear about the last moments of her son's life, but now it was here for the telling she was not so sure if she did want to hear about it at all.

Going back into the room she found the poor chap had fallen asleep. She thought he must be totally exhausted. She said gently, 'Sid, lad, here's your tea. Get this down you and you'll soon feel better.'

Being a Yorkshire woman she was of the belief that a good cup of tea cured all ills. Keeping her impatience at bay until he had finished his drink, she finally asked, 'You said you'd come to tell me about my John, how he died.'

'Aye that's right. John and me hit it off straight away, you know. I suppose it was with us both coming from the same area.'

Here Edith interrupted, 'I'm sorry, I never asked where you come from and if you'd come out of your way coming here to see us.'

'No, I don't live too far away, only at Cleckheaton, so you see straight away John and I had something in common.'

'What do you do for a living? I mean when you're not in the army, Sid. I hope you don't mind me calling you Sid, but any friend of my son's is a friend of mine.'

Here Edith saw his face relax a little and he suddenly looked much younger and at ease. 'No, of course I don't mind being called Sid. Again John and I had something in common work wise. I'm in the works of an engineering firm selling locomotives. Not cars but of similar backgrounds. Aye, as I said we hit it off straight away, so when the going became rough in France, as it did, and we were retreating to the coast we stuck together. We didn't know where the rest of our fellow troops were most of the time. It was really every man for himself. All we knew was we wanted to reach the coast but how great our chance of escape was we just didn't dare think about. Then we didn't even know how fast the Germans were advancing from the south. Finally, totally exhausted we poured on to the beaches at Dunkirk after making our way through the burning rubble of the town. Then all we could do was stand about and wait, we had to dig in the best we could, under a hail of shells and bombs from the dive bombers until somebody came to rescue us.'

Here Edith interrupted, 'So John did actually make it to the beach at Dunkirk?'

'Oh aye he did that, and once we were there we thought we'd make it home. But as I said there were the bombs. Supplies and rations were running out fast and we were all becoming demoralised and hungry so all we could hope for was that rescuers would arrive at any time. I saw the best of them snap under the stress. They'd start fighting each other and try to jump the queue to get into the boats when they came. It was only because they no longer knew what they were doing. Sometimes it had to be at gunpoint that the orderly ranks were eventually formed. But you could still sense the fear. It was as if you could smell it. There was an underlying sense of panic at the thought of facing imprisonment or massacre if they lost the race against time.' Here Sid paused and Edith saw the look on his face as if he was re-living it again. She felt really sorry for him as if he were her own.

'Don't carry on lad, if it's upsetting you too much,' Edith said kindly, while all the time hoping he would go on as she desperately wanted to hear about the last moments of her precious John's life.

'No, I want you to know and understand.' Then a thought came to him, 'You do want to know, don't you?'

'Yes, lad, of course I do,' Edith replied forcibly.

Here there was a short silence as both became engrossed in their own thoughts. Finally, Edith seeing his empty cup picked it up, 'Let me get you another cup of tea before you continue.'

'Thanks, I won't say no. That'd be right grand.'

This time as soon as Edith was seated Sid plunged in. 'The bombs were coming down thick and fast. Before you knew where you were one would make a crater and next thing you knew a bloke would fall in it and the next bomb would cover him over.'

Seeing the immense pain on his face Edith asked gently, 'Is that what happened to John?'

'Yes, there was nowt I could do. As soon as I saw him disappear in the crater I ran to try to get him out, but before I reached the crater another bomb dropped and it was as if it had never been disturbed. There was no hole, no trace of John,' he said with his voice trembling.

By this time tears were streaming down both their faces. 'Thanks, lad, it's been a great comfort to know what happened in those last moments of his life. At least my poor lad was buried, rather that than bits of him left all over France.'

Neither of them had heard the door open and had not realised there was anybody else there until a voice asked sharply, 'What's going on here?'

Edith saw Alfred have a look of shock on his face as he saw Sid sat there. She could tell that for a moment the same thoughts had gone through his mind and that their John had returned to them. As soon as he realised his mistake he instantly held his hand out to take Sid's, 'Well, who have we here then Edith?'

Jumping quickly out of her chair Edith turned to Alfred, 'Ah Alfred, this is Sid. He was a close friend of our John's and was with him at the end. He's been telling me all that happened.'

At hearing this Alfred was not sure if this was a good or bad thing after how Edith had been behaving of late. 'Has he now!'

Edith could sense these thoughts of

Alfred's by the look on his face. 'It's all right, Alfred. It's done me no harm. In fact it's helped me. I know he really is dead and at peace now. I feel a lot better for knowing.'

'I'm glad. Thanks, lad, for taking the trouble to come to see us.'

'No problem, as I explained to Mrs Taylor I only live at Cleckheaton and John and me were real good friends. I'm pleased I've met his family. He always said he'd bring me here to meet you all. That was if we both survived. But I wanted to come in any case as he'd described you all in so much detail that I felt I seemed to already know you all.'

'You'll stay to have a bite to eat with us won't you?' asked Alfred kindly.

Jumping up Edith put her hand to her mouth. 'Food, I'd forgotten all about tea, we've been that busy talking. You go and talk to Alfred now Sid whilst I see to things here before they're all in complaining they're hungry.'

'If you're sure as I don't want to put you out?'

'Nay, lad, the rest of them will never forgive me if I don't keep you here to meet them. 'Sides there's usually somebody extra at our meal table, they're always arriving home expecting me to feed one friend or another.'

'Thanks, that'd be great. My family don't

know I'm on my way home, so they'll not be watching out for me.'

Edith felt as if she had known this lad a long time as she heard him chatting away to Alfred whilst she made tea. He showed no embarrassment as each of them came in from school and had a good look at him.

Just then the outside door slammed once more, 'You've not met all of us yet,' Edith laughed as her eldest daughter walked in.

Martha stopped in her tracks and stared at Sid with open mouthed amazement. Finally she managed to get the words out, 'Who's this, Ma?'

'Sid, a friend of our John's and he's been kind enough to call to tell us what really happened to John.'

'Oh, I wish I'd been here to hear what he'd to say.'

For the first time since Martha's entry into the room Sid spoke. 'It's all right; your Ma's invited me to stay to tea. I'm going to tell it all again to your Pa afterwards so you can listen in if you like.'

'Thanks, I'd like that. I'll just go and get changed out of my work clothes. I've time before tea, haven't I Ma?'

'Of course, lass, off you go.'

Edith noticed Martha give a quick look at Sid as she went out of the room. She knew it was unusual for her daughter to bother changing out of her work clothes if she was not going out. Already she could sense an attraction for her daughter from Sid.

Sid chatted well into the evening repeating all he had told Edith. She listened to it all once again, as he re-told the tale. Somehow it seemed to bring her closer to her lost son, yet it also helped the healing process. Edith was conscious that Martha held on to every word Sid said. But her other daughter, Ethel disgusted her; she behaved as if she was far older than her thirteen years. Edith knew she was trying to flirt with Sid. She worried Edith, what would happen to her she did not know but she was afraid some lad would take advantage; she was such a forward young miss. At times it was hard to tell who the eldest daughter was, Martha or Ethel. Martha still had a young, fresh look about her that made her appear younger than her actual years. Edith had made sure early on that Sid knew how old Ethel really was and all her coy glances and suggestive actions were like water off a ducks back with him. She could see it was Martha that held the attraction.

By the time he finally ran out of steam, telling the tale, Edith realised how late it had become, 'Your family aren't expecting you tonight, you told us earlier. You could stay here now it's so late and use John's bed for the night then get off early morning to go home if you like. Besides, I doubt you'll catch a bus now, they'll have finished running for the night.'

With no hesitation he accepted the offer. 'Thanks that'd be great; as long as you're sure it'd be no trouble for you?'

'Nay, lad, none at all, besides the bed's already made up,' then Edith added sadly, 'It was all changed ready for John coming back home.'

'Thank you Mrs Taylor. If you don't mind I'd like to hit the sack. It's been a long day.'

'Come on, I'll show you the way,' Martha said quickly, already moving towards the door before her mother could make a move.

After she had taken Sid out Edith and Alfred exchanged a knowing look.

When she came back in the room Edith said, 'Nice lad.'

'Aye, he's okay.'

'Um.'

'Well, I suppose it was good of him to trouble to come and tell us all about John,' Martha admitted.

'Course it was, he'd no need to do that.'

'No, I suppose not. Anyway I'll go up myself now.'

As Sid parted company in the morning he

gave his thanks to them all, then looking around all their faces asked, 'Would it be all right if I wrote to you when I go back? It'd be nice to have somebody to communicate with besides my family.'

'Of course you can, lad. That'd be real nice.' But inside her Edith knew it was really Martha he wanted to write to.

Martha realised this and felt a glow of happiness within. She had dreamt all night long about him. Eh, he was a nice lad; she did hope he might fancy becoming her young man. Her spirits were even more uplifted when he said he would walk her part way to work as it was on his way to his bus stop.

He did not say much as they walked along but it was not an uncomfortable silence. As they parted company he turned to her, 'Next time I'm on leave would you like to go to the pictures with me?'

'Oh yes, thanks and shall I'll write and let you know what's coming on at the cinema and what's probably any good to see?' Then suddenly realising she might have been too forward she added, 'That's if you'd like me to?'

'I would, it keeps you going receiving letters from home. It makes it all seem as if there's something worth while to come back to.'

Martha seeing the time had moved forward, 'I'll have to go otherwise I'll be late for work.'

'Aye, you do that. We don't want you to be late, now do we?'

'See you soon then.'

'Hope so, bye.'

'Bye.'

Her feet barely seemed to touch the ground as she ran the rest of the way to work feeling so elated because he wanted to see her again.

Yet at home Edith was in a troubled state. She liked the lad well enough but she was afraid if owt came of it between Martha and him, he might be taken away from her like Edward had from her all those years ago. Then all Martha would be left with would be a broken heart, nothing else.

22

Contentment settled on Edith that she had never expected to feel again. She had put her son to rest peacefully after Sid's visit. She could not imagine anything else could come along to rock her boat. She should have understood by now that it was another calm spell before the storm.

Martha had seemed settled in the textiles. Because the firm she worked for produced material that was used in the making of the soldier's uniforms she was allowed to stay in that job. At the same time, she was not prevented from moving to other employment so long as it was connected with war work. It was not long after her eighteenth birthday in 1941 that she made her bold announcement.

As they were all eating their tea, and for once all of them were silent, Martha broke that silence with her shock announcement. 'I'm leaving the mill on Friday. I'm starting at English Electric on Monday.'

'You're what?' Edith choked between mouthfuls of tea.

'I'm going to be working in the new works at Low Moor where they make some of the components for the Halifax bomber.'

'That's what you think, madam,' snapped her mother.

'Ma, just listen to me. John felt he'd to do his bit. He did and there's nobody sorrier than me how it ended. Well I feel the same; I've got to do what I can to help the war effort. Anyway, it's not as if it's dangerous or anything.' Then she gave a little giggle, 'I suppose some of the men could be.'

'What exactly do you mean by that remark, young lady?'

'Well I'm going to be on inspection. I'll have to check what's been manufactured for faults, so I suppose the men won't be too pleased if I reject any of their work particularly seeing as how I'm only a mere young woman.'

'Alfred, tell her, she can't go and work amongst all those men,' pleaded Edith.

'Come on, Edith, be sensible. Think about it, now wasn't there men in the weaving sheds when you worked there?'

'Well yes, but that was different.'

'How was it?'

'I don't know, it just was,' Edith still persisted.

'Look the lass is only trying to do her bit. There's nowt wrong with that. Just leave her alone and let her get on with it.'

'Have it your way, but you do know Martha once you start there, you can't leave if you don't like it. That's it; you'll be there for the duration of the war.'

'I'm fully aware of that but I've no plans to leave. As I said before I want to do my bit and that's what I mean to do. I'll stick it out there whatever because as you said once I've taken the plunge there's no way out again.' Then laughing she added, 'Unless I find some nice young bloke to wed me and I have a baby, and then I'd be able to leave.'

Her mother snapped at her, 'Martha, enough of that. I'll have none of that talk at the meal table with young ears listening.'

'Don't take on so, Ma, I'm only joking. I don't intend that to happen, at least not for a while yet.'

'I should hope not.'

Here her father butted in, 'Come on, Edith, loosen up a bit. Martha was only having you on.'

'Well all I can say is just you be careful and don't do owt daft, that's all I ask,' begged her mother.

'I will. After all, Ma, it's you who's taught me all I know so far about life.'

Edith kept quiet after this comment; she was not really sure how to take it.

Martha did cause her to have a few rather

bad moments about some of the tales she brought home and recounted once she started her new job. Men being men they could not help themselves resenting, at times, that it was a pretty young lass inspecting their work. Being a factory there were plenty of mice around. They saw this as a great source of amusement. Their idea of a joke was for Martha, or indeed any of the other female inspectors, to suddenly come upon a dead mouse where they least expected it. If there was one thing Martha really disliked it was a mouse, dead or alive. She came home many a night looking white and shaken and Edith would straight away want to know what had been going on.

Now if it had been Ethel that would have been different altogether. A right case she was. Edith thought back to how, when Ethel was much younger, her grandpa had caught some mice and left them on one side in his shed to get rid of. Who did they find but Ethel, stroking those dead mice? Aye, she was a right one she was. When Edith saw Martha's white face she would try to offer her sympathy, 'What is it, lass? Have they been up to their antics again?'

'Aye, Ma, but you know what men are, really just little boys at heart.'

'Well done, that's the way to look at it.

Don't let them see you're afraid. They'll soon stop it if they're getting no more fun out of their little games.'

'I know that, but it's hard not to react when you hate mice like I do.'

'Just try to shut your mind off from what you're seeing. Think of something nice instead.'

'I do.'

'That's the way.'

At other times Martha would recount tales that brought her pleasure. Probably one of the most important events in her life was when on January 12th 1942 Her Royal Highness, The Princess Royal, and her younger son visited the works. Martha even managed to catch a glimpse of them. That was a memory she carried with her for many a year. Unusual though it was, that was one of the rare few good moments of her working life during the war. Mind, Martha had a happy look on her face most of the time, as Sid had written as promised and on his last leave they had gone out every spare minute they could together.

Edith liked him, as did Alfred; he seemed a nice enough lad. Martha certainly thought a lot of him, already that was obvious for all to see. Edith only hoped the poor lad made it through the war. She did not want to see the light extinguished in Martha's eyes as it was for so many young lasses. But why was she worrying only about this lad being killed, she should be worrying about all her family's lives as the bombing had started on Bradford.

She had never felt more pleased about the fact her parents lived in the country away from the town centre, than she did now. At least they were well out of it all or at least she hoped so. Not that Bradford suffered as badly as many places but what bombs that were dropped on the town were bad enough and did plenty of damage. She fair felt for the folk of the other towns that suffered constant bombing, particularly when the first bomb dropped on Bradford August 27th 1940 and she had a real feel for what it was like. She knew from the newspaper reports that windows were blown out in Leeds Road and two churches in Rooley Lane were damaged.

Then on Saturday 31st August 1940 one of the big stores in Bradford centre, Lingards and Rawson Market were blown up. Not so far away from them, at Laisterdyke, there was terrible damage and a lot of people had to be evacuated. The sky was lit up that night. Nothing was sacred; the New Catholic church was bombed and it was said the damage there alone came to £20,000.

Aye, her parents were well out of it, as it

really was becoming so frightening.

The lads only thought of it as good fun and complained because the damage was not nearer home so they could go and help. Edith thanked her lucky stars there were no bomb sites near by for them to play on. She could well imagine one of them easily hurting themselves if there had been.

Alfred, at last seemed settled in his job. He was kept busy both with work and the home guard. At least she had no longer to worry on that score, there seemed to be no temptations, whatever there had been, for him.

Considering everything, and now she was coping with the loss of her son, life did not seem too bad taking into account there was a war on, not as bad as it was for some folk. That was what Edith thought but as usual something happened to shatter her peace once more.

She could not believe it when she heard her father's voice; it was so early in the morning. He called out as he entered the house, 'Are you there, Edith?'

'In the front room, clearing up, come on in. Is Ma with you?' Edith called back.

There was no response, she turned around from dusting the sideboard and gave a gasp of shock as she saw her father stood there pale faced and starring with vacant eyes. Quickly she asked, 'What's up, Pa?'

Still he stood there and the words just would not come.

'Pa, what is it?' Edith wanted to shake him. Then comprehension dawning she sobbed, 'Is it Ma? Is she ill?'

Finally her father spoke, 'Yes, it is your Ma.'

'Why didn't you say so straight away? I'll just get my coat and we'll go to see to her. I'll look after her don't fret.'

'There's no need, lass.'

'What do you mean there's no need? Of course there is, she needs looking after.'

'She's passed away, went quietly with no fuss in her sleep.'

'No! She can't have. Tell me it isn't true,' screamed Edith.

'It is, lass, I'm sorry,' murmured her father.

'But why, why Ma, when she's never done anybody any wrong?'

'That's the way it is, lass. She'd not wanted to tell you because she thought you'd had enough to worry about. But she's had a weak heart for a while now, that's why she's been getting so tired lately. It's just finally given up, it was worn out.'

'I can't believe what you're telling me. Tell me it isn't really true.'

'I can't, lass, because it is true. I'm sorry.'

'But Pa, what about you, how will you manage?' Edith finally thought to ask.

'I don't know. It hasn't really sunk in yet that she'll not be there any longer. There's so much to do and organise. I never really fully appreciated how well your Ma organised everything. I feel all at sea worrying about her funeral.'

'I'll help you Pa.' As the full implication struck home she asked, 'Have you been to see the undertaker yet?'

'Aye, but they ask so many questions about what you want to do. I just can't think straight to plan anything.'

'Do you want me to come with you now?'

'If you would as I'd like it all sorted out proper like. She deserves that, a good send off.'

Here Edith could hear a break in her father's voice. She had never understood that he cared so much for her mother. Somehow she thought he had just taken her for granted, at her being there to serve his every whim. But for the first time ever Edith saw a look of love on his face.

Never in her wildest dreams had Edith realised it could hurt so much loosing a parent. She had thought when she was much younger that she had suffered terrible pain loosing Edward and Elsie, but it had been nothing like this. The pain had been acute at the loss of her eldest son, John, but that was a different pain again. She suddenly realised her own vulnerability on how much pain her passing would no doubt cause her own children. She had never thought of it in those terms before.

All the family were heartbroken as she broke the sad news to each of them in turn. They had all thought a lot of their Grandma Thompson as she had been a very special person.

'Oh, Ma,' wailed Martha, 'I'll miss her so much.'

'I know lass; it's the same for me.'

'I'm sorry, Ma, it must be terrible for you. After all, you've lost your mother.'

'Yes, lass, I have and I realise now you never really appreciate what you've got until it's gone.'

Martha was not sure if this comment was partly aimed at her, 'But I do appreciate you, Ma.'

'I know, lass, I meant myself, not you.'

Edith could not believe that her father seemed to shrink before her very eyes. She had always thought of him as a strong, commanding figure but it seemed as if he was suddenly leaning on her to take charge.

Edith could see he had tears in his eyes as

he said to her on the morning of the funeral, 'Aye, lass, I do miss her so already.'

'I know Pa, so do I.'

'Yes, lass, but at least you've all your family around you. I feel so lost now.'

'But you've all of us. We're family.'

'I know that, lass, but it's not the same. It's those moments when you talk together like only man and wife do.'

'I see what you mean. There's nowt I can do about that I'm afraid, only say we're all here for you at any time.'

'Thanks. Anyway I'd best get ready now, times marching on.'

Sarah was laid to rest in the same grave as Elsie, her youngest daughter and Edith's sister. There was no ease from the pain. This woman, her mother, even though she had only been a small woman had been big in love and kindness. Edith had never appreciated how many people her mother had known but the chapel was full, a sea of faces wishing to pay their final respects to their friend. It was not until she was no longer there that Edith realised how much store she had set by her love and influence. Now who would she turn to, that could give her that so often much needed guidance to put right all her wrongs? Her mother had always listened to her and helped her to do that.

Edith did not know what to do about her father; he seemed so alone and lost without his partner in life. But contrary to her belief that he would come to live with them when she offered, he was adamant he would stay in his own home. After all, he said that was where all his memories were. No amount of persuasion from any of them could change his mind. In the end Edith relented, really as she had no choice and so organised a local woman to go in daily to make sure he had a cooked meal and do his general housework. That seemed to resolve that immediate problem; she only wished they all could be sorted out as easily as that.

She did not know how to stop her own heartache. Many a time, whilst she had a quiet moment on her own, she would shed a tear for the memory of her mother. She even took to talking aloud to her as if she could still hear and even though there was no reply it seemed to offer her a peace of mind. Because somehow, as was her usual way, she had to carry on because her family depended on her, just like she had depended on her own mother without consciously realising it.

23

Irrational fears started to gnaw at Edith that she would loose more of her sons to the war. She could not voice these thoughts and she felt as if she was slowly going mad with the agony of worry. By some miracle, both George and Fred had found themselves in work at a munitions factory so she knew she would keep them at home out of harms way, or so she hoped. But by the beginning of 1945 she was concerned that if the war went on much longer, Harry would indeed be old enough to enlist as he had voiced his hopes so long ago. Knowing his love for danger she knew instinctively that was just what he would do - join up and look for as many hazards as he could find with no thought whatsoever about the consequences.

She had never known such a sense of relief go through her when they all heard the news on May 7th that Germany had surrendered unconditionally. She knew she had been right in having her concerns when Harry let out a great moan at hearing this. 'Oh! Why'd they to go and do that now when I'm nearly old enough to join up and fight? Meanies, I wanted to go and help us win, couldn't wait to get in a few shots at those Jerry's.'

Edith could not believe her ears, because for the first time in all the years of knowing him, Alfred's temper flared up instantly, 'Shut up, Harry. I'll hear none of that talk in this house. Don't you think we've suffered enough from the war by losing John? Our family has given more than enough towards winning.'

Harry was quickly deflated at his father's tone of voice. 'Sorry, Pa, but I did so want to be a soldier.' Then brightening as if another thought had struck him he added, 'Never mind, maybe next time.'

Edith could see Alfred was still angry as he shouted back. 'Don't you understand a thing I've said to you about all the horrors and wasted lives of war? Anyway, let all of us hope and pray there won't be a next time. I never want to live through another war and I'm sure that goes for your Ma as well. Twice is more than enough for anybody to have to cope with.'

Before any more could be said, as usual Harry's mind moved on and flitted to the next thing. 'Do you think there'll be celebrations then?'

Edith looked hard at this lad of theirs, who had already caused her more heartache than the rest of them put together. Finally she said, 'More than likely, lad, aye more than likely.'

She was right. The weather might have been miserable with a light drizzle but the grey skies could not prevent the elated crowds from streaming into the streets of London from an early hour.

At three o'clock Churchill broadcast to the nation then went to Downing Street and to the House of Commons in a car that was pushed along Whitehall by the pressure of the cheering crowds. For the first time since the outbreak of the war, the lights were switched on all over Britain. Everything seemed so much brighter and more cheerful in that light. Even the old dirty stone buildings no longer looked dark and grey with their soot covering. Edith could understand the feelings of the children who had grown up never seeing the lights on outside. They must surely feel they were seeing a whole new place. She felt as if a light had been switched on inside her.

She still had sad moments by the deep pain of the death of John and her mother and when she was least expecting it the heartache crept back. It only needed some simple act to cause the upset. Seeing a small, grey haired lady walking in front of her with the swinging gait of her mother, was enough to remind Edith of what she had lost in her mother's death. Many a time she had to stop herself calling out, 'Ma.' Then she would remember; no more would she suddenly see her and feel uplifted in her spirits from her mother's unselfish kindness. Panicking in case a passer by noticed she would feel a small tear of sorrow run down her cheek. Often having her hands full with shopping bags she could not discretely wipe it away.

But having the street and store lights on again helped, it dispelled some of the gloominess within her. Now the dark pit felt as if it was slowly moving away, she no longer stood on the edge ready to fall into it. At last she could try to live again, the rest of her family were safe from the dangers of war.

She could see Martha's joy as she realised Sid would soon be home safe and sound. It was hard not to notice how close they had grown to each other when he came to visit during his last leave home. When they thought the others were not looking they would touch each other tenderly. Not that Edith minded as he was a nice enough lad. She had just been afraid of him being taken from Martha as all those long years ago Edward had from her. But not this time, it was all over now. Suddenly the full impact hit her and she said aloud to nobody in particular, 'It's over!'

'Are you all right, Ma?' Martha asked looking at her with a concerned expression.

'Aye, lass, I've not felt like this for years. It's suddenly hit me, the wars over and all my worrying for everyone has gone with it.'

'I know, Ma. I can't wait for Sid to be home for good.'

'I understand that, lass. Anybody can see the way the winds blowing there.'

'I hope so, Ma. I really like him a lot. He's so much fun to be with but he's kind and generous.'

'Well, what more could you ask for?'

'You couldn't. I suppose inside I've tried to suppress some of my feelings just in case he didn't make it. But now I can let them all go.' Suddenly she burst into tears of happiness with the relief she felt.

'Come on now, don't take on so. At least you know he'll be safely home soon.'

'I know. I think it's just the reaction of letting go all the worry I've felt for him. I do feel happy, I really do.'

Edith felt herself relax more and more as the war receded and life began to get back to some normality. As Harry was approaching school leaving age she questioned him on what he wanted to do with his life. 'I've already told you, I'm going into the army,' he replied looking very pleased with himself.

'Nay, lad, surely you want to get an apprenticeship like your brothers, that'll lead you into a good job,' she tried to ask persuasively in the hope of setting his mind on another track.

'No, I've told you what I'm going to do. I don't want to do nowt else.'

Edith felt a pain go through her heart at the thought of him in the army. What if there was another war? Despite whatever they hoped, he would be one of the first to have to go.

Alfred could see what was going through Edith's mind and quickly butted in before an argument erupted. 'Leave it, Edith, it'll all sort itself out. He's not leaving school just yet. Time enough yet to have other thoughts.'

In a petulant voice Harry shouted as he ran out of the room in annoyance at his parents not listening to him, 'You'll not get me to change my mind. I'm going in the army and that's that, so there.'

Edith called after him. 'Come back here you cheeky young monkey,' but he was gone and well out of earshot.

In no time after he had been demobbed, Sid asked to speak with Alfred and Edith. It took no guessing, with the radiant look on her daughter's face, to know what it was all about.

As soon as they were seated, Alfred not being one to beat about the bush asked, 'Well, Sid, and what can I do for you?'

Edith had to keep a smile from her face because for the first time since she had known Sid she saw he was at a loss for words. 'Er, um, it's like this.'

Suddenly Edith was back in her parent's lounge with Alfred at a loss for words then stuttering to ask the same question of her father.

'Yes, well spit it out, lad. Whatever you've got to say can't be that bad.'

Edith could see Martha frowning at Sid as she was loosing patience with his slowness in saying what he had to.

'No, no it isn't bad. It's like this you see, I'd like to ask for your daughter's hand in marriage,' he at last managed to stammer.

Alfred laughed, 'You're welcome to it, be glad to get her off my hands.' Then, seeing that he had maybe gone a little too far in his fun and upset Martha, added, 'No I don't really mean that, we'll be sorry to see her go.'

Then it was Sid's face that changed at the thought he was not getting the required consent after all. 'No, I mean you can have my daughter's hand in marriage, but we'll be sorry to lose her. I'm sure Edith will agree with me on that. You're getting a grand lass, I'll tell you.'

'Pa!' Martha said feeling herself blushing bright red.

'What's wrong, Martha? Am I embarrassing you? But it's the truth. Anyway, I don't think a celebration drink would go amiss, do you Edith?'

'No, I'll just get the glasses.' In the latter years they had taken to keeping some sherry in the house for moments of need. Up until now it had been only needed for sad occurrences. Even Alfred had a drop which was a very rare event for him.

Edith's mind was starting to worry how on earth they would afford the wedding and manage at home without Martha's wage coming in. She made a quick decision that the wedding would have to be kept simple and that was a fact. What with the rationing it would take some time to prepare.

'When do you plan to wed?' Edith enquired of the couple, as her thoughts ran on.

'Oh, it won't be for quite a while yet. We want to save up a deposit for a house of our own. We're young enough, so there's plenty of time. In any case I've to get used to being a civilian again.' Edith could see by the look on her daughter's face that she did not want to wait too long. They would sort themselves out, she was sure of that. At least her own panic of organising the event was stilled.

Alfred seemed to be doing well enough in his job, although there was never any money to spare. Edith fretted herself about the cost of a wedding. In the end she suggested, as they had room to spare, she bought a table and became an outworker burler and mender. At first Alfred did not seem too keen but in the end relented when he saw how determined she was. Also he could see, despite the more happy moments, she was still grieving the loss of her mother and John and was really in need of something to occupy her more as the family needed her less now.

The thought of a wedding set Edith fretting and grieving because her mother would not be at the event. She had never given a thought to it before; she had always imagined she would be there on her granddaughter's wedding day.

As life moved on and Edith almost forgot her daughter was to be married, out of the blue much sooner than expected Martha and Sid were telling them they had set the date. Apparently Sid's parents had come up trumps by saying they would pay the deposit on a house as a wedding present. It had been a huge relief to the happy couple as they had come to the conclusion they would be in their dotage before they could tie the knot. Edith had made no concession to the amount of money Martha had to tip up each week out of her wages. Martha was lucky if she could manage to save a few coppers each week.

When Martha was on her own with her mother, she expressed her happiness and surprise about this. 'Isn't it grand of them, Ma, to do this for us? Sid was so determined we were going to have our own house to start our married life in; I'd begun to believe the wedding would never happen. We've been saving this past year and are still a long way off a deposit, never mind the furniture. Anyway, we're going to start looking at houses this weekend, ones that we can now afford with their help. His parents are coming with us. I suppose it's only right seeing they're paying the deposit. Mind, I hope they don't interfere too much but let us choose what we like. After all, it's us that have to live in whatever we get.'

'I'm sure they will,' Edith had to agree reluctantly because they had already had a meeting with his parents after the engagement and they had seemed pleasant enough. 'I suppose we'd best start talking about wedding arrangements now. Sid had better come to tea on Sunday then we can get ourselves organised.' Edith had a laugh here thinking about Martha's previous comments about her future in-law's possible interference. She did not want to be accused of the same thing. 'I'll let you have your say about the wedding arrangements. Well at least within reason. I'm not saying we can afford the earth, we can't but somehow or other we'll have a nice do.'

'Thanks, Ma.'

Edith only wished she could feel as happy within herself about spending all this money. There again she did not want any shame brought on her family by people thinking she was mean and this was her eldest daughter's wedding. Never having much all her marriage, what little she had now, she felt she wanted to cling on to it in case of another rainy day. Yes it always seemed to have to be spent on one member or another of her family, never herself, which made her feel resentful.

When Edith next saw her father, she was quick to tell him the news. 'You'll soon be going to a wedding.'

'Oh aye, let me have one guess. I bet it's Martha's.'

'That's right, mind I could do without the expense at this time. We just feel to be getting on our feet at last,' she moaned.

'Never mind that, I'll help you out.'

Now Edith wished she had never opened her mouth, 'Oh! I didn't mean that, we'll manage. I've worked hard this last year and managed to put a little bit by ready.' After all, they had their pride and she considered it their duty to look after their own.

'Nay, lass, I've told you before I've more than enough money for my simple needs.' Here he gave a small laugh, 'She's my grand daughter after all.'

'Thanks, Pa, that's ever so kind of you,' she conceded, with a feeling of gladness that it had worked out this way. 'I just don't know what we'd have done without you all these years,' she added as an after thought.

'Well, I'm glad I can still be of use to someone,' he replied in his usual sarcastic manner.

'Now don't be like that, Pa. You've been a lot of use to a lot of people in your life.'

'Maybe so, but I feel a spare part at times now, since your Ma passed on and that's a fact,' he said with sadness in his voice.

'I know, I do try my best to help but nobody can replace Ma. She was special.'

Seeing her father was getting upset she quickly changed the subject.

'They're both coming to tea on Sunday,

we're hoping to get organised then. Do you want to come as well and help us discuss the arrangements?'

'Why not, I've nowhere else to go.'

As Edith sat listening to them discussing the wedding proposals, it brought back once again memories of that evening all those years ago when Alfred and she had sat talking about their marriage with her parents. She was glad this was in different circumstances and Martha was not pregnant. She seemed to be brooding on the past more and more.

'We'll never get together enough coupons to buy you a new wedding dress,' Edith put in.

'I realise that, Ma. I'll have to look around for a good second hand one.'

Here Edith's father joined in, 'But we'll have a good reception. I'll pay for that.'

'No, Pa, you can't possibly do that.'

Edith saw some of her old father as he angrily said, 'Don't tell me what I can and can't do Edith. I said I'd pay for it and that's the end of the matter. Martha, you and Sid have a look around and let me know where you want it, then we'll get it all booked.'

'Thanks, Grandpa, I never expected this.' Then with a beaming smile on her face she turned to Sid, 'That's great isn't it?'

'It is, thanks ever so much. As I'll soon be a

member of the family is it all right if I call you Grandpa?'

'Why not, what's one more calling me that?' This comment brought sharply to Edith how much her father had moved in his letting go of his stiff and starchy manner.

'Well, I'm glad we've managed to get it all sorted and are in agreement. Now the hard work begins of getting it all booked and organised, I suppose,' sighed Martha.

24

Martha had been right in her assumption that there was plenty of hard work in organising the wedding in readiness for their big day. They all seemed to be here and there checking out one thing or another. There were all the wedding arrangements, and then the house they had finally settled on to be sorted out and furnished. Even the lads were willing to help them with that. They all pooled their resources and coupons and managed to get together what they could to furnish it.

It was a bonny house for them to start their married life. It even had an inside WC and bathroom much to Martha's delight. She had become so used to the inside toilet at home but the years of suffering having to go outside in her young days were still strong enough not to want to endure it again. Aye, she had to admit she was doing well for herself and that was a fact.

Edith was glad when the day dawned clear and bright for her daughter's wedding. As soon as she had woken them all, although Martha needed no waking as she had been up with the larks, it was all go for everyone. There were great arguments who should use the bathroom first. Mind, Edith had never known the lads to be so concerned about their washing habits before. Still, she had to admit she was pleased they were going to be groomsmen and Ethel was one of the three bridesmaids. Sid's sister was another and a work friend of Martha's the third.

They had been lucky to find some nice material in a turquoise colour and Annie had helped Edith in the making up of it into bridesmaid dresses. Annie and Edith had stayed good friends all these years and even though they lived a distance apart had never lost touch with each other. Edith felt it was a comfortable friendship with Annie. They had no need to say a lot in each other's company to be happy. Martha had always stayed the most regular of Edith's children to visit Harry and Annie, and at times it seemed as if it was Annie's own daughter getting married as she was so taken up with the preparations.

For Martha they had found a lovely dress that a young woman, just the build of Martha, was selling. It had only been worn the once then put away very carefully so nobody would know it was not new for this great day of Martha's.

At last, much to the relief of everyone, after

the hectic preparations, the wedding cars were waiting for them. The lads had already gone on ahead to the church so they were there in good time for when the guests started arriving and could give seating directions. Now it was time for Ethel and her mother to go to the church. It all felt very strange to Edith, just the two of them going together. Edith was so used to her large family around her most of the time. Ethel was still rather a wild one and Edith found it difficult to communicate with her. A silence prevailed in the car as each was locked in their own thoughts.

As soon as they arrived at St. Matthew's Church in Bankfoot, Ethel was whisked away from her to join the other bridesmaids having their photographs taken. Sadness came over Edith; she suddenly felt very lonely and missed her mother desperately. She still suffered so many mixed and confused emotions that at times it was difficult for her to know what she did feel about events.

She felt a gentle touch on her arm and turned in amazement to see her youngest son, Harry, at her side. At the last moment he had managed to get leave from the army which he had eventually joined despite all the family protests to the contrary. 'Come on, Ma,' he said cheerfully, 'let me escort you down the aisle to your seat.'

She was so taken aback she let out more sharply than she intended, 'Well wonders will never cease, what's brought all this on?'

'This is what I'm supposed to do isn't it, as a groomsman?' he asked looking innocently at her.

Gently smiling at him now she linked arms with him, 'Aye it is, lead on.' Edith decided maybe going into the army was not such a bad thing for him after all. He seemed far more settled in himself than she had ever seen him.

Edith noticed as soon as she walked in the church that it looked packed, and each face became a blur as she walked down the aisle. She could not have told anyone who was there. Then she saw one face that stood out from the rest and it came into focus. She saw her father watching for her and seeing her gaze on him he gently patted the pew beside him, 'Come on, lass, sit here and we'll look after each other.'

Suddenly thinking she had best make sure Sid was there she had a quick look around. She felt a sense of relief when she saw him sat at the front on the right, though why she had ever doubted that he would be there she did not know. She saw how calm and relaxed he looked as he sat waiting for Martha to come down the aisle to him. Aye, they would make a grand couple.

At last the organist started to play the Wedding March. Edith turned to glance back and felt tears of pride prick her eyes as she looked at her eldest daughter and husband. She could see the look of sheer happiness and pride on Alfred's face as he lead Martha down the aisle.

As Ethel walked past her, going down the aisle behind Martha, Edith had the impression that Annie had been a bit skimpy of the material in her bridesmaids dress for her. It was straining over her hips and stomach. She was sure they had bought plenty of material for all the dresses. 'Oh well!' she sighed quietly, 'too late to do anything about it now.' But she did wish she had noticed it before, and then they would have had time to alter the dress to have made it a better fit. At least the bouquet of flowers she held in front of her hid the tightness quite well.

Tears sprang to Edith's eyes as she heard the couple repeat their wedding vows. She felt her father gently get hold of her hand and give it an affectionate squeeze. This brought to mind how much he had mellowed over the years. Why she had viewed him as some sort of ogre all those years back she really did not know now. He had helped them so much with his kindness, throughout her marriage. At that moment in time she felt closer to him than she ever had before and started to understand he did love her. He just was not one for wearing his emotions on his sleeve.

Quietly she heard him ask, as she watched the happy newly weds walk up the aisle after the signing of the register, 'Are you all right, lass?'

'Aye, fine. They make a grand couple.'

'That they do. I'm glad she's met a good young man like that. Let's hope Ethel does as well for herself.'

'Aye, we'll see. I'm not holding my breath on that score. There as different as chalk and cheese her and Martha.'

'I know, lass, but she's still yours whatever happens.'

'M'm. Come on it's time to make a move,' she said abruptly as she did not want to have to think about Ethel on this happy day.

Alfred was walking beside Sid's mother up the aisle and Sid's father came to Edith's side for her to join him.

'Grand wedding,' he whispered to her as they moved up the aisle.

'It is that. It all seems to be going to plan so far. I'm right glad the weather's turned out so good. You can just never tell in May what it'll be like. After all, they do say never cast a cloud until May is out.'

In what seemed no time they were out of the church, 'Come on, I think they're waving for us to go over there and have our photograph taken with the bride and groom,' Sid's father motioned.

Edith said with some relief now that she could get back to her own family group, 'Aye they are.'

From that moment on the day seemed to pass in one hectic rush after another. First they were moved this way and that for their photographs to be taken, then rushed off to the reception party. It seemed one constant round of small talk and banter.

When it was finally all over and Alfred and she were alone getting ready for bed, Edith had to admit to him, 'I'm exhausted. I wouldn't want to go through that too often. At least we've only one more daughter and she'll not wed for quite a while yet. After all she isn't even going steady.'

Once everything settled back to normality Edith could not believe how much she missed Martha being around the house. Her mind seemed to want to believe she was just away on a short holiday and she would return soon. Every time she remembered this was not the case she became quite tearful. She started to ask herself, 'Whatever's the matter with me, I'm not the kind of person to be brought to tears so easily?' But it was not long before her mind was distracted from all this by another shock in their lives.

Ethel marched in one evening with her latest boyfriend, Sammy. Both Ethel and Alfred found it hard to keep up with her men friends as she changed them so rapidly. Being surprised at her bringing Sammy home, as this was quite a rare event, Edith blurted out without thinking. 'This is a surprise, what brings you both back here?' Normally Ethel seemed to like to keep her boyfriends well away from her parents, as if she did not want them to see who she was associating with.

'We've something to tell you both,' Ethel said abruptly not beating about the bush.

Edith was totally at a loss to imagine what they could have to tell her and Alfred that was so important that they needed to come together. 'Well sit the pair of yourselves down then, if you're staying a while. I'll just put the kettle on and then you can fire away with what you've come to say.'

She saw a glance go from Ethel to Sammy as much as to say, 'I told you so.'

For once Alfred seemed at a total loss for words. At the best of times he found it not very easy to converse with this difficult daughter of theirs, but usually managed to say something. Both Ethel and Sammy sat there silently making no attempt at any conversation.

As Alfred saw Edith start to bring the tea in, he said with relief in his voice, 'Do you want me to carry anything through for you, luv?'

'No, only one more trip to make, then it's all in here.'

Finally when Edith had finished and sat down she turned to the young couple, 'Well then, what do you want to tell us?' All the while she was trying to hope and believe it could not be anything that important.

Ethel was the first to speak, 'We'll have to be wed as I'm pregnant.'

Both Edith and Alfred exploded together, 'You're what?'

'I'm pregnant,' she said once again quite unashamedly.

First to recover Edith asked, 'How far gone are you?'

'About five months.'

'Five months!' shouted Edith, and then realisation dawned on her why her bridesmaid's dress had been so tight. It was not Annie's fault after all for making it too small; it was Ethel who had expanded. What a fool she had been not to recognize the fact. As a mother herself she should have seen the signs and she would have thought Martha might have noticed something amiss, particularly as she had shared a bedroom with her. But both of them had not noticed anything out of the ordinary. Mind, Ethel was a sly one; she had certainly kept this well hidden from them all.

Edith was taken aback when Alfred questioned, 'I didn't know you'd been seeing Sammy that long?'

In a sulky voice Ethel answered, 'Well, I must have mustn't I? How else would I be pregnant with his child?'

Again before Edith could say anything Alfred demanded, 'I take it he is really the father?'

'Of course, what do you take me for?'

'What do I take you for you ask? I'll tell you, a very deceitful young woman keeping us in the dark about this until now. You must have known for a good while. What did you think would happen, that the problem would simply go away?'

'No, of course not but I just wasn't sure.'

At last Edith had her turn to speak, 'Wasn't sure? What on earth do you mean? You're either pregnant or you're not. I can't see the difficulty there and in any case you could have seen a doctor, he'd have confirmed it.'

'Well you know I've always been irregular. I

just thought it was worse than usual and I'd put on a bit of weight.'

'A likely story and what did you think the morning sickness was caused by?'

'I haven't been sick.'

Edith gave a sniff as if she did not believe this for a tale but then remembering her own circumstances of her own marriage she tried not to sound too harsh, 'Where do you think you'll live then?'

She knew Ethel had no money saved up. When she had left school she had found a job in a ladies clothing shop, saying the mills were not for her. But she did not earn good money, not as much as she could have earned if she was in the mill and any money she had ran through her fingers just like water. Now Ethel lost some of her bashfulness, 'We thought you might let us live here, as there's plenty of room now Martha's married.' Then becoming a bit braver again she added, 'After all, you lived with Granddad and Grandma when you were first wed.'

Aye, she was right there Edith thought. They had, but to Edith the circumstances seemed different. She knew they'd had to get wed because she was pregnant with John, but at least they were engaged and planning to get married in any case. Besides which, her parents already had known Alfred by then.

But there had been no talk of marriage before, between Ethel and Sammy. In fact they hardly knew Sammy and what they did was not too good. If she was to be honest Edith was not too keen on his family. He did not come from a particularly good area and if what she had heard about his family was true, they were a bit on the rough side and not against going outside the law if the opportunity arose.

But that did not alter anything, their daughter was pregnant with his child and at least the lad was willing to wed her.

'What do you think, Alfred?'

'Nay it's not up to me. It's you who'll get the extra work if they live here. What she says is true, there's room enough.'

'I don't suppose we can refuse then, you'll have to live somewhere. We'd best discuss everything else seeing as you're both here and time is running out with you being so far gone. I take it Sammy's parents don't know yet?'

'No.'

'Well they'll have to be told as soon as possible because there's no delaying the wedding as time is getting short now if we're to make sure you don't have an illegitimate baby.' It had never entered Edith's head not to agree to them being married. That was the only thing to do.

'We don't want a big do like Martha's. We just thought at the registry office would be fine.'

At these words Edith could not stop a sarcastic comment coming out, 'I'm glad that is all you want, because the way things are that's all you will get. Well, if it's the registrar's office you should be able to get that booked quickly, hopefully in a few weeks time. I think you'll have to make do with a small reception here. What do you think Alfred?'

He laughed, 'I leave all that kind of thing to you, dear.'

'It's money. We've none to spare for an outside do.'

Deep down Ethel was feeling hurt. She always seemed to have everything second best in comparison to Martha. Although she would not have admitted it for the world she would have loved a big wedding like Martha's. Still, she realised beggars cannot be choosers and at least her parents were agreeing to it all. It had been easier than she thought it would be as there had been much less argument. Not that she felt excited by getting wed, it was simply a case that she had to have a father for her baby. She felt no love for Sammy, maybe affection, but that was all.

She was only too aware of the scorn poured on unwed mothers and she wanted none of that on her. It was up to her to work on Sammy and mould him into what she would like him to be. She was already determined she was going to get something out of this marriage and life. He owed her that much.

So instead of everything settling back to quiet and normality after Martha's wedding as Edith had expected, it was all rush once again organising another wedding as best she could. Of course, everyone in Wibsey would know it was a shot gun job and tongues would be wagging.

Her father could not believe his ears when Edith told him what was happening. This time there was no offer of money forthcoming to help with the wedding. There was only disgust from him. Not only that, he quite clearly stated his opinion that he felt she was far too young to be wed, but Edith knew there was no choice and they were stuck with the situation, like it or not. At the end of the day she was their daughter and they had to try to do right by her.

25

Edith did what she had to do to get the wedding organised with no satisfaction or enjoyment. She did it purely out of a sense of duty. When the actual day arrived there was no great feeling of excitement in the air as there had been at Martha's. Annie had kindly used her sewing skills once again and managed to make a nice suit for Ethel with a smock effect blouse and loose jacket. She was too far gone to disguise the fact she was pregnant but at least she still did look bonny as a bride.

Never having been to a register office wedding before, Edith did not know what to expect but she could not believe how quickly it was over. It seemed a mass production process, one couple came out and another straight in and so on. No photographer had been hired this time, but Alfred had brought his camera along so he took a few pictures of the group stood in front of the registry office, but it was not a particularly attractive setting.

Neither of them felt really at ease with Sammy and his parents as they had not had time to get to know them well enough before the wedding. They had actually only seen Sammy's parents a couple of times and felt they had nothing in common with them whatsoever. Edith could see it was going to be difficult getting a conversation going when they went back to the reception, as they had not seemed to want anything to do with the preparations. They indicated by their comments that they were relieved to be getting Sammy off their hands.

It had been decided by Edith and Alfred only close family was to go back to their house for the do. This time Harry had not been able to get leave and Edith was surprised how much she missed his company. At one point they thought they were going to have to book the wedding for a week day as the registry office was fully booked at weekends, but as luck would have it they suddenly had a cancellation on a Saturday morning so they managed to get their booking for then. It was a good job it had worked out like it did for them. Otherwise, if it had been a weekday, there would have been even less guests than there were. Most of who they would have wanted to invite would not have been able to get the time off work during the week, including Alfred.

Martha had not much patience about the predicament her sister found herself in and as they had shared a bedroom at home was more than surprised she had not noticed anything amiss. She felt quite cross with herself about this. Still, Martha had to admit Ethel had always been a sly one, so untidy and dirty that it was difficult to know whether it was her time of month or not. Soiled pads would emerge at any time and Martha never knew whether it was recently used or one of last month's just emerging.

Alfred and Edith had relented and paid for the newly weds a few days away at Bridlington. They knew it was not a very exciting place for a young couple but it was the best they could afford for them under the circumstances.

As Edith had expected, the reception had been a strain on all of them, what with the lack of conversation because it had been hard to break the ice, and the general atmosphere of animosity. Thankfully, at last, the couple were on their way. Edith only felt relief that she would be able to have a few days peace for her and Alfred giving her chance to recharge her batteries. Edith thought sadly that their house looked as if a bomb had hit it. She worried that it would take forever to get it back to normal, if ever.

Sensing how her mother felt Martha said softly at her side, 'I'll come and give you a hand tomorrow. We'll soon get the house back ship shape.'

'Thanks, lass, that's kind of you when you've your own house to see to now.'

'It doesn't matter; I'll soon catch up with that on an evening. You're looking a bit tired yourself. Two weddings so quickly are a bit much for anybody.'

'Well they're over with now and I hope this is the last for a while.'

'I'm sure it will be, I can't see any of the lads marrying quickly.'

'No, I must say I agree with you there. As long as they've got their heads screwed on the right way and don't get a lass into trouble.'

'You never know with anyone do you? But I think Ethel's predicament will have taught them a thing or two.'

'We can only live in hopes. Anyway, I can see Sid waiting for you. I'll see you tomorrow then.'

It was as well that Edith made the most of those few days' peace. It was soon shattered when Ethel and Sammy were back. She had never realised, when her daughter was at home on her own, how loud she was. Or maybe it was the combination of her and Sammy together.

She knew she should not be pleased at them going out spending money most evenings but at least for a short while peace reigned in the house, with them out of the way.

Much to her immense surprise Alfred aired his views, 'They should stay in more on an evening and be saving up for a home of their own instead of gallivanting off to the pictures or dancing nearly every night. It all costs money and besides that it can't be good for the baby. By the way does she help you in the day? I mean when she's on her own with you, does she do any of the housework?'

Not liking to paint too bad a picture of their daughter Edith toned down what she said. She knew it was bad enough for Alfred with what he saw and heard when he was at home. It was getting on his nerves. 'Well a little bit. You know how it is. We all have our own way of doing things and I like to do it my way in my own home.'

'Well, just make sure she pulls her weight,' said Alfred in a voice as if he did not really believe her and with an unusual anger as he showed consideration for his wife.

Edith did not like to admit she wished Ethel was still going out to work each day and away from under her feet. Despite going into a shop to work rather than the mills the shop owner had been less understanding of her situation, than the mill owners would have. In fact, as long as the work was done they did not care if a woman was pregnant. But it did not take the shop owner long once she knew of Ethel's pregnancy to dismiss her. Most days she did not climb out of bed until near lunch time, and then she would slop around in her nightwear until even later still. Funnily enough, Edith had never smoked while Alfred just had his pipe now and again. But Ethel and Sammy puffed away like chimneys. As soon as Ethel managed to get out of bed, that was the first thing she did, light a cigarette. Edith kept asking her, 'Are you sure you're not harming the baby with those things?' She said this in the hope that Ethel would give up smoking. She was fed up herself of living in a fog in the house. The smell seemed to get everywhere; she could even smell it on Alfred. She had noticed some of the white paintwork turning brown. She was sure it was with all this smoking because it had never happened before. She was rather concerned that if it could do that to the paintwork then what was it doing to them all as they inhaled the smoke.

Instead of apologising Ethel would just look at her with contempt. 'Cause I'm not harming the baby. Do you think I'd do anything to harm my child?'

But Edith was not sure about that. She did

not think Ethel really wanted the baby. She was certainly making no attempt at preparing for it. If Edith and Martha had not done some knitting and sewing of baby clothes she did not know what the poor mite would have to wear when it was born. No, Edith had to admit it, even though she was her daughter, Ethel was a slut.

She knew it was having an effect on the rest of the family. It all came to a head when George dropped his bombshell that he had found another job, but it was down in Birmingham so he would obviously be moving away from home.

Luckily, as usual on an evening, Ethel and Sammy were out when George informed them of this. Alfred asked, 'But why move so far away? Couldn't you have found a better job around here if that's what you're after?'

'If truth be known, Pa, I just have to get away from here if Ethel and Sammy are going to stay on. I can't stand living here with them any longer. They're so loud and I'm sorry to say Ethel's dirty. She doesn't care about her own cleanliness or where she leaves her dirty washing. I can see she's no help to Ma and that upsets me. No, it's best if I move away before I say too much and permanent harm is done.'

'But do you want me to suggest to them

that they get their own place?' Edith pleaded, but knowing at the same time his mind was already made up to move. It warmed her heart to know one of her lads cared about her well being.

'No, I'm quite happy to be trying somewhere new and it's not too far away from Harry's army camp, so happen I'll be able to see him a bit more.' Laughing he added, 'It'll do me some good, after all you never know who I'll meet and it's a very good job with prospects.'

It seemed the final straw to Edith that Ethel and Sammy were driving the rest of her family away and it made her feel really despondent. Yet Edith knew with the birth so near she really could not tell them to go. She would just have to accept the situation as it was for the moment, but she was determined after the birth things would have to change.

A greater depression fell on her once another one of her family had left the nest. Despite never showing any outward show of affection for them all she did care very deeply for each one of her brood. She knew Fred was lonely without George and only hoped he did not decide to move away as well. But at least she did know he was a home bird at heart and did not think he would really do that. Also he was the only one of them that could get Sammy into any kind of conversation, so he had some companionship there.

All too soon she saw the early warning signs that the birth was imminent. No sooner had Ethel started her labour pains than she was grumbling and swearing how much it hurt. Edith could see she was going to have fun and games during the day as the house was already echoing with screams of pain from Ethel and Edith knew this was nothing to what it would be before the baby was born. Losing her patience she snapped at Ethel, 'Pull yourself together, girl, this is only the start. You've a long way to go yet and the road will be a lot harder before you get to the end of it. No good making such a do about it, it'll not help anyone, least of all you; only get on all our nerves. We've all been there and had to go through it.' Then she could not stop herself adding, 'If you want the pleasure then you've got to have the pain that follows.'

'Don't say that, Ma, it hurts like mad, it really does hurt,' she pleaded. 'You must have been lucky and it was a lot easier for you, otherwise you'd have never have gone through it six times.'

Once more her daughter was only thinking of herself and this riled Edith no end. 'Don't talk nonsense girl, it hurts every woman. Mind over matter, that's what you need.

329

Relax yourself then it'll help, the more tense you are the worse it'll be,' Edith said in a no nonsense tone of voice.

She might as well have talked to the wall for all the good it did. If Ethel was suffering then she certainly made sure her mother suffered with her. Edith was sure the whole of Wibsey must have heard her screams and even worse the abusive language against Sammy and life in general. But finally her efforts produced a lovely bouncing girl, which, as far as Edith could tell had in fact been a relatively easy birth. Certainly there had been no complications.

When she saw the little lass Edith felt the first stirrings of the joy at being a grandma. The realisation suddenly hit her, that Alfred and she were grandparents now. Here was another generation newly born and part of her and Alfred.

She was amazed how indifferent Sammy was at the birth of his baby girl. Alfred had shown great joy at the birth of all their children and he showed no less joy at the arrival of his first grandchild.

Sammy just looked at her and sniffed in contempt, 'She's more like a wizened prune with all those wrinkles than a baby.'

'Nay, lad, she's right bonny for a new born. I've seen a lot worse straight after birth than she is.' Here Edith paused then asked, 'What are you calling her?'

'Oh I don't care, any old name will do. What do you want to call her Ethel?'

'Oh, I rather like Daisy.'

'Daisy it is then,' stated Sammy then dismissed the subject without any real consideration.

Silently Edith was miffed at this choice of name, yet pleased it was not too horrific. But it was just as she might have expected from the pair of them, no proper thought to why they had chosen the name.

Ethel played her part to the full moaning and groaning she could not get up, she hurt too much. Finally the midwife lost all patience with her and told her in a no nonsense voice to get herself out of bed. 'Who do you think you are, Royalty, young lady? Lying there like that with your poor Ma having to run around after you and Daisy. Come on, there's nothing wrong with you that's stopping you getting up and doing a few light jobs around the house.'

'That tells her,' thought Edith rather pleased, but little did the midwife know that even when she was up and about there was little chance of her doing much helping out, not even little odd jobs. Still, at least if she was downstairs it would stop her calling to her mother to keep running up and down at her demands.

Edith was wrong that it would be easier; life became even harder as she seemed to be constantly stepping over dirty nappies that were left around. The house smelt of baby, not a very pleasant smell, a mixture of dirty nappies and the sick smell of milk. If it was not the smell then the family had to listen to the cries of Daisy until one or the other went to pick her up to soothe her. But it was never Ethel who went to cuddle her own child.

However much Edith or Alfred chastised her to go to see to Daisy she would stay put with a cigarette hung out of her mouth and manage to say, 'Oh leave her be, she'll stop soon enough once she realises she can't have attention all the time. The more you go to her the more she'll cry.'

'Now that isn't quite true, Ethel. Don't you think I've had enough practice with six of my own to bring up to recognize the difference when Daisy needs seeing to and when she's just crying for attention,' scolded Edith, but all to no avail.

Things were becoming so bad Edith felt sure the whole family would break up. Without meaning to Edith, Alfred and Fred kept snapping at each other. Not really sure what to do about it, Edith was more than glad when the problem resolved itself.

After the usual arguments between everybody Ethel suddenly said with more conviction than usual, 'Will you all be quiet and listen to me.'

There was an instant hush as they were all so taken aback. 'Go on then, say what you've got to say,' Edith said after a few moments of silence and nothing had happened.

'We're getting a house.'

Alfred stuttered with shock, 'You're what?'

'We've been given a house. Sammy put our name down, a while ago, for one of those new council houses they've been building around the back. Seeing as how we've a young un and no home of our own, we've been given priority. It'll be ready to move into next week.'

'Oh! That's grand for you,' muttered Edith feeling a rush of relief. Then really brightening at the thought of peace again in her home she added, 'Anything I can do to help you get it ready let me know.' Already Edith had grave doubts how Ethel would ever manage in a home of her own. But who was she to grumble when she saw the look of delight on the rest of the family's faces, that their home would become their own again as they had known it.

Alfred was quick to reiterate what his wife

had said, 'Aye, I'll help you if you need, decorating and such like.'

It was Sammy who actually said, 'Thanks, Pa, that's most kind and we might have to take you up on that offer.' Then he added rather embarrassed, 'I've not had much practice in the decorating department.'

Alfred did not altogether voice his true thoughts as he replied, 'Nay, lad, it's not kindness, you are family and we must all pull together.' He felt it prudent not to add what he really wanted to say, 'We just can't wait for peace to reign here again.' Even then he felt guilty at himself for maybe he had still appeared overly keen for them to move out, but the pair had not noticed as they had been so taken up with themselves and their plans.

26

On the day of them departing Edith sighed happily to herself, Sammy, Ethel and Daisy had gone and they could now get back to normal. She was pleased at the thought, despite the hard work she knew was to come for her as she needed to clean the house from top to bottom to make it feel back like her own, instead of total chaos.

It suddenly struck Edith that with only the three of them in the house they would rattle around with so much space. But the peace, Edith could not start to imagine it. At last, maybe this was the life she had been waiting for so long. Surely nothing else could happen to them? Her father was keeping well and still came to see them despite his age. No, he had probably still a good few years left in him yet, much to Edith's relief. She was much closer to him now than she had ever been in her childhood.

As usual life was not just as she expected it to be. When Edith was at her happiest, thinking she was getting everything back together, but then fate was persistent in dealing blow after blow to Edith.

Busy upstairs trying to get the bedroom that Ethel and Sammy had used looking like it belonged to her house, she heard an agitated voice, 'Edith where are you?' Despite the agitation she recognized her father's voice.

'Up here Pa, cleaning. Hang on a second and I'll be down with you.'

'Hurry up then, I must talk to you this minute.'

This really set Edith worrying. Had something happened to Alfred and they had let her father know so he could tell her. Willie could easily have done that seeing as how he knew her father. It amazed Edith, in what was probably only seconds, how many thoughts went through her mind.

'I'm coming, Pa,' she called out as she ran down the stairs. 'Now what is it? Let's go in the kitchen and I'll make a brew whilst you tell me.'

Before they had even gone through the kitchen door his impatience got the better of him as he quickly said, 'He's gone and done it again.'

'Pa, slow down. What do you mean? Who's done what again?'

'Alfred!'

Edith felt her stomach begin to churn as that old familiar feel of fear took hold.

'Alfred! What do you mean he's done it again?' she asked, yet dreading the response.

'Girl, do you have a problem understanding what I say?' her father asked impatiently.

'No of course I don't. But how can I understand if you haven't explained to me what you mean.'

'Money's gone missing again. Now do you understand?'

Inside she was crying, 'No, no,' but she did her best to keep calm in front of her father. 'Money's gone missing? From where and what's Alfred to do with it?'

'Gone missing from the firm he works for, of course.'

'Look, don't you think it'd make more sense if you started the tale at the beginning? Let me make us this cup of tea then you can explain it all clearly.'

'If you really must make a drink, but don't take long about it, I'm impatient to get this off my chest. It's making me ill not sharing it.'

Edith was glad he had agreed to the tea because she felt in need of a few minutes to get over the shock of what he had said and have a chance to pull herself together. 'But not again,' she cried silently, she could not take it happening again. All these years now things had seemed to have settled down. She knew she was making a mess of getting them the tea as she split milk and sugar everywhere but she could not stop herself shaking with the shock of what her father had just said.

Trying to sound not too perturbed by what was happening, as she walked into the room she said, 'Right here we are. A nice brew, I wasn't long was I?'

'I don't know. Stop nattering on girl. But I must tell you what's happened or I'll bust.'

'All right, I'm ready, fire away then, tell me as I'm all ears.' Edith only wished she felt as calm as she was trying to sound.

'I'd not been up two minutes this morning when Willie came knocking at my door. As soon as I saw him I knew he was agitated. He couldn't stop himself. Before I could ask him he started to tell me, he was that upset. Apparently there's been money going missing for quite a while and he's had his suspicions, but he didn't want to be unjust to Alfred. He knew of his past money troubles and how easy it would be to lay the blame at his door again. So he watched and waited and finally his suspicions were proved correct. Only because he's my son in law is he keeping him on and not reporting him to the police. But in no uncertain terms he's told Alfred what he thinks and he's got to pay the money back. They've agreed upon a small amount each week from his wages.' Then seeing the tears running down Edith's cheeks he said, 'I'm sorry, lass, truly I am. But I'd to tell you because I'm sure Alfred wouldn't and I felt you were entitled, as his wife, to know what's been going on.'

'I realise that, it's just I thought for once all was going well for us, at last.'

'Well don't say anything to him, lass, if you don't want to. At least it's all out in the open. I just had to tell you.'

She was not a believer in secrets being kept between man and wife. Then her thoughts quickly turned to Edward but there again that was not really a secret to harm Alfred as it was all long before his time. 'No, I'll have to mention it as I don't like things not out in the open,' she said after pondering on it.

Then she carried on talking before her father could answer and gave a rueful laugh, 'I don't know why I'm worrying about keeping secrets. Alfred seems to have no conscience on that score.'

'Don't get me wrong, lass, I like Alfred a lot. He's kind and thoughtful, and in many respects you've got a very good husband and father. But taking care of money seems to be one of his failings.'

'I know, maybe he's just too kind and generous to other people. I don't know what it's all about and I'm not sure I'll ever get it out of him now, if I haven't managed to over all these years. I know one thing for certain it makes me both angry and upset that there's nowt I can do about it which doesn't help take the pain away. Anyway that's enough of going on about it. How are you keeping, Pa?'

'Oh fine, you know me, but I'm a lot happier now I've got that off my chest. Martha and Sid came to see me last week. They invited me to tea on Sunday. I must say they seem to be settling down well together, they make a good pair.'

'Aye they do that,' she replied with pride in her voice. 'I'm glad all seems to be working out there. I had a letter from George last week and he seems happy enough working away from home and he's seeing a fair bit of Harry.'

'What about Ethel and Sammy and the little lass of theirs?'

'Don't mention them. I thought we were talking about cheerful things now. Have you seen that house of theirs, a tip, an absolute tip.'

'Nay, I've not been invited and I don't want to intrude.'

'Well I wouldn't bother about it if I was you. I don't like to admit it because she's my daughter, after all, but who she takes after goodness knows. As I said the house is a tip and doesn't look as if it's ever been cleaned from the day they moved into it and it reeks of stale cigarette smoke. They've never even got around to decorating most of it. Things are still packed in boxes - how they find anything I don't know. I just don't know what to do with her, I really don't. Ma brought me up to be clean and tidy and I hope I have been. I've tried to instil that into all of mine but something went wrong with Ethel.'

'Of course you are clean like your Ma brought you up to be. You've always kept a house to be proud of.'

'I've brought both my daughters up to be the same. Martha's like me in that respect, but goodness knows where I went wrong with Ethel.'

'Don't blame yourself; it's just one of those things that sometimes happen in families.' Then laughing he added, 'Happen she's a throw back.'

Edith joined in the laughter, 'At times I wish somebody would throw her back somewhere.'

'Aye, happen so. Any roads I think it's time I let you get on with your jobs. I'll make tracks home now.'

'Thanks, Pa, for troubling to tell me; because I'm sure as you say if you hadn't Alfred certainly wouldn't have said owt.'

'Aye, but don't be too hard on him,' he said as if defending Alfred much to Edith's amazement.

'I won't.' Although she said these words to her father she knew she was like a simmering volcano waiting to explode with anger at Alfred's actions once more.

Saying that, she tried all the rest of the day to calm herself down but as soon as Alfred came through the door she pounced on him.

'Well, come on explain yourself, what have you been up to this time?'

Trying to look as if he did not know what she was on about he said in a jovial voice, 'Now what have I been caught out at this time? Am I doing too well with my sales with the young house wives?'

'Be serious a minute,' his joking about the situation was making her temper rise even more. 'You know full well what I mean, money!'

'Money, don't I give you enough?' he asked innocently.

'Of course you do, nobody could fault your generosity. That's just the problem. As I understand it, money's gone missing from your firm.'

'Now I wonder who's been telling tales, maybe I can guess. I bet it was your Pa. Am I right?'

'Does it really matter how I know? Isn't it enough that I do?'

'Now fairs fair, you want me to tell you things.'

'All right then, it was my Pa. But he only told me because he's concerned for us. No other reason.'

'I'll accept that. Anyway it's no great shakes; I was always bad at sums. I must have made a few mistakes giving change,' he replied calmly.

'Oh, come on pull the other one. You've always been all right with sums, and why now suddenly giving wrong change. You'd have been doing it for years if that was the case.'

'Well, that's all I'm saying on the matter, so you'll just have to accept it as that.'

'Back to that are we, evading the truth.'

'No, I'm not, but I'm not prepared to say anymore so you'd best just leave it at that,' he replied with a firmness which was unusual for him.

At that Edith had to be satisfied because she knew from past experience that no matter how hard she tried she would get no more from him. But it left her feeling deeply angry and hurt inside.

At least this time there seemed no repercussions for her; they hardly felt the loss of the small amount he paid back each week.

So again life seemed to be on an even keel for them. Then a couple of things happened that seemed to reinforce this idea to her. First of all Fred announced he was getting engaged to be wed. By, he had kept that quiet, they had only met the lass a couple of times and not really taken it as anything serious. Mind Edith had to admit she had appeared a nice enough woman. After his announcement Edith decided they had better get to know the lass if she was to be part of the family.

'Bring her to tea on Sunday, Fred. I'll ask Pa, Martha and Sid to come as well then she can get to know some of us.'

Fred frowned at his mother as if pondering what to say next, 'Well actually she does know Martha and Sid.'

'Oh and how's that?'

'Well, we've called a time or two to see them.'

'Who's the dark horse then? You've kept that well quiet. Never mind, I'll still invite them in any case, she'll happen feel more comfortable with some faces around her that she knows.'

'That's great, Ma, because she is a bit shy. She's an only child and not used to a large family like ours. I think the thought of meeting most of us at once overpowers her.'

Laughing, his mother asked, 'Now you're

not saying we're that frightening are you?'

'No, of course not, don't tease, Ma, you know what I mean.'

'Of course I do. Don't worry she'll soon feel at home here.'

It seemed they were in no great rush to wed; they wanted to save a nice nest egg before they did, so they could buy a house of their own and furnish it. Edith did not mind that because, although she was happy for him that he had found a nice woman, she also felt rather sorry that he would be the last one to leave home. There would only be her and Alfred left. Funny to think they had never actually lived on their own together before. There had always been somebody else with them. But Edith realised regretfully that was what life was like, everything moves forward. She soon received her next piece of good news. After the Sunday tea, which went very well and Fred had left to take Ruth a walk then home, Martha and Sid hung on.

'Ma, I've got some good news for you,' Martha said.

'You've been promoted at work.'

'No better than that, in fact I won't be working much longer.'

'You're expecting?'

'Yes,' Martha replied proudly.

'Oh! That's grand. Alfred come here. I've

just had some wonderful news. Martha's expecting.'

'Aye that's excellent news.'

Edith knew they were already grandparents but they did not really feel it, as they did not see Daisy very often. No close attachment seemed to have formed there. She hoped it would with this next baby because somehow she thought she could enjoy being a grandma given the chance.

Both Martha and Sid looked as pleased as punch. Edith suddenly realised they had been wed over two years now, so she had really expected this news before.

Aye, at times life seemed good, Edith decided. This was maybe because it was the time she had been waiting so long for. She was a great believer in the saying that things come in threes so maybe she was due another piece of good news soon.

27

Edith stirred restlessly in her sleep. There was something wrong, it was all too quiet. For a long while now Alfred had been a noisy sleeper, either snoring or making deep breathing sounds. It annoyed Edith so much, and disturbed her sleep that she had threatened often enough to move herself into one of the spare bedrooms. But each time this had been an idle threat as she did not really relish the thought of nobody to cuddle up to on the cold nights. She was cold now, there seemed to be a coldness initiating from somewhere in the bed. By, she had never known Alfred sleep so quietly for a long while. She gave him a gentle dig in his ribs to make sure he was all right. Panic started to set in as she received no response, 'Alfred, Alfred, answer me. What's wrong with you?'

Still nothing, she moved over his face to see if she could feel him breathing but there was no gentle waft of air on her face. Finally she plucked up courage to touch his face. It was icy cold. 'Oh no, no,' she said quietly, 'Not this. No please God, not this.'

Jumping out of bed she started to run out

of the bedroom shouting as she went, 'Fred, come here quick. I think your Pa's been taken bad.'

She heard a moan from Fred's room as she came near to it, 'Fred, do you hear me,' she shouted with a touch of hysteria in her voice.

'What is it, Ma?' a sleepy voice called.

'Your Pa, something's wrong with him,' shrieked Edith.

Now she could tell the last remark had brought him fully awake as she heard fumbling noises from his room and he quickly shouted back, 'I'll be with you in half a mo.'

Edith stood on the landing shaking in fright waiting for him to come out of his room; nothing would induce her to go back into the bedroom on her own. It seemed forever before his door swung open.

'What is it?'

'I don't know but he seems too still and quiet to me. He doesn't appear to be breathing.'

'Oh my God,' shouted Fred as he rushed forward into his parent's bedroom shouting, 'Pa, wake up, talk to me.'

But Fred's voice still brought no response from Alfred. Gently he touched his father as his mother had done and felt the same coldness and noticed the lack of movement. Fred stood upright with a look of despair on his face, 'I think he's dead, Ma.'

'No he can't be, he'd so much to look forward to. He was so excited at Martha's news that he was going to be a grandpa again and at yours that you're to be wed. No he can't be, maybe he's had some sort of attack and he's in a coma.'

'I'd best get dressed and go to the phone box to call the doctor,' Fred suggested for a lack of anything else to say.

'Aye, do that, I'm sure he'll know what to do. Hurry now we can't waste precious time.'

'Honestly, Ma, I don't think all the hurrying in the world will help him now. But I'll be quick just in case there is something the doctor can do, just as you say.' He only said this to try to calm his mother but deep down he knew his father was past anyone's help.

Edith had never thought of herself as deeply in love with Alfred but now at the thought of him gone from her forever she realised how that love had quietly crept up on her over the years. She could not bear the thought of not having him with her, despite his slight lapses with money. Now why was she thinking that way? The doctor would sort him out and all would be well again.

It was no time before Fred was back although it had seemed forever to Edith, 'The doctor's on his way Ma, he says he won't be long.'

'Oh that's good. He still hasn't moved yet.' Edith had found the courage to stay with Alfred wanting to be the first face he would see when he came around.

'Ma, I don't think he's going to move again, you've got to accept it. He's dead.'

'No, don't say that, you just wait 'til the doctor gets here and then you'll see how wrong you are.'

'All right, come on let me make you a cup of tea whilst we wait for the doctor.'

Suddenly she wanted to leave the bedroom as the coldness of the room was frightening her again. 'Aye that's a good idea. It makes a change you making me a cup. Happen when your Pa comes around he'll want one too.'

Looking at his mother sadly Fred tried to pacify her, 'Yes, Ma, don't fret I can soon make him one if needs be.'

He was relieved when he heard the knock on the door, but before he had chance to get there his mother shot up and opened the door.

'Ah doctor, I'm glad you've come. Alfred's had a funny turn.'

Looking puzzled the doctor asked, 'I thought Fred said it was more than that?'

'Nay, I'm sure you'll soon put him right.

Come on this way doctor.'

Fred followed quietly behind and it was not long before the doctor stood up from looking at Alfred and turned around to gently take Edith's hand, 'I'm sorry Mrs. Taylor, there's nothing I can do for him. I think he's had a massive heart attack. At least he died in his sleep, he'll not have suffered.'

'No, no, tell him Fred. There's some mistake he can't be dead,' Edith screamed.

'There isn't, Ma. That's what I've been telling you.' Fred was stunned by his mother's reaction to his father's death. She had always seemed to cope somehow and he had always had the feeling their love was rather one sided with his father being the one giving out the most affection.

Now the doctor turned to Fred, 'Look, lad, I'll give you something to quieten her for the rest of the night.'

'Thanks doctor,' he replied with relief because he did not know how to cope in a situation like this.

'Can you get hold of Martha?' asked the doctor.

'I will in the morning. There's no point disturbing them now as there's not much of the night left, but they'll all have to be told. But if you can give her something to help her now I'll put her to bed and then get a neighbour to sit with her when morning comes whilst I go to tell Martha and sort things out.'

'Aye, that'd be best. I'm sorry, lad, this has happened to your Pa. He was such a nice man, but I did warn him.'

'Warn him, about what?' asked Fred puzzled about this remark.

'He came to see me a while back because he wasn't feeling too grand. I did various tests and told him what the problem was. I warned him to slow down and take life easily. Didn't he say anything to you or your Ma?' the doctor asked looking dismayed.

'No, not a thing, and I'm sure he never told Ma. Just like him trying not to cause her any more worry,' Fred replied sadly.

'Hm, well it's too late now. If only he'd taken notice of what I said. Look will you be all right on your own if I leave you? Your Ma has settled now, she should be asleep for quite a while yet. But if you need me to come back to her don't hesitate to call me again.'

'I won't.'

'You'll need this for the undertaker,' said the doctor as he handed Fred the form with his father's cause of death on it, 'and you will have to take it to the registry office to get the death certificate. Once again all I can say is I'm so sorry, lad.'

'Thanks doctor, bye.'

Fred did not get any more sleep that night, he was that upset himself. He thought a lot of both his parents and loved each of them in his own way.

★ ★ ★

Fred did not like to have to do it, but he knew it had to be done. He would have to let Martha know and of course his Grandpa and Grandma Taylor, who would be heartbroken at loosing a son. Grandpa Thompson would have to be told, he would surely want to come to console his daughter.

As soon as Martha saw Fred at the door she sensed there was something amiss. He never normally called this early on in the morning. 'Come in quick, Fred. What is it? Has something happened to Grandpa?'

'No, not Grandpa,' he said with slight trepidation not wanting to do anything that could upset her enough to harm the unborn baby.

Letting out a sigh of relief her face relaxed, 'Oh, thank goodness for that.'

It hurt Fred to think how upset she would be in a minute when he had told her the sad news, 'Let me finish Martha. It's Pa.'

He saw her face blanch with the shock of

these words and he put his hand out to steady her as she reeled with the news. For a moment he thought she was going to collapse.

'I'm all right,' she said steadying herself, 'Go on, tell me everything.'

'Ma woke up in the night and thought it was very quiet, you know how Pa lays snoring at the side of her. So she tried to wake Pa but there was no response from him. She woke me to go and phone for the doctor, but one look at him before I went to do that told me all. He was dead. Ma just wouldn't believe it, not even from the doctor. I've had a terrible time from her. I just didn't know she cared that much about him.'

'What about her now?' Martha asked hastily as she went out of the room as if to get her coat.

'Hey steady on, remember your condition. Mrs. Wilson's sitting with her, but thankfully the doctor has sedated her so she was still asleep when I left to come here.'

'Oh Fred, I can't believe it,' moaned Martha in despair. 'Pa can't really be dead; he was so looking forward to being a grandpa again.'

'I know, sis, but according to the doctor he'd been warned that he'd a dickey heart, but just like him he said nowt to any of us. I can't take it in myself even though I've seen him. I'm sorry I'd to come to tell you this sad news Martha, I really am.'

'I know, Fred, but it's not your fault, it's nobody's fault.'

'Will you be all right on your own if I leave you now?' he asked knowing Sid had already left for work. 'I'd best get on my way as I've to tell our grandparents and so many other things to organise.'

'Yes, don't worry about me. I'll sort out having the day off work then I'll get across to Ma as soon as I can to see to her. You go and tell whoever you have to. Are you going to see the undertaker?'

'I'll have to although I suppose it should really be Ma or George, as he's the eldest. But I don't know when he'll be able to get here, besides he doesn't even know yet. I've still to get in touch with him and let him know. It'll be a shock to him and Harry. I don't suppose Ethel will care one way or another, there only seems to be herself that she cares about. She'll have to wait until last to be told, there's no hurry there it seems to me.'

'Don't say that, I'm sure she will be upset really. Aye, you've a lot to do, you'd best get on your way and I'll get round to see Ma as soon as I can. Don't fret about me; I'm tough you know, I'll be all right. I'll take good care of Ma as well.'

'Thanks, see you later and you remember to take care.' Fred felt much relieved that he had Martha there to give him moral support at a time like this.

'I'll take care don't fret, this baby's very important to me. But you also look after yourself, you've had a nasty shock as well seeing him like that,' Martha replied kindly to her brother.

Edith woke up in a sweat after the nightmare she'd had that Alfred was dead. As she opened her eyes her heart started to beat faster as she did not recognise where she was. This was not her bedroom. Then it all came flooding back, it was reality not a dream. Alfred was really dead and she was in the spare room away from their bed where he still lay.

She cried silently to herself, 'No, not this and just when things were going our way at last.'

Suddenly she saw a shape move and she jumped with shock and fright.

'Ssh, dear, you're all right I'm here.'

In the darkened room she could not see who was there and she did not recognise the voice. 'Who is it?' she asked sharply in panic.

'It's me dear Lucy Wilson from next door.

You're all right I'll stay with you as long as you need me.'

'Where's Fred?' she asked now getting very agitated.

'He's had to go and tell the others the sad news. Then there are all the arrangements for him to sort out.'

Edith made as if to get out of bed but fell back with weakness. 'I should be doing all that.'

'Now don't you go and fret yourself, he's a capable young man. He'll soon have it all done. Now how would you like a nice cup of tea?'

'Oh yes that'd be nice,' Edith replied automatically with no real interest in the tea.

As soon as Lucy Wilson had gone out of the room it all came back to Edith with such a force. She just could not believe it, three loved ones being taken from her. First there was her son, John, then her ma, now Alfred. Suddenly she realised where her thoughts had been, how she really did love him and now understood this was really the first time she had actually thought like this or acknowledged the fact. She cared for him, of that there was no doubt, but she had never said she really loved him. Maybe it was the shock of his loss that was putting thoughts like this in to her head, or had the love slowly grown and crept on her over the years? She certainly knew there seemed a void already where he should be. He might have made her cross at times, to say the least, but now she could not imagine life without him.

A moan escaped her as she thought about that, just at the precise moment that Lucy came back into the room. She nearly dropped the tea at the shock of hearing that sound as she thought Edith was having some kind of attack herself. Quickly she rushed to her side, 'What is it dear?'

'Alfred!'

'Yes, dear, he's left this life now.'

'I know, but how am I to manage now without him?'

Such deep reaction shocked Lucy as she had always thought there was not much love lost between the two of them. Somehow they had never seemed close.

'You've all your children dear, to take care of you. You're luckier than some in that respect.'

'Maybe, but it's not the same, they've their own lives to lead. Oh I don't know I really don't,' she groaned.

'What don't you know, dear?'

'How I'll carry on without him.'

'Come on now, you will. God will give you

the strength to get through it. I'm sure of that.'

'But why'd he to take such a good man like that?' she pleaded.

'Surely you've heard it said before, he needs the young as well as the old and the good as well as the bad.'

Edith gave a bitter laugh as this brought back her mother's words when they had lost their Elsie. 'You sound just like my Ma, she used to say that.'

'Well there you are, dear, we can't all be wrong. Now come on drink up this tea before it gets cold. I've put plenty of sugar in, to help with the shock you've had,' she said kindly.

28

That was all Edith felt she was given until the funeral, endless cups of tea to help her keep going. But she did not want all this attention. She wanted to be left alone to think on her memories. Her mind was so confused. Suddenly Alfred had become this person she loved. She did not know how to cope with these longings. When he had been alive she had not realised that she'd had such deep affection for him. Now her mind seemed to be telling her she loved him, it made his sudden death all the harder to bear.

Somehow she managed to carry out the normal daily functions but her body felt as if it was slowly dying off from inside. She felt numb with shock and wished she could die, so she could now join Alfred and say the words she should have told him, 'I love you.' She might have said them in the past but if she had chance to say them now they would be said with sincerity in her voice.

Fred and Martha had sorted out all the funeral arrangements. Alfred was to be buried, but he could not join his son, John, as he had been lost in France and no trace of him had ever been found. He had no grave, only the beach at Dunkirk. But the two of them could be united in death and Edith could not wait for her time to join them.

Martha's voice broke into her thoughts, 'Are you ready, Ma? It's time to go now.'

'Time to go where?' her mind asked and then she remembered she had been getting herself ready for the funeral of her beloved one. Waking out of her reverie she quickly pulled herself together. This was it then, their final parting. She checked herself carefully over because it would never do to let him down on this day. Finally satisfied, she called to Martha, 'Aye I'm ready. Just give me another minute on my own then I'll be down with you.'

Quickly she picked up the photograph nearby and gave it a kiss and whispered the words, 'Good bye my darling. I'm sorry I never said how much I loved you whilst you were here but I hope you're still around me in spirit and know that I really do love you.'

Brushing a tear away from her cheek, she gave a final check in the mirror then braced her shoulders and set off downstairs to face one of the saddest days if her life.

Quietly the undertaker came up to her, 'This way Mrs. Taylor, we'll take the lead.'

The party followed them out to the various

cars. Slowly the procession of vehicles moved on to Alfred's final resting place.

Edith had been brought up not to show her emotions in public and despite her resolve to stay dry eyed the tears poured down her cheeks. She felt proud as she heard the Minister's words outlining Alfred's life and it brought home to her just what a kind man he had been in many respects. It had only been his weakness with money where his fault had lain. But there was no mention of that to-day, only the good things about him. Her mind distanced her from what was happening. It all felt unreal, her body did not feel anything. Soon she would wake up from this dream, but another part of her knew she would not. Would she ever come out of this nightmare again?

She heard gentle sobbing and turned to see Alfred's mother wiping tears from her cheeks. Poor woman, she had lost another son. Edith knew what that felt like. But at least, for this other woman her son, Alfred, had lived long enough to have some life, children and grandchildren of his own. More than Edith's own son John had. Suddenly Edith felt very bitter by all she'd had to suffer. Then she remembered Alfred's brother who had died all those years ago in the Great War.

She felt her own father touch her arm,

'Come on, lass, it's time to move now. Alfred's coffin is going to the grave.'

She stood and watched another one lowered into the ground. How many more times would she have to go through this? Hadn't she already seen her sister and her mother laid to rest? But it was only his body. His spirit would stay with her, of that she was certain.

That was it. Now they would all go and have some food and be merry. How easily most people forgot they were at a funeral and managed to laugh again.

Her father had insisted on paying for the funeral meal. He said she had enough to cope with. Besides he said he would like to do this as his final parting gesture for Alfred, because, despite everything he had always liked the bloke.

Her body developed a will of its own. It went around the different people attending the meal, chatting and thanking them for coming. Was this really her doing all of this? At last they had all gone, now she could relax and show her true feelings.

'How are you, Ma?' Martha asked with deep concern in her voice.

Before she could stop herself she answered sharper than she intended, 'How do you think?'

'I know I just can't believe he'll not walk through this door any minute, with his usual cheery greeting.'

Then to Edith's dismay her daughter broke down in front of her. For a moment Edith came out of her own self absorption, 'Come on, lass, don't take on so. Think of that baby inside you. You'll be upsetting it. We don't want to have a melancholy baby, now do we?' This brought home to Edith just how much this man had been loved by his family and a moment of resentment flashed past her that it was him that had received all their love. But then it was replaced with a feeling of gladness that it had been this way as he deserved it.

Finally her sobs subsided. 'I'm sorry, Ma. I didn't mean for this to happen but it just came over me unawares how much I'll miss him.'

'I know, lass, and there's really nowt I can say that can take the pain away. Only you've still got me, if that's any good to you.'

'Of course it is,' replied Martha giving her mother a hug.

'Good, let me find Sid, it's time you were both off home. You've had a hard few days particularly for someone in your condition.'

'Get on with you, Ma. I'm young and healthy.'

'That's as maybe, but you've still to look

after yourself, if only for the baby's sake.'

'What about you? Will you be all right if I go now seeing as how Ethel's already taken herself off home?'

'Aye the lads are here so I'll not be on my own.'

'But, Ma, are you sure they'll look after you? More like you'll have to see to them.'

'Away with you, lass I've said I'll be all right.' She turned to Sid who was now at their side, 'Sid, just get her home. She's had a long day and she's wilting on her feet, I can see it. In fact she's had a hard few days and a bad shock for someone in her condition. Her Pa would never forgive me if anything happened to her or the baby. He was so happy about it.'

This thought brought a deep sadness back to Edith, but she now wanted to be on her own with her thoughts and memories.

'All right you win,' conceded Martha, 'We'll go but I'll be back tomorrow to see how you're getting on.'

Despite her sadness Edith managed to give a weak smile. 'You make me sound as if I'm in my dotage.'

★ ★ ★

Martha did come the next day as promised and continued to constantly see her or keep in touch. Edith was glad of this, because life became even more difficult for her than she could ever have imagined. She knew she was luckier than some widows; she had her own home and no fear of being turned out of it. But it was the loneliness, never in her wildest dreams had she imagined that she could be so lonely. Not that her family neglected her, it was not that at all. It was just the loneliness of those intimate moments that any caring husband and wife share.

She was so unhappy inside, that at times she did not want life to go on for her. She just wanted to shut herself away inside the house and not see anybody. At this time her deepest wish was to join Alfred, yet at the same time she knew her family still depended on her to help, if they had a problem. This gave her something to live for as she knew she was at least needed by somebody.

Fred was all for cancelling his wedding in the circumstances out of respect, but Edith was adamant it must go ahead as planned. Alfred would have wanted that. He had stressed often enough that he believed that life must still go on as usual even when a loved one had just died. He had believed so much in life.

For a short while the wedding plans took Edith out of herself giving her something else to think about. Not that she was really deeply involved with the organisation as Fred's future in laws was seeing to all the arrangements. But when it came to the actual wedding it was very hard for Edith to cope with it. She felt an odd one out being without a partner and it brought back Alfred's loss with renewed pain. At least at Martha's wedding she had known once Alfred had given the bride away, he would be back at her side. But not this time, she was really all on her own. Mind, she did feel cheered that he had, at least, had the opportunity to give their girls away for marriage. Funnily enough, once again the trouble of her family, Harry, was the most sensitive to her distress and tried to be her companion much of the time. Maybe she had misjudged him all along, or it was simply that the army was doing a good job on him. Whatever it was, Edith was glad he had turned out a good lad after all her worries, because in the past he had caused her many a sleepless night with concerns about him. But however hard he tried it just was not the same as sharing the little laugh and joke with a son as with a husband. She was glad it was accepted that the mother of the bride or groom could shed a few tears. But it was not Fred's marriage that caused hers.

What she had not given much thought to

was the fact that after the wedding she would be totally alone in this great big house. After having so many people in it she had never imagined what real loneliness could be like. At times she thought she would go out of her mind at the lack of conversation. Not that her family did not try to keep her company, they did, but she could still go long spells without seeing anyone. The mornings and evenings were the worst, waking up and knowing there was nobody there to even say good morning to. Aware of their mother's loneliness, one after another they kept coming up with suggestions about what she could do with her life.

Martha was the first one to come forward with her idea, 'Ma, Sid's been talking and he says his firm are recruiting a lot of engineers from out of town, and they're looking for places to live. You've so much room to spare why don't you take in lodgers? It'd give you company and some extra income.'

'No thank you. I think I've done enough skiving in my time. Anyway, I don't fancy that kind of company; you don't know what they're really like.'

'Well I think it'd be a good idea. After all, they'd be out at work all day so there wouldn't be so much to do for them and it'd bring you in a nice bit of money. It'd also be some company on an evening. At least think on it.'

'All right, I will but I'm sure the answer will still be the same.'

Then when George came on his next visit he brought with him his bright idea, 'Ma, I've been thinking about what you could do. You've a lot of money invested in this house. You could sell it and get yourself a little shop with living accommodation above. You enjoyed having the shop before, didn't you?'

'I think that was slightly different then. No, I don't want to be tied day in and day out in a shop. Unless I had someone work with me I'd never have any time off. Then to employ somebody would beat the object of having the shop. No, I really don't think that's a good idea at all.'

He was not the only one of them who came up with this idea; Fred brought it up as well. But Edith was sure they were all conspiring together to get her to agree to this notion of theirs.

Finally she came up with her own thoughts; she would be an out worker burler and mender again. Not that it would give her company but at least she could earn money because she did worry about not having enough to live on. She could do the work when it suited her best to fit in with any other plans. After all, Martha's baby was due any day and she wanted to be on hand to help her if the need arose.

As with all the best laid plans things do not always work out as expected. What she had never given a thought to was the weight of the rolls of cloth. She set herself up in a spare room — that was no problem as she had plenty of space. She could manage the work well enough but when she came to the end of the roll she was dependent on one of the lads being there to help her move it and put the next roll under the table. Sometimes she would have to wait days before anybody strong enough called to help her. She started to feel very cross about her own inadequacy.

Although her father was a regular visitor she felt he was too old to be humping heavy rolls of cloth around. Not that he put up much objection himself when she told him, 'No, Pa, I won't let you risk straining yourself helping me with these. Let the younger ones do it when they call.'

What he did say was, 'I just don't know why you don't move in with me. I've plenty of room and I know you fret yourself whether I get fed well enough and looked after. Why don't you sell this rambling house then you'd have plenty of money and not have to do this work. It'd kill two birds with one stone. I'd be looked after and you'd have company and money in the bank. What do you say?'

'I'll think on it. It's a big decision. We might not get on living together after all these years of each of us being independent.'

'Don't be daft, of course we'll get on together and don't forget one day you'll have my house when I pass on.'

'Now, Pa, don't start that topic.'

Edith did not take his point lightly and gave it a lot of thought but decided she needed to talk the idea through with somebody else. She thought long and hard on this and decided Martha, out of all her children, was the best person to discuss it with.

As soon as she had outlined the idea to her Martha was all for it. 'It makes sense to me Ma. You'll give Grandpa some company and you can keep your eye on him at the same time. I know how you worry so about him, but at the same time you'll have company yourself. It would be ideal.'

'Aye that's just what your Grandpa said. But I don't know going back to living with him after all these years. I just don't know. 'Sides, I didn't really get on with him that well when I lived at home.'

'Yes but a lot of water has passed under the bridge. That was then. It's up to you, of course, but I can only see the sense of it. This is a big house for you to live in and look after all on your own. You must feel lonely in it and you don't need all the space.'

'I know I do feel lonely, I'll admit that, but there are so many things I can do here and most importantly there's the memories. It's so difficult to decide so I really don't know. Maybe I'll sleep on it then it'll look clearer in the morning. Anyway how about you? How's that baby coming on? Getting ready to be born yet?'

'It feels like it. I'm glad I've only another couple of weeks to go now. It's very tiring when you get near your time.' Then laughing she added, 'I'm sure I don't need to tell you that.'

'No you don't, I can still remember. Just wait until it's your sixth.'

'Not likely, two's the most I want.'

'Well you'll just have to wait and see what happens. Sometimes we end up with more than we intend.'

Martha looked hard at her mother, 'Maybe so, who knows, but times have changed so we have more control of family size.'

In the end Edith did not get much chance to ponder on her father's idea as Martha had the baby earlier than expected. But all was well. She had a beautiful baby girl, just perfect, who they named Sarah. Edith had to wait to see her as there was a flu outbreak so no visitors were allowed at the hospital. She was a little bit on the small side being early and for some reason she seemed to pull at Edith's heart strings far more than any of her own had done, or for that matter more than Daisy. Straight away an attachment seemed to grow between them, or at least Edith thought so.

Then when Edith went back to her own home after staying with Martha and Sid to help them out, she felt even lonelier than ever. Her father sensing this added a further enticement for her to move in with him. 'I know I live a little bit out of the way, but if you come and live with me I'll arrange it so you can have some driving lessons, then you can have the car to use and you'd be able to go and see Sarah as often as you like. After all, I am getting old and I think it's time I gave up driving and was chauffeured around, so how about it then?'

Finally Edith relented. In any case she was not managing to get much burling and mending done, one or other of her family seemed to need her help. Her small reserve of money was rapidly running out. She could do with the money from the sale of the house.

'All right you win, but it'll take me a while

to sort everything out. I suppose I could let the children have some bits and pieces of furniture. I'll only come on the proviso you let me bring my favourite pieces of furniture along. I'm not getting rid of everything, all my memories.'

'Of course, that goes without saying.'

'Right, I'd better get on with it all. I'll have to let them all know what I'm doing. They'll be pleased with my decision, I'm sure,' she said in a business like manner.

She wished she felt as certain as she sounded that she was doing the right thing for herself, as she was moving further away from her family by going back to Denholme, but yet again she was giving herself some companionship. Because who knew how many more years she would have to enjoy her father being around. Then she would really be on her own and that did not even bear thinking about.

29

All too soon for Edith's liking everything was arranged and she was moved in with her father. When she had agreed to join him, for some reason, she imagined her house would take a lot of selling but a buyer was found the first week it was on the market. Then she had a panic wondering why on earth she had not suggested her father live with her. But she soon calmed down as she remembered his stubbornness and pride and he would not have left his smallholding for the world.

As good as his word, her father sorted out driving lessons for her. She had thought herself too old to do anything as adventurous as driving but she took to it like a duck to water. In no time at all she was a fully competent driver and had passed her test much to her family's amazement. She loved the freedom of being able to get out and about and was free to go to see Sarah on a regular basis. She had not felt a real grandparent to Ethel's child but with Sarah an instant bond had been formed from birth and that stayed as she grew from a baby into a little girl. Before she knew where she was

Fred was a father and she had another grandchild. But however hard she tried none became as special as Sarah. It was her who helped Edith keep her sanity whilst living with her father.

Never in her wildest dreams had she imagined it would be so different to live with her father than seeing him on a regular basis. She could not ever remember him being so demanding when she lived at home as a young girl, but she soon realised her mother had no doubt taken the brunt of it then so she had not noticed.

Maybe old age was making him worse. For some reason, once she was living with him he seemed to start giving in to his age and became less active, in fact he expected Edith to do everything for him. She was at his beck and call. It seemed far worse to her than bringing up six children. At times she bitterly regretted the move and only wished she had taken on board some of the other suggestions from her children.

Even Martha began to wonder if she had encouraged her mother in the right move as she saw what was happening. Her mother certainly did not look as happy as she had expected her to be at this stage in her life. 'Are you and Grandpa getting on all right, Ma?' Martha asked with concern.

'Whatever makes you ask that?' Edith snapped back.

'Well to be honest you just don't look that happy and you are a bit irritable.'

'Well I'm sure you would be living with a cantankerous old man like he is nowadays,' Edith snapped back.

'But Ma, he is your Father,' Martha protested all the while thinking of her own gentle father.

'Sorry, he's just a bit difficult at times, I've to admit. I'm sure it'll all sort out given time. At least I do hope so,' Edith sighed.

Edith was not quite as confident as she tried to sound. Not that there was not some good moments because there was. Her father seemed to settle best on an evening then they would sit and listen to the radio and have a meaningful discussion, if sometimes heated, afterwards. Now and again she thought she would go mad living with him yet at the same time she did realise, as Martha had pointed out, that he was her father and he was getting old. She understood enough to know when he had gone she would miss him deeply, despite her annoyance with him at times.

Yet without even looking for it she found what she thought sounded the solution to her problem. Browsing through a copy of 'The Lady' magazine she noticed advertisements for housekeeper posts. She paused and studied them in more depth. She felt like that with father, a housekeeper more than his daughter. Not that she was really interested in exchanging one housekeeping job for another. But there again some of the advertised jobs were seasonal, in different parts of the country, so she could go somewhere else for a short time, yet be earning. This seemed an ideal way to see other parts of the British Isles. Then when she came back after a break from her father she might be able to tolerate him with more patience. It seemed the answer, when it all became too much for her, to look for a job away, short term. Studying the job advertisements she found the one that looked the most appealing to her was in Scotland.

The position was as housekeeper to a Colonel during the grouse shooting season at his lodge there. To apply a letter had to be sent to his permanent housekeeper in London. Well, she might as well apply, after all nothing ventured nothing gained.

Edith gave a little laugh as she wrote the letter at the thought this was the first time she had applied for anything like this despite her many years experience of running her own home. In her heart of hearts she did not think she would stand that much chance of success, since she did not really have much of an employment record. But it was a nice dream to keep her going in the hopes she would get away for a while. Mind, if she did not get this post there was nothing to stop her keep trying for something else. In the end she wrote, putting all her attributes down of looking after a large family and she made mention of the shop hoping this made her appear a responsible person.

Each day she watched for the post, so she could get to the letter before her father did. She did not want him to know what she was up to. When the reply was not in each day's post she felt more frustrated and disappointed as each day passed. Yet when she saw the envelope and guessed what it was she could barely open it as her hand was shaking so much with excitement, although she expected it only to be a rejection.

She could not believe her eyes when she read the words that the job was hers without even having to be interviewed. Her experience of bringing up a family of six must have certainly impressed. Apparently the housekeeper from London would meet her in Scotland and give her the once over and all her instructions. In was incredible to her that it had been as easy as that for her to get the job.

When she read the name of the gentleman she was to work for, her heart gave a quick flip. It was a Colonel Mitchell. That name of all names, still, her Edward Mitchell had been dead many years now.

Her family were amazed when she broke the news what she was going to do. Even more so that she'd had the initiative to do it all on her own without hinting to them what was going on. Inwardly they felt proud of her that she had been successful against what must have been other competition.

Of all of them Martha understood her motives the best. 'I'm glad you've got this job. It seems like a good idea to me to get away for a while and then when you come back you might be able to cope better with it all. Don't worry, I'll look after Grandpa and I'm sure, at least, Fred will go and see him regular like.'

'Aye, I'm fair excited at the thought. It's given me a challenge again in life. I only hope I can make a success of it when I get there. It'll be quite different looking after the gentry than my own brood. The Housekeeper said in her letter, there was the Colonel, his wife and three children. That'll give me a fair amount of work and keep me out of mischief. The good news is she did say others worked at the lodge, but gave no further details. I'll just have to wait and see.'

'You'll cope, you always do,' Martha replied confidently.

'I suppose so, but I'm starting to wonder what had come over me when I applied. Still, it'll get me away from Pa for a while and then as you say once I get back I'll probably have missed him so much that I'll enjoy being near him again. Do you know, I think if this works out I might think of doing it on a regular basis when I get fed up here. Now I've only Pa to break the news to. That's the hard bit, worse than coping with the new job, I think.'

She actually had butterflies in her stomach as she broke the news to him. Surprisingly enough he took it better than Edith had thought he would and actually encouraged her to go. She decided maybe she had been getting on his nerves as well. It seemed to her now as if she were doing both of them a favour by going away for a while. It actually shocked her, this realisation and made her understand how selfish she had been in thinking of only how she felt. Then even more so when her father had opened his house to her in her hour of need, with no apparent apprehension on his part.

There had been no mention of any uniform in the correspondence so she decided she had better get herself some very practical, dark and plain dresses ready. Before she knew where she was, it was time for her to take her leave of them all. At that moment in time this seemed to become the biggest adventure of her life. She had never been so far away from home on her own before. Not that she had really been away anywhere on her own, when she thought about it. It made her acutely aware how much of a good companion Alfred had been to her. She became very nervous and sure she was going to make a complete mess of the whole thing.

Her father had said she could take the car if she wanted, but she decided it was enough of an adventure just going to the job without driving that distance for the first time. She enjoyed every minute of the train journey as she watched all the different people getting on and off the train. Plenty of them had a chat with her. Finally on reaching her destination, as promised, there was the gardener come chauffeur waiting with an old car to take her to the house. She tried to say tactfully that she could drive if needs be whilst she was there but she just received a dark look of disbelief from this man, that a woman was capable of such a thing. She was seething with his arrogance. But on reaching their destination she let out an exclamation of delight at the house and its setting.

Grumpily, Tom, as she now knew he was called, spoke, 'Best make the most of it now. Once the shooting party arrives you'll have no time to spare to admire the view, they'll keep you that busy.'

'I see. Are there a lot of them going to stay here?'

'Who knows, the Colonel never thinks to tell us. Mind, I don't think he rightly knows himself as he has a habit of throwing out invitations then forgets who he's given them to. He's too generous by half, if you ask me.'

Edith was not so sure he should be talking about his employer in such a manner, particularly to a stranger at that.

As soon as she entered the house the London housekeeper rushed up to her, 'Ah, Mrs. Taylor. You have had a good journey I trust.'

'Yes, thank you.'

'Good, I'll show you to your room and let you get settled in then I'll go through everything. I want to get on my way as soon as I can as it's my holiday now. I always have it when the Colonel and family are up here. They'll arrive the day after tomorrow, so not that much time to get everything organised. Come on this way then.' Edith followed the short plump figure up the stairs.

She led Edith to a charming attic bedroom with an adjoining sitting room.

'This is nice,' exclaimed Edith, then she walked to the window and looked out. 'What views, it reminds me of living in the country when I was a lass.'

'Yes, well I'm sure by the time you finish here you'll be fed up of the country. Give me London any day.'

Edith said no more; obviously this was a born and bred city dweller.

The housekeeper's voice interrupted her thoughts, 'Right, if you've got all you need I'll leave you be. When you've finished come down to the kitchen and I'll give you a meal and we'll talk. It's nice and cosy in the kitchen. It is much better than some of the large draughty rooms.'

As Edith unpacked she began to ask herself what she was really doing here. What on earth had possessed her to leave her family even for this short while? Then the fears of whether she could really cope came back to her, particularly when she thought of the London housekeeper and how efficient she seemed. Edith only hoped she would be able to run the house to the standard that was obviously going to be expected of her.

What she had always taken for granted suddenly seemed like climbing a mountain without Alfred behind her giving encouragement. He had been her support through so many things in life. She felt as if a mist was beginning to clear from her eyes and she was seeing what she should have seen all those years ago. Alfred had been a wonderful husband and father. Well, apart from his little problem but that seemed of no real importance at this moment in time. A tear slid down her cheek as she would have given anything to have him with her now. Then calmness came over her as if Alfred was near by and watching over her to protect her from harm.

Suddenly she looked at the time and realised she better get a move on, she did not want to make a bad first impression by being so slow unpacking. No, that would not do at all. Wiping her face dry she put on a forced cheerful expression. Hoping she could find her way to the kitchen through the maze of corridors without too much difficulty, she left the cosiness of her bedroom. Surprisingly, it was not as complicated as she had first thought to find her way around. As she walked in the kitchen the London housekeeper turned to the cook, 'Ah here she is then, nicely on time. You can dish the meal up for Mrs. Taylor now.'

'Yes, Mrs. Sharply,' replied the tall thin

cook. Edith had to control a smile as they both looked as if they had been placed in the wrong job.

'Come on, Mrs. Taylor, sit over here near the stove and keep warm. If you don't mind I'll chat whilst you eat as there's a lot to tell you.'

Edith was quite taken aback, she seemed much friendlier now than she had first imagined. 'No not at all. I'm well used to being talked to whilst I eat.' Then seeing the puzzled look on Mrs. Sharply's face added, 'With that family of mine, there was always one or another with something to say.'

'I see, yes you did mention you'd brought a large family up, in your application letter. Am I right in saying you've never worked as a housekeeper before?'

'Aye, that's right.'

'What did you do before you were married and had your family? Were you in service?'

'No I worked in the mills as a burler and mender.'

'Oh I see, I can't say I've actually heard of that job. Of course in London itself there are no textile mills and that's where I was born and bred and have spent most of my life.'

'Yes, this is new to me, travelling to Scotland. I've not left my birth place often.'

'Anyway we'd best get on with the matter in hand regarding what will be your duties over the next few weeks.'

'When do the guests start arriving?'

'Colonel Mitchell and family arrive the day after tomorrow, as I said before, but I'm afraid he's not very good at letting us know when and how many guests to expect. That's why I suggest you have all the rooms ready and always have more food cooked than the amount you need. Usually somebody unexpected turns up at meal time. Mind, cook has been coming here the last few years so she's well used to what can happen. Aren't you Cook?'

'I am that; always have a pot of something simmering just in case.'

'You'll not see a great deal of them as they all go on the shoots, even his wife and children. When I say children, Henry is actually seventeen, Samantha sixteen just and Freddy fourteen. Mrs Mitchell will leave the menus to your choice as long as the food isn't too fussy and is well prepared. But, in any case she knows how well cook prepares the meals. It's a blessing them being out so much as it'll give you chance to get on in peace.'

'Will there be help to clean the rooms and make everything ready?' Edith asked worried at the thought of what was to do in this huge place.

'Yes, some girls are coming from the village tomorrow. It's up to you how long you need them and how many to keep on after the main preparations are done. As I said, you've a free hand really in the running of the place. The main thing is to be ready for the unexpected and then you'll be fine. Anything else you need to ask?'

'Only can you show me around so I get my bearings where things are kept. By the way have the girls worked here before?'

'Some will have so they'll show the others where everything is. Right, if you've finished your meal I'll take you on a tour around.'

As Edith moved to leave the kitchen she turned to the cook, 'Thanks for the meal, it was excellent and most welcome.'

'No problem, dear, talk to you later.'

It did not take Edith long to get herself sorted out in her mind. She actually amazed herself how easily she adapted to the new environment and work. Mrs Sharply left the next day for her annual holiday quite happy in her mind that she had made a good choice in Mrs. Taylor and that she would be able to manage well enough even with all the unpredictability of the Colonel and his family. Edith had lost her anxiety of being unable to cope and soon settled down to the task in hand, having everything prepared for when the first guests arrived.

30

Most of the other staff, as Mrs. Sharply had indicated, had worked the shooting seasons there before so were well versed in what to do. Edith found that everything more or less ran like clockwork, with her just overseeing that all went along smoothly. In actual fact they all got on very well together. All of Edith's initial home sickness soon vanished.

The same lady had been housekeeper here at the lodge during the shooting season for many years prior to this, but she'd had to retire due to ill health. The other staff willingly accepted Edith as her replacement.

When Edith first saw Colonel Mitchell she was pleasantly shocked by what a nice friendly person he appeared, with no airs and graces. He chatted to her as an equal. Prior to this she had received the impression, from what the other staff had said, that he did not give a hang who worked for him as long as his house ran trouble free. This appeared not to be the case at all. It soon became apparent why he left them so much to their own devices. He thought of them as equals — not servants and as such trusted them to get on with the job allocated to them. Edith appreciated how the misunderstanding had come about. In fact, it was rather strange but in many ways he reminded her of Alfred, a kind and gentle man.

Then Edith convinced herself it would be too good to be true if his wife was equally as easy going. It was with a slight reluctance that Edith made herself known to Mrs Mitchell the first time she needed to discuss a menu for an important dinner party.

Edith was rather taken aback when Mrs Mitchell spoke. 'Don't call me Mrs Mitchell that's much too formal. Call me Millie.'

'Oh, er, yes right. I've brought these menus for you to approve for tomorrow night.'

'If they're fine by you then that's good enough for me as I trust my staff and I don't like to stand on ceremony. If you've a problem come to me but otherwise anything you organise will suit us.'

Edith left the room slightly open mouthed with shock at somebody like Mrs Mitchell or Millie, being so friendly and easy going towards her. She had not imagined it would be like this working for the rich.

Surprisingly she saw more of the family than she had first imagined and it brought a great sadness to her own heart to watch what a happy and close knit family they were.

Colonel Mitchell treated his children in much the same way as Alfred had theirs. It was obvious he adored his wife but it seemed to be a reciprocal thing as adoration shone out of her eyes whenever she was near him.

Edith was not unhappy for them; it was a joy to see the love. It was sadness for her own waste of life that hit her. Nothing could have brought home more sharply to her the years she had wasted by not giving Alfred the love he deserved and she now knew she had for him.

A sob escaped Edith as she sat alone in her room brooding. Why had she not seen it before what a good, kind, loving and generous man she had married all those years ago? Now it was too late. She had never used any of the opportunities she'd had to tell Alfred how much she really loved him, which she began to appreciate because this family had shown her what real love, was all about, giving and sharing with each other. It was the love that had been between her and Alfred, not this imagined love she'd had for Edward all these years.

Her sadness at all the waste of both her and Alfred's life was immense. If only she had found all this out whilst Alfred had still been alive, then she could have really shown him her love. She wept bitter tears in the privacy of her room at the thought that this was no longer possible.

But was it? She still had her father, children and grandchildren. It came to her like a bolt out of the blue; she could give them all the love and attention they deserved. Not that it would put things right between her and Alfred but there was no need for them to suffer any longer. She knew at times she had been reserved with them, held her love back because of resentment, blaming them because she felt her life was not as it should be. Not that she thought she had been a bad mother to her family. She had simply not shown a great deal of love and affection in a demonstrative kind of way. But it was not too late for her to change and give them the love that was now welling up inside her. It had not been their fault that she had thought that life would have been so different if she had been married to Edward. This thought made her appreciate that her six children would not have been the ones she had, had she married Edward. The good part of Alfred would not have been in them. She might not even have born six children to Edward and now she had brought them up she would not have wanted it any other way. She began to think it had been God's will that she had conceived so easily so many times. He had brought her through the last pregnancy with the baby so she survived to bring up her family.

Now, at last she understood the love between her mother and father, it was so great it did not need the words. That was why her father had been in such a state of grief when he lost his wife. Tears rolled down her cheeks as she realised by her own stupidity what she had missed by following a dream, not cherishing what she had with Alfred and the family.

Alone with these thoughts a sense of peace and contentment washed over her and she imagined Alfred's voice in her head, 'I always knew you really loved me, but it didn't matter if you did or didn't. I'd love enough for the two of us.'

'Oh Alfred, what a fool I've been,' she moaned out aloud. But it was just like him to be so unselfish.

Edith stayed in her room and shed bitter tears at the waste, all because she had held on to a dream. Now that dream had been shattered in a matter of days. Tidying her hair and face she braced herself to move forward to her new life. A life where she would not be frightened of sharing or giving love to the people who meant the most to her and deserved it. She only hoped the damage she had done was not irreversible.

We do hope that you have enjoyed reading
this large print book.

Did you know that all of our titles
are available for purchase?

We publish a wide range of high quality
large print books including:
Romances, Mysteries, Classics
General Fiction
Non Fiction and Westerns

Special interest titles available in
large print are:
The Little Oxford Dictionary
Music Book
Song Book
Hymn Book
Service Book

Also available from us courtesy of Oxford
University Press:
Young Readers' Dictionary
(large print edition)
Young Readers' Thesaurus
(large print edition)

For further information or a free
brochure, please contact us at:
Ulverscroft Large Print Books Ltd.,
The Green, Bradgate Road, Anstey,
Leicester, LE7 7FU, England.
Tel: (00 44) 0116 236 4325
Fax: (00 44) 0116 234 0205